The Last Time I Saw Jane

KATE PULLINGER

PHŒNIX

A PHOENIX PAPERBACK

First published in Great Britain
by Weidenfeld & Nicolson in 1996
This paperback edition published in 1997
by Phoenix, a division of Orion Books Ltd,
Orion House, 5 Upper St Martin's Lane,
London WC2H 9EA

Grateful acknowledgement is made for permission
to quote from the following songs:

One Of Us Cannot Be Wrong
Written by Leonard Cohen
© 1967, 1995 Bad Monk Publishing
Used by Permission. All Rights Reserved.

Famous Blue Raincoat
Written by Leonard Cohen
© 1971 Leonard Cohen Stranger Music, Inc.
Used by Permission. All Rights Reserved.

A CIP catalogue record for this book is available
from the British Library.

ISBN: 1 85799 864 2

Printed and bound in Great Britain by
The Guernsey Press Co. Ltd,
Guernsey, Channel Islands

For Adrian and Christine,
Derek and Jessica,
Sarah and Jennifer

Catherine Tekakwitha, who are you?
Are you (1656–1680)? Is that enough? Are
you the Iroquois Virgin? Are you the Lily
of the Shores of the Mohawk River? Can I
love you in my own way?

Leonard Cohen,
Beautiful Losers

PROLOGUE

Audrey's father killed her mother in a car accident. She did not die immediately, but in hospital seven days later. Enough time for Audrey to fly from London to British Columbia and see the damage for herself.

The telephone rang at six a.m., like an alarm hurled across the room. It was still dark outside. Audrey had always known the call would come while she was sleeping; very bad news has a way of arriving in the night.

The accident was muted and sober as far as car accidents go, slow-moving, metal and chrome remaining intact. Audrey's father had been an excellent driver at one time, able to negotiate the mountain passes and narrow roads where they lived, in winter snow piled high as an overpass, but since he retired, his sight and his reactions had dimmed. He had a tendency to sit behind the wheel slumped to one side, as though he wasn't driving but watching television. Audrey's mother said she worried that he would pull out into oncoming traffic one day. But he kept on driving, and she let him; it was too great an affront to have to give up that as well as all the other passions that had slid from his grasp with age.

As she packed Audrey remembered the last time she had been to visit. Instead of flying to Victoria she had taken the ferry from the mainland across the Georgia Strait to Vancouver Island. She had seen an eagle floating in the airstream above Maine Island in Active Pass – the sight was so familiar, even though it had been years since she was last on the boat. She couldn't help but think of Jane. In fact, she had given herself a fright when she looked out the window and saw a pregnant woman standing by the railing. But, of course, it wasn't Jane.

The ferry had docked and she walked down the covered ramp towards her parents, fraught with ambivalence and love. She could see them in the waiting throng. They looked tiny, as though they'd been shrink-wrapped by the ageing process. Oh God, Audrey had thought, old age. Can there be anything as unexpected, as demanding?

But it was not an ill-judged corner turn that killed her mother. Audrey's parents had been out to dinner with a group of friends, couples who, like them, had been married for decades, and the widowed remains of couples, gamely joining in. They had gone for Chinese food, and all the men made jokes about going home to eat a real meal later. By the time they left the restaurant it had begun to rain, so the husbands went to get the cars while the women waited in the foyer out of the damp. When Audrey's father was trying to explain to her what had happened, he said, 'The damn rain, the air smelt of the sea, fresh, there was a bird – a heron – standing in a puddle in the parking lot.' Audrey's father brought his car in close to the kerb, so 'the girls', as he called them, 'would not have far to walk'. As he came up to the entrance the small group of women stepped forward, his wife, Audrey's mother, leading. He went to brake – he said this very carefully, as if getting the sequence of events correct would somehow make it better – but he had got so clumsy, he had so little control, his foot slipped to the accelerator and the car leapt forward, onto the pavement, knocking Audrey's mother down, one wheel moving over her abdomen, her chest, as she lay stranded on kerb and pavement, the sound – her little cry, rubber tonnage on flesh and wool – both muffled and clear. Their friend Dorothy Jones – Dorothy Jones, her father used to say, as batty as a softball team – was clipped by the vehicle as well, she fell and broke her hip. The other women stepped back, and then ran forward, shouting, waving their hands, slapping the windscreen of the car. When he realized what was happening, in that slow moment when his wife had disappeared, Audrey's father suffered a heart attack in front of the steering column. It was mild, but served to debilitate him even further.

Because of the speed and skill of the emergency services, Audrey's mother took seven days to die. The nurses put the couple in the same room – Audrey's father on a heart monitor, her mother on a respirator, wires, tubes and bandages covering every surface of her frail body, her old body with its lovely folding skin. They had to shave her hair, her clean white hair that he said reminded him of snow, snowy mountain passes, snow unwalked in, untouched; she had dyed it blonde for years before revealing this whiteness, this shining curtain, to her husband, who told his daughter that he had loved her all the more for it. Audrey's father recovered from the accident, physically, quite quickly. He spent three days sitting and staring at his wife, watching her machine-driven breathing. The hospital staff did not have the will to remove him from the bed. She never regained consciousness, not even when Audrey, her one child, arrived. Audrey looked at her father and wished her mother could speak, if only to forgive him. But she did not.

When her mother died – in the night, after Audrey had taken her father home for the first time – Audrey conspired with her father to have him incarcerated. There was no question of criminal or civil proceedings – the family of Dorothy Jones was angry about her broken hip, but felt that Mr Robbins had been punished thoroughly – but Audrey's father did not want to continue to live on his own in the home that his wife had made for him. He wanted to go into an institution, an old-age home, 'a cheap one', he said, meaning, send me to prison, please. Audrey discovered that the standard of care for the elderly on southern Vancouver Island was extremely high, possibly the highest in the world, and the home Mr Robbins eventually went into was as pleasant as homes full of the old and alone can be. Then, in one of his last moments of lucidity, Audrey's father told her to go back to London, go back to her life there, and to forget about him, to live as though he too were dead.

And so Audrey went back to London, shocked and shaking with grief. She had already lived many years in the city, years that had passed in a minute. She found London was a place she could sink deep into, sink everything, and yet not drown. When she first left Canada she thought it easy to forget all about where she had come from. And after she buried her mother and locked up her father she believed that forgetting was complete.

But at night when Audrey slept, regardless of whether she shared her bed or not, she dreamt of her parents, she dreamt of British Columbia. She dreamt of her days, long past, at university in Vancouver, her uncovering and devouring, her flesh-eating desire for the past. She'd given up the ghost on a degree in History, three-quarters of the way through. At the time, dropping out wasn't a failure, it was a liberation. She had left Canada then, and gone to live in London, like a little chick of Empire returning home to roost.

And now Audrey dreams of James Douglas. In these dreams, she follows James on his journey. Water laps against the side of the ship. The year is 1819.

James Douglas was anxious to get away from Lanarkshire, to leave behind his father, and his father's family, and to arrive in the new world, a vast uncharted place he had read about in school. At age sixteen, Scotland held nothing for him, except reminders of what he was excluded from, what he was not allowed to be. At the port in Liverpool there was no one to wave him off. He stood on the far side of the ship and looked towards the sea. This voyage was to take him

4

north to north, the Atlantic grey and choppy as land and summer faded from sight. At night in his ship-bed he remembered another journey he had made, ten years earlier. This new migration was of his own volition. He was leaving Britain for a fresher place.

After four weeks crossing the Atlantic, rocking storms and steamy calms, the ship reached Newfoundland, sailed on past Cape Breton, through the Strait of Cabot, into the Gulf of St Lawrence. Their passage was smooth. The Captain told Douglas one morning that they had entered the St Lawrence Seaway, but the young passenger did not know where he had arrived, the seaway so wide and tidal that neither north nor south shore could be seen. And then, when it finally did come into view, the land was strange and wild, a barrage of colour where the forest came down to the river-sea, as the leaves changed with the season, many more shades of red and gold than James could have imagined. Some days later, through the glass James saw small boats low to the water, close into the bank, swiftly paddled by people he took for Indians. Other days there was nothing for mile after mile, no human sign, no break in the trees.

And James, James Douglas, was heading west, as far west as he could go without falling off the land-shelf into the Pacific. This journey would take many years, and by the end of it he would be entirely remade, not one inch of his skin, not one hair on his head, of his former self would remain. Not one speck of the boy he might have been.

Audrey did not know why she dreamt of James Douglas now, why he had come back to her from books and papers she had read years ago, at university. But he had come back, and he was going to linger, and she saw that she had better get used to it.

PART ONE

A la façon du pays

In the custom of the land

*Our sons shall wed your daughters,
and we shall be one people.*

Samuel de Champlain
to the Algonquins, 1603

I

London, five years later

They met at a lecture. A mutual friend had written a book. At the party afterwards Audrey drank arts corporate sponsorship whisky; she downed glass after glass, neat. Shereen was drinking beer. They collided at the drinks table.

'Don't I know you from somewhere?' said Shereen.

Audrey steadied herself. She thought she would have remembered the other woman's face, sharp, fine features, cropped black hair, a yellow dress vivid against her skin.

'I've never met you before,' Audrey replied. 'Audrey Robbins,' she offered her hand in compensation.

'Shereen Bannerjea. But I recognize your name – you're a journalist?'

Audrey nodded.

'I'm sure I remember your face.'

'People often mistake me for somebody else,' said Audrey, feeling a little whisky-philosophical, 'as though my face is generic somehow. A face everyone recognizes.' She laughed, 'Mum and Dad wanted to make sure I'd be able to fit in anywhere.'

'Do you?'

Audrey laughed again. 'I suppose so. In a way.'

Shereen persisted. 'What part of America are you from then?'

Audrey paused. This question always came, eventually, whenever she met anyone new; she was accustomed to it. It used to make her bristle, ten years ago she would have

9

enunciated, 'I am not from the US; I am from Canada,' smoothing down her indignation. Now, after all these years away, the question gave her the mildest, most benevolent annoyance. What part of America are you from? 'Canada.' She took perverse satisfaction at the idea of Canada as the fifty-first state. Canada, the blank white page.

'Oh, I'm sorry,' said Shereen. Everyone always apologized then, as though they had made some terrible *faux pas*, like asking after a parent who was recently deceased. Audrey brushed it away.

The two women talked, not saying much, telling jokes at their own expense, Shereen recovering quickly from her embarrassment. Audrey liked her right away, and wanted to know her, but held herself back. You can't be best friends with everyone, even if that is your first impulse. Shereen's conversation was measured, her accent posh and modulated, and this itself Audrey found alluring. Then someone interrupted, a friend of Shereen's who launched into a complicated piece of gossip. Audrey knew none of the people involved and could not follow the convoluted tale. She excused herself and wandered back in the direction of the drink.

Jack Campbell was standing near the door. Audrey had noticed him when she first arrived, and smiled at him now; she knew who he was. American, black, good-looking, works in TV. He had the kind of social notoriety people attract without ever having to do anything. It followed him, like expensive aftershave, turning heads. That leather jacket, Audrey thought as her gaze met his.

She poured herself another whisky and looked around to see who else was at the party. The same people were always at these things; she had a whole set of acquaintances from drinks parties, people she could mumble to once she was half-cut. As she raised the glass to her lips she felt a hand under her elbow. She turned.

'Jack,' he said, his hand now shaking hers firmly.

'Audrey,' she replied, returning the grip, slightly alarmed.

'That's a nice dress you're wearing.'

Audrey looked down at herself; she felt long, bony, and as though she sagged slightly. She had worn this dress – low-cut, tailored – vaguely hoping someone might like it, but men don't give outrageous compliments as often as they might. She looked at Jack. 'Just an old . . .' She could not continue.

'Just an old thing . . . I don't believe you.'

'It's not true.' She smiled.

He returned her smile. 'And what do you do for a living?'

She explained, then asked the same question herself.

'I hang around at parties looking for women like you.'

Audrey blushed, then blushed more deeply when she realized she had coloured. They continued to talk. After a while she said, 'Well, I haven't met a man as flirtatious as you in years.'

'It's good to flirt,' Jack said, 'good for morale.' He flashed his broad smile at her once again.

They left together a bit later, Jack in his leather jacket, Audrey in her raincoat. It was January, very dark and damply cold. He walked her through Camden – through the debris of the market, past the dark pubs and their malty spillage – to the underground station. He said he was going to get a bus. For some reason she wondered if in fact he had a car parked somewhere nearby. He gave her his telephone number and told her to ring. She put the bit of paper in her pocket and then, later, touched it with her fingers as the train travelled beneath the city.

But it was Shereen whom Audrey rang several days later. She was writing an article for a glossy women's magazine; it was a 'Lifestyles' piece about inter-racial relationships.

Lifestyles, she thought as she dialled Shereen's number, how did I get into this?

'You're asking me if I've ever dated a white man?'

'Yes, you know . . . or any kind of non-Asian?'

Shereen paused down her end of the telephone line. Audrey panicked. Perhaps she had misjudged her.

'How many women are you interviewing for this piece?'

'Five.'

'Why would anyone be interested in who I've gone out with – anyone who didn't know me, that is?'

'Oh hell, Shereen, everyone is interested in this kind of thing, you know that.'

'It's so . . . voyeuristic.'

Audrey took a drag on her cigarette. 'Come on, you're a lawyer, you're used to prying. You know what these magazines are like.' Audrey smoked only when she was drunk and when she was making these phone calls. She kept a packet of rolling tobacco in a jar by the telephone, expressly.

'Oh well, you've got me there.' Shereen paused. 'The question should really be have I ever gone out with another Indian.' She laughed and Audrey relaxed, stubbed out her cigarette. Shereen gave her what she wanted, a nicely bite-sized version of her relationship with someone called Phil, the man her mother had loved to hate. 'She made such a lot of fuss, and it seemed to have more to do with him being Jewish than anything else. My mother has a thing against Jews, it's part of her anglophilia. She was much happier when I brought home nice boys from Church of England families, that was okay with her.'

'But the relationship with Phil ended anyway?'

'He was a wanker. As much as I enjoyed winding up my mother, I'm afraid he was a creep.'

Audrey finished her article. Several months went by before she ran into Shereen again. Another party – more mutual friends, as though London had been transformed into a small town suddenly. They stood in a corner and talked about their work while other people danced.

It was getting late when Shereen went off to find the toilet. Audrey felt awkward on her own. 'Aren't we supposed to come to parties to meet men?' Shereen had asked earlier, both of them a little hysterical with drink and dope. Yeah right, thought Audrey now, surveying the room full of gay couples, straight couples and single women.

At that moment Jack Campbell appeared, taking hold of Audrey's elbow, reminding her of his name.

'You never rang,' he said.

'Hello Jack,' she replied, thinking: I didn't believe you wanted me to. She smiled.

He looked directly at her, his face bare and frank, brown eyes wide, smiling. He wore his hair cropped close to his head, his temples shone, his skin both burnished and rosy. Her hand grew warm as he held it.

'So you're a journalist,' he remembered. 'What kinds of things do you write about?' He held her gaze, as flirtatious as he had been the first time they met, and Audrey, suddenly nervous, was uncertain of how to respond.

'The arts. Women's issues. You know.'

Jack nodded. 'You mean *Cosmopolitan* orgasms and *Elle* sex things?'

'That's the basic concept.'

'How exciting.'

'Don't take the piss out of me.'

'Audrey,' he chastised, 'I'm not taking the piss. Someone's got to write for those magazines. Better you than me.'

Audrey found herself wondering if Jack wasn't just a little bit of a jerk.

'I've got some good ideas for a feature on women's underwear,' he said, taking hold of her elbow again. 'I'll tell you all about it if you'll let me.' He smiled, he really did have a wonderful smile. His leather jacket smelt terrific. Oh fuck, thought Audrey, why else come to these parties?

13

On the way out the door Audrey thought of Shereen – she had not said good-bye. She would ring her tomorrow and they could have a laugh about it, Audrey swept away by a man.

Jack's flat had huge windows, blank polished wood floors, a white linen square on a round polished table, clothes and books all neatly hidden away. Very modern, encased within a Georgian façade. Jack shut the door and pulled Audrey close. As they kissed, he made a few jokes about underwear but when Audrey slipped off her skirt – I'm not letting him fumble with zips and buttons, she thought, I'm too old – he stopped being trite and grew serious. They got into bed and didn't fuck, but fooled around, talking, hands lingering. Audrey felt fine, just fine. Her body tingled beneath Jack's fingers. In the dim light his skin was smooth and dark. They slept. In the morning Audrey woke early, saw Jack, and felt besotted, as if during the night a spell had been cast.

Shereen did laugh when Audrey rang a few days later to apologize for disappearing. 'So who was Mr Whisk-Away?' she asked.

'Jack Campbell. American,' she added as if that would explain everything. Then, as an afterthought, 'Black.'

'Oh,' said Shereen. She paused.

'You know him?' Audrey's heart slipped lower in her breast.

'We haven't met. I know of him, you could say.'

Audrey decided not to pursue it. She gave Shereen a few of the details, rendering the encounter slightly comic. It felt important to keep Shereen entertained. 'He'll probably dump me tomorrow.'

'Oh no,' said Shereen politely, 'of course not.'

Audrey had a fleeting thought – Shereen is masking something – but she pushed it away. 'Well, I hope not. I could use a bit of male companionship.'

'Couldn't we all,' said Shereen. 'Don't make me jealous.'

Audrey's last boyfriend, Michael, had left her over the course of a weekend. It was August and unusually hot; at night everyone in the city had their windows wide open and sex was in the air, like pollen. Michael met someone else one Friday night, did not come home until late Saturday. He moved out on Sunday afternoon, after he and Audrey had had a lengthy, bitter discussion about what went wrong. Before he left Audrey had always considered herself young. The younger woman liberated her of that particular confidence.

Audrey thought she was in love with Michael; she was accustomed to his being around. Later she decided that this was what drove him away, this as well as her wrinkles. Their relationship had lost its lustre of newness, it had become comfortable, like an old armchair. Michael got up and left, suddenly, and Audrey felt bad for a while, sat upon, frayed.

James Douglas, who had begun to re-inhabit her dreams after her mother died, flickering on Audrey's bedroom wall at night like film noir, returned with greater strength after Michael dumped her. It was as though there was something about James Douglas she had not deciphered, as though he had something to tell her. He was sending her messages, oblique and personal, from another century. Audrey was a heavy sleeper; unhappiness made her nights even more leaden.

Nothing in Lanarkshire had prepared him for Fort St James, and yet it was as though he knew his way. The Hudson's Bay Company post was situated at the source of the Fraser River, the southern tip of Stuart Lake in the watery, harsh interior of the Pacific region. The land is rolling, the high, knotted stomach of the province raised between the coastal mountains and the Rockies. Stuart

Lake, Babine, Takla, Tezzeron, Chuchi, all feeding into the Fraser. Salmon come to spawn here, torn, hump-backed and spent after their journey from the mouth of the river hundreds of miles to the south. On a summer's day the dry-brown earth stretches tree to tree, tree to tree, good land for horses. At night, you hear the loon. On a winter's day, snow, the frozen lake, darkness, the northern lights, wind.

The fur trading post was islanded; outside the stockades lay dense and perpetual wilderness. Children died in infancy more often than not. Men travelled by trapper line, canoe, and horseback, 'close to civilization' meant less than one week upriver from port. The post was dependent upon trade with the native population for food as well as fur. At Fort St James, too far north for crops and vegetable cultivation, the staple winter diet was salmon, dried, candied, smoked, powdered, and the women, native wives – there were no white women – were employed in its preparation, storing it in the salmon shed.

James Douglas was a tall young man, broad-shouldered, able-limbed, and he knew well how to use his body to impress or intimidate. He saw clearly the important links that made the fur trade possible – links between the Company and the Indians. Without the indigenous people the tenuous trade network could not have existed, could not have suffered across the tundra, through the trees. The Indians supplied their skills, their knowledge, and their guidance, at a price. James was quick to recognize the importance of paying, and this bargain – all there was of western Canada at the time – suited him.

And at Stuart Lake James saw other kinds of transactions taking place. Many of the white men there in the snow, in the trees, had taken as wives women from the country *à la façon du pays* – in the custom of the land, a practice as old as the fur trade itself. At Fort St James, Hudson's Bay Company Chief Factor William Connolly was married *à la façon du pays* to Suzanne Pas de Nom, a Cree woman. They had many children. One day James's gaze came to rest on the Connolly daughter, Amelia. She was twelve years old; he was twenty-one. Amelia was not shy and she walked up to James Douglas and said, 'What is your name?'

He replied slowly, flattered by her tone, and watched her stroll away.

Amelia and James began to court, James taken with Amelia's petite and lively ways, Amelia with James's fine eyes, very dark and lustrous. They conversed in Chinook – a made-up traders' language composed of the native tongues Chinook and Nootka, English and French. They lived inside the secure wooden walls of the fort, James and the other HBC men trading with Indians who travelled from all directions bearing fur to the post. 'My little Snowbird', James called Amelia.

In winter, with little to do during the short afternoons and dark nights, the women and children often fell asleep huddled round the fire, and this was where James and Amelia did their wooing. There was little privacy but Company men were adept at ignoring each other, even in close proximity. Amelia regaled James with Cree myths that her mother had told her, and she talked to him about herself. Although she had not ventured far beyond the wooden stockades, her life held stories that were riches to James, of the forest, of the Cree. And of life in an inland trading post.

'One year, when I was a small girl, a box arrived from the distant world, England, dresses for us, the girls and women of the Company.' She spoke in a low voice, so that none of the others gathered to the fire would hear. The men were passing Company rum back and forth, caught up in their own web of tales. 'My sisters and I put on the new frocks. Oh, they were beautiful, with lace, and ribbons, and fine straight hems. We ran around and around and around the great room until we were dizzy.'

James smiled at Amelia's recollection, and went to speak, but he saw her face had darkened.

'Then Elizabeth, my youngest sister – ' Amelia paused and looked hard at James – 'she ran too near the fire. Her dress caught the flames.' She closed her mouth sharply, as though to swallow the words. 'She was wrapped in a rug and rushed outside and rolled in the snow, but it was too late. She died. Elizabeth died.'

James's heart stopped at her words, and his own sorrows bullied up behind him. He pulled her close. Amelia told James she was not fire-shy, she could not be. 'Sometimes even now when I look into the flames I see my sister there.'

Amelia asked James to tell his own tale but he said that as far as he was concerned his life had begun with his voyage to the new country. He had come west to leave those stories behind. Amelia did not find this peculiar – his life in Scotland and before was beyond her reckoning.

They waited until she was sixteen before they married *à la façon du pays*, witnessed by Amelia's parents and other traders and Indians at the fort. The ceremony itself was very simple, more Cree than HBC. James did not hesitate over his 'country marriage'; he did not pause at the threshold thinking of another, better, union he might make elsewhere. He had left Scotland intending to stay away. He knew his father had not wed his mother, he knew that she had been left behind for another, more favoured, marriage, and James despised his father for this. He felt no dubiety.

Amelia was very young but she recognized in James a certain steel-eyed determination that she knew she could match. She had grown up in this cross-bred world, a place struck at the brink of modernity. Hers was a moment of great flux and change, for her mother's people, her father's Company. She and James would make a new world and live in it. Their marriage was utopian, ecstatic and timely.

Two years on her own after the break-up with Michael –

hardly a lifetime – Audrey had not given up on the idea of men but she hadn't done anything about meeting any either. Jack Campbell was a surprise, a bonus, like winning the lottery without buying a ticket. She couldn't quite believe he existed.

Jack worked in television which was good news – as the song goes, you've got to have a j-o-b if you're gonna be-with-me – and bad news: he worked long hours and was away a lot. He was a producer, part of a medium-sized independent company called Eye to Eye. Jack produced nature programmes, and dabbled in documentaries and drama.

'I like making deals,' he told Audrey the next time they met, several nights after they had first gone home together.

'Deals?'

'Finding money, putting together co-commissions, matching directors to projects . . . it's the producer who's really in charge and I like that.'

'Sounds good,' said Audrey. She didn't want to ask too many questions; she wanted to appear interested – she was interested – without turning their date into Interview With a Boyfriend. He was intelligent, she thought he was sexy, he seemed to like her too. That was enough; that was a good start. They could proceed.

After eating they went back to his flat. Jack peeled off Audrey's clothes while Verdi's *Un Ballo in Maschera* played. She couldn't help thinking that opera suited the flat, and wondered if an interior designer had chosen the CDs too, then reprimanded herself for such bitchiness. Jack left Audrey in the middle of the room while he took off his own clothes, and then he stood behind her, his fingers light upon her skin. Audrey had had her hair cut short recently, close around her ears and slightly longer on top, a little butch, but she liked it. 'Your neck's so long,' Jack murmured. Audrey had goosebumps, she suppressed a shiver. He ran his fingers down her back. She felt examined, scrutinized, and was excited by that. He pulled her to him and she felt his body, very warm, hard and soft, the sharp smell of the day upon him. She started to speak, thinking of HIV tests, wondering if he could match her three, then cleared her throat and stopped. Shut up, Audrey, shut up, she thought. Jack touched her breasts. They moved onto his white sheets. He had a box of condoms in the drawer beside his bed. They would have safe sex. Two questions flashed through Audrey's mind: 1. A box of condoms, does he fuck a lot of girls? 2. A box of condoms, did he buy those just for me?

The next day, after she'd gone home and put the night away with several cups of coffee, Audrey's phone rang. 'Let's meet,' said Shereen. They arranged to have a drink.

'Tell me about Jack,' she demanded once they found a table. They were in a groovy bar that was full of groovy people.

'He's sweet.'

'He doesn't look sweet.'

'No?' asked Audrey. 'Well, I don't know, we've only just met. I like him so far. I'll keep you posted.'

'What's he do?'

'He's a television producer.'

'Can't be too many black producers in London. And American to boot.'

'No,' said Audrey. 'I suppose not.'

They had another beer. Audrey admired Shereen's shoes.

'Do you like being a journalist?' said Shereen.

'It's okay. I've got my patch. I'm well enough established that if I keep having ideas for stories I'll be all right.'

'Why do you write about . . .' Shereen made a slight pause, '. . . the things that you do?'

'What do you mean?'

'Well, since we met I've been watching for your name. I

read a lot of newspapers and magazines, I'm a print junkie. Why do you write about race so often?'

'Race?' Audrey repeated as though unfamiliar with the word. She blushed. 'Colour?' she said, although she didn't like the sound of that either. 'I don't know. You thought that? I'm embarrassed. I've never been asked that before.'

'Haven't you?' said Shereen. 'I don't object, I'm just curious.'

'That's okay.' Audrey felt unable to answer. 'I don't know.' Her brain was empty. 'These things interest me. It's that intersection of cultures that London provides . . . The magazines love it, it's easy to sell, "Inter-racial love", "Inter-racial sex", "Inter-racial parenting". For white readers it's like going on a cultural safari, isn't it? An experimental tour. Editors especially like anything they think is exotic or strange. There aren't enough black journalists? It's easy to sell. I think I write responsibly. It's – I don't know.'

'But how did you come to it, how did you come to make that your area?'

'It's not *my* area,' replied Audrey, feeling slightly defensive. 'I write about a lot of more general issues as well, and I write about the arts too. Haven't you seen any of those pieces?'

'I suppose – but it's the others that stick in my mind. Like the one you interviewed me for.'

Audrey shrugged and spread her hands, hoping to deflect what she wasn't sure was a criticism. 'I've got to make a living somehow.'

Shereen seemed happy enough with that for the moment but Audrey felt she had been coy, dishonest even. There was more to her choice of subject-matter but it was difficult to explain. The two women talked about other things, the high street law firm where Shereen practised. She looked depressed when Audrey mentioned conveyancing.

Later Audrey felt a little drunk. She lit a cigarette and returned to Shereen's original question. 'White people who are interested in racial politics are regarded as weird, voyeurs, cultural interlopers. Aren't they?'

'By whom?'

'Black people. White people . . .'

'I wouldn't know,' Shereen interrupted. 'I'm not an expert.'

Audrey ignored the rebuke and ploughed ahead. 'I'm interested in . . . difference. The English invented foreigners, it's a national obsession. And yet, we're expected to stay in our own corners, aren't we?'

Shereen gave a polite nod and Audrey let the conversation veer away to other things.

★

Audrey spent her adolescence beside the sea on a rural patch of housing on its way to becoming a suburb, twenty miles outside Victoria, BC. In England she once met a woman who, when she said she came from British Columbia, commented, 'You speak very good English for a South American.' Downtown – cinemas, hippie shops, coffee bars, tourists, Chinese restaurants – is a fifty-minute drive along roads that, to begin with, are closed in by the forest.

The northern sea has a kind of melancholy to it, the Pacific so grey and unhappy, foghorns lamenting endlessly. That was part of what Audrey couldn't stand as a teenager. Her parents had friends who lived up island in a place called Desolation Sound, the mood of most of the west coast in winter. Sometimes, Audrey thought, it felt as though the sea muffled everything, it numbs you, it reduces you to nothing with its endless tides, pounding your heart like a pebble on the beach, smoothing you into shape. Walking on the beach always made her feel depressed, the sky dark and low, the shore lined with piles of silvery wood, flotsam from distant log booms. Audrey used to identify with the driftwood. She longed for the big wide world out there, she was waiting to put an ocean between herself and that place.

And then Audrey got to know Jane and things improved a little. They made friends in grade twelve, the last year of high school. Jane was part of the in-crowd, cool, cars, weekend jobs, sex, dope, alcohol and cigarettes. Audrey was school smart, part of the good student university-bound crowd – not complete nerds and rejects, but not universally admired either. Jane was beautiful, sloe-eyed with long, loose curly hair; she had one of those slinky, curvy, shocking bodies that some girls manage to acquire. She looked amazing in her pink cardigan and her faded baby-blue jeans, enigmatic, sophisticated, intelligent but bored. To boys their own age she must have seemed completely unattainable and, in fact, she did have an older boyfriend who had gone off to Mexico or somewhere.

They became best friends, surprising everyone, themselves included, escaping their tight cliques and joining forces, like members of warring tribes gone AWOL. They started sitting together in class, catching each other's eye, laughing. Suddenly they were talking together at lunch, after school. It was like falling in love, which Audrey had never done. They began to share secrets, there was an enormous amount of vital information that neither had ever told anyone else. Audrey learned to drive and she took her mother's car to pick up Jane, out to Metchosin, navigating the dark road as it bent through the trees. They'd go downtown on Friday nights, lights getting brighter as they drew near to the city, choosing a bar where they thought the management would let them drink without questioning their age, still under the legal minimum. Audrey used to think she would be allowed in anywhere with Jane; she had the kind of looks that encourage men to drink.

They'd get paralytic, brushing off barflies with mixed success, making confessions, telling jokes. Then Audrey would drive home again, both of them either depressed and maudlin, the world's weight unbearable, or singing loudly along with the radio, unconquerable, weaving back and forth on the empty roads. Audrey's parents must have guessed at what they did, her mother's car arriving home smelling of beer, vomit even, but Audrey imagined she was keeping it all from them, her secret life. She and Jane drank more and more, smoked dope when they could get it. There weren't any other drugs around but if there had been they would have used them.

Jane brought out a kind of reckless wildthing in Audrey, a side of herself she had not known existed. She discovered it was good to be bad. Suddenly desperate to be adult, to do grown-up, dangerous things, she abandoned the studious girl with spectacles firmly wedged behind a pile of textbooks.

From the outside, it was hard to see what they found in each other. Jane was smarter than anyone had ever given her credit for and Audrey acknowledged that. When they became friends Audrey felt as though she had come to life, as though she had lain dormant until then. It was a true friendship, teenage, confessional, full of experiment, revelatory and dramatic. Not to be repeated, as lost to the adult world as childhood itself.

*

Jack and Audrey looked good together, tall and North American, black and white. On the street, in the city, people mistook them for tourists, obscuring the fact that they had both been in London for years. 'I pay my taxes,' was her usual retort, but Audrey didn't mind being taken for a visitor when she was with Jack. She liked the picture they made together. He made her feel a tourist in her own life somehow, an illusion she enjoyed. And besides, she was an alien in many ways; the flip-side of being perpetually foreign was that Britain's problems were never her own.

Audrey had not slept with an American before – somehow, she mused, I missed out on that particular nationality. But Jack was like her, his American-ness dulled by his years away. Sometimes Audrey thought her own sense of herself as Canadian had become anglicized, romanticized. She could become Ur-Canadian when the need arose, displaying national characteristics like a performing dog. Yes, I can ski, I can paddle a canoe, I speak French badly, 'oot and aboot', I adore ice hockey. Jack could do his American thing, his African-American thing, but, for the most part, he did not. He enjoyed confounding expectations. English people wanted him to be West Indian and, when he was not, they didn't know what to do.

Audrey's female friends were suspicious of Jack for reasons she pretended to find difficult to understand. She knew that beneath their talk lay a mistrust of his being American. And the fact that he was single – there had to be something wrong with him, there were no single men. And the inter-racial business – some of her friends, white and black, felt uneasy about that, although few of them would admit it. Audrey wasn't completely sure what to think of it herself. When she was younger, she'd gone out with a few black guys, although never for long, never more than a couple of weeks, a month. She had gone out with all kinds of men. But she was excited about Jack, and she didn't think it was just because he was black, although she admitted to herself now that that – his skin against hers, their flesh together – turned her on. 'It's the kiddies I worry about,' she could hear her father saying. Well, there are no kiddies, there would be no kiddies, and anyway, what if there were? Her mother wouldn't have liked it either, Audrey couldn't fool herself there. But none of that mattered – Audrey had lived without her parents and their opinions for a long time. Besides, they were wrong.

Audrey tried to defend Jack against her friends and their worries, despite the fact that, as yet, she had not gone beyond besottedness. In the cold hard light of the afternoon, she saw he was a stranger. She was getting to know him. But it was not easy. He kept himself hidden, using first impressions as a kind of shield: I am like this, there is nothing else.

'I like things simple,' he said one Saturday afternoon.

'Hmm?' replied Audrey, reading the paper. They were sitting in a café and outside the sun shone weakly.

'I don't like things to be complicated.'

'Things are complicated—' Audrey almost added 'sweetheart'. She had not tried out any endearments on him yet and thought this not the right moment.

'I don't like it when things get fucked up and complex.'

'Okay.' Audrey didn't know what to say. 'Neither do I.'

'All right, then,' he said, and went back to his paper.

Audrey tried to return to the paper as well, but could not. What did he mean? Was he saying he didn't like to get too involved? Or was he saying he liked to be sure of things, that he wanted commitment, contracts? Audrey suspected it was the former, but she didn't ask. They would get to that eventually, no use rushing it. They could have that discussion some other time.

'He's a bounder,' Gina said. Gina was Audrey's oldest friend in London. Other friends had disappeared, propelled by underground trains to distant parts of the city, never seen again, new ones in their place. Gina was English, a Londoner – yes, really, but not really – her father was Irish, her mother English. Her parents had divorced long ago, but their uneasy alliance was calm

26

within Gina; she liked to say she was all things, they were all her people, 'my people', Catholic and Protestant Kilburn Irish and the jelly-faced Englishman who was Chancellor of the Exchequer, 'although I wouldn't vote for him'. Gina did not vote for anyone, she had lost her right to vote in the poll tax fracas and never bothered to get it back. Now she was married and respectable, working in health-care management, one child. She and Audrey saw less of each other, but they used the telephone, their fax machines, and e-mail to communicate. Jack's race was not an issue with Gina, but she had found other reasons to complain.

'A what?' Audrey adjusted the phone against her shoulder.

'A bounder. I know all about this kind of bloke and believe me, Audrey, he's no good.'

'But you've never met him.'

'Yes I have, at a dinner party at what's-her-name's, Miranda Johnson, two, three years ago.'

'Really?'

'Yes, and even then I thought this man is bad. He's so flirtatious! It will drive you crazy.'

Audrey cut off Gina before her friend could give her advice. She did not want advice about Jack.

When they met in a pub a couple of nights later the first thing Gina said was, 'He's too handsome for you.'

'What?' Audrey felt appalled. She turned away and studied the wallpaper, a print of shelves crowded with leather-bound books; the complete works of Dickens followed the complete works of Hardy followed the complete works of Shakespeare in an endless repeat. No wonder she didn't like pubs any more.

'He's just . . . well, be careful Aud. He's not to be trusted.'

Again Audrey steered the conversation away.

On the way home she thought about what Gina had said. Did the whole world know something she did not? Did

Jack Campbell have 'Heart-breaker' tattooed on his forehead, had she somehow managed to miss the clues? Not that she had ever been all that adept at interpreting signals in the past; she was frequently amazed by the unexpected, unexplained things that happened. The death of her mother five years earlier had confirmed it. She felt as though she had spent her life murmuring I can't believe it, I can't believe he/she/they/you did what you did.

The next time she saw Jack she tried to sound casual. 'What did you say your last girlfriend's name was?'

'I didn't.'

'Hmm?' Audrey smiled sweetly.

'I didn't say. We haven't talked about my last girlfriend.' Jack pushed his chair away from the table and leaned back, lifting the front legs off the floor. Audrey noticed this made it impossible for the waiters to get past. They were in a restaurant where the tables were glass-topped so that between courses you could examine each other's knees. 'You must be confusing me with one of your other boyfriends,' Jack said.

Audrey could feel her blush rising. 'Well, who was your last girlfriend then?' She had blundered into this.

He brought his chair back down to the floor and edged forward so their knees were touching. 'You've never met her, I'm sure.' He kept his voice low. Jack was calm, Audrey was not.

'You never know.'

'We will not discuss this,' he said firmly, taking her hand.

'No,' said Audrey, after a pause. 'I guess not.' She felt a little baffled by his – what was it? discretion? paranoia? obstreperousness? – and wondered if he had something to hide. A string of girlfriend suicides, a battery of angry hens? Was this what he meant by 'keeping things simple'? Audrey did not try any harder, did not push him, but she felt cheated. She had always enjoyed that process of 'I'll-tell-you-about-mine-if-you-tell-me-about-yours in new relationships. Perhaps he was right to refuse to disclose and exchange these stories. Their lists of failures were bound to be tellingly long. Besides, she had stories of her own that she would never tell; that is the advantage of living away from where you come from, there is no one to remind you who you are.

Audrey liked her freelance life – she never had problems with ideas for articles, she always had dozens stacked up, waiting to be trotted out to her editorial contacts. She had been offered a column in a women's magazine a few years back, but she had turned it down; she could not bear the thought of churning out opinions every month, despite the fact that a regular gig would help stabilize her erratic income. She had no opinions, things changed so quickly, opinions were for the opinionated, there was always another side to the story. She preferred flux. In work, if nowhere else in her life.

On Friday evening at his flat – already they'd got into the habit of nearly always going to his place – Jack asked Audrey what she had done that day. She told him: finished a feature, faxed it off, secured two new commissions, had lunch with the deputy editor of a Sunday colour supplement whom she had known for a long time, sucked up to two other editors over the phone. Had a bath, ironed her dress, and taken the bus to his place.

Jack's list of accomplishments was just as long; he had had four meetings, signed two new contracts, dealt with his assistant's personal crisis, slipped out to Marks and Spencers to buy some new socks, and had lunch with one of his partners. 'And I have to work tomorrow.'

'Really? On Saturday?' Audrey had hoped they might spend the day together.

Jack nodded.

'Are you free on Sunday?'

He refilled their glasses and sat back, stretching his arms

over his head. 'Nope. Got to work then too.' Jack looked away and the fine taut lines of his throat and neck became apparent.

Audrey kicked off her shoes and brought her feet up onto the couch, slipping them between the cushions. For a moment, looking at Jack, she found it difficult to think straight, his face compelled her so. She thought him incredibly attractive, every moment she spent with him underscored this. She wanted to kiss him. She restrained herself. 'Sunday?'

He nodded. 'You will find that my work always comes first.'

She laughed uncomfortably, thinking about what he had just said. Jack wasn't laughing. You will find that my works always comes first. Always.

'Oh yes,' said Audrey, 'so does mine.' Didn't it? Where would she be without her work? She thought of her father, on his own in Victoria, hadn't his work always come first? She felt unhappy.

They sat in silence. Jack reached over to pull her closer, lessening the distance between them. 'But when I'm not at the office I'm going to devote myself to giving you sexual pleasure,' he said, 'My Life's Other Work.'

Audrey let herself be kissed. That was, after all, what she wanted.

When Gina invited Audrey and Jack to dinner Audrey figured she was trying to make amends for all she had said the other evening. Jack was not keen – 'I'm going out with you, not your friends,' he complained – but he acquiesced eventually. Audrey did not mention that Gina had called him a bounder. She wanted him to have a chance to prove himself, even if he was unaware of this challenge.

They arrived on the dot of eight. Gina wasn't ready, still putting the baby to bed. Bob was in chaos in the kitchen, surrounded by bowls and pots, piles of dirty laundry.

Audrey and Jack sat alone in the sitting room with their drinks.

The evening passed awkwardly. Jack didn't say much; he was not responsive when Audrey tried to include him in the conversation nor when Gina asked him pointed, inquisitive questions which Audrey thought a little too nosy. When Gina reminded him they had met once before, he said he had no recollection of that evening. At around half past ten he yawned openly. Audrey was mortified, but the others didn't notice. They left shortly after that.

In Jack's car on the way back to his flat, she did not speak.

'You're too English, Audrey,' he said after they had driven around Regent's Park, 'liable to freeze with embarrassment.'

'What?'

'You're too concerned with what other people think.'

'I don't like to be rude,' she paused, dampening down her anger. 'They're my friends.'

'I wasn't rude, I just don't know them.'

'Well, you certainly don't seem interested in getting to know them either.'

'I'm not,' he said shrugging. 'I'm too old for this.'

'What?'

'The business. You start seeing someone, it's nice, you have a good time, sex, talking – I'm interested in you, not your friends.'

'But they're part of my life.'

'Not the part that I'm concerned with.' He put his hand on her thigh. She clamped her knees together, regretting the move as soon as she had made it. He put his hand back on the gear stick.

Audrey rang Gina the next day. 'He seemed nice,' Gina said blandly.

'Did you think so?' she asked, surprised.

'Sure. A bit reserved maybe. Different from how I

remember. Quiet. But he doesn't know us.'

'No. Nice meal.'

'We were all tired.'

2

This story has been harped in variations by almost as many authors as have given us gunpowder plots.

H. H. Bancroft,
History of the North-West

Dear Audrey Robbins,

I was given your address by Carol Lumbank at the Canadian High Commission in London. She suggested you might be available, on a freelance basis, to conduct some research for me in the British Library. Although I am unable to travel to Britain myself, I have been granted a travel bursary by the Social Sciences and Humanities Research Council and they have agreed to allow me to use it to hire someone like yourself. The tasks required of you would be simple – I will send lists of books, articles and documents I want to see, the researcher will photocopy the information, then post it to me. I realize that, in our age of computers, this system might seem antiquated, but I prefer to work with hard copy, and – correct me if I'm wrong – the new technology has not filtered through to the deepest of the deep stacks of the British Library.

I will pay by the hour for your time, and reimburse your expenses.

I look forward to hearing from you.

Yours,
Professor Shula Cronin,
Dept of Social Anthropology,
University of Toronto

Audrey read the letter over breakfast. She had met Carol Lumbank in London on many occasions, at Canadian High Commission cultural events. Over the years Audrey had interviewed a number of Canadian writers and film-makers; she had given chocolates to Alice Munro, and roses – big, thorny red roses, roses to make you bleed – to David Cronenberg. But she grew weary of being pigeon-holed by her expertise – publishers sent only books by Canadians, film interview commissions had been offered only for Canadian films – and had lowered the Canadian content of her journalism during the past few years. Now she did race things, sex things. Those pigeon-holes were more exciting.

But Professor Shula Cronin and her offer: Audrey liked the idea of being paid to wander around the library, and she wouldn't say no to a bit of extra income. Payment by the hour, expenses reimbursed, it sounded as though Shula Cronin wanted to hire a private eye; Audrey had always fancied herself a private dick, and what was academic research if not a kind of detective fiction? She rang Carol Lumbank, who apologized for giving out Audrey's address without first asking.

'I hope you don't mind – I thought of you, or at least thought that you might know someone who could do that kind of work. Has she been in touch?'

'Yes she has. Who is she – what's she like?'

'Like? Well, she's older, at least sixty I'd say, perhaps sixty-five. Very distinguished. Had a struggle with cancer – breast cancer I think – a few years back. And an unfortunate . . .' Carol paused, 'mishap over one of her books around the same time.'

'Oh?'

'She wrote a book about Haida mythology – a good book by some accounts. I haven't read it. But it transpired – or so it came out – that at the beginning of her career she taught in a residential school in northern BC for a few years. Before she went on to university. Way back in the dark ages, after the war.'

Residential schools, Audrey hadn't thought about residential schools in years. At the end of the last century the government had established Christian missionary schools for native children throughout the west. Because of the initial failure of efforts to convert and assimilate the Indians, many schools became residential. Children were taken from their parents, their families. They were sent to board hundreds of miles away, kept separate from their communities for years at a time. At school, they were not allowed to speak their own languages, and were punished severely – beaten, whipped and worse – if caught doing so. Their traditions were outlawed as well, dismissed as savage. Family and tribal structures were decimated. The policy was considered enlightened and progressive right up into the sixties, before it became unfashionable with the boards of education, the Ministry of Indian Affairs.

In the intervening years, it had gradually been discovered that, within the schools, sexual abuse of the children was endemic. The perpetrators were their teachers, most of whom were missionaries, priests and nuns. The legacy of the residential schools was still keenly felt, a source of great sorrow, pain and bitterness for First Nations people. Audrey could remember the old school near where she grew up. Even then, windows boarded, abandoned, it had been a scary place.

'This connection to those wretched institutions destroyed her credibility,' Carol said, 'even though she had been there as a novice teacher, not a missionary, for less than one year. It was very unfortunate – she got tied up in the whole "authenticity of voice" debate and made some enemies when she said she believed that writers must be free to write about whatever they please – that history is not the property of any one group.'

'Oh,' said Audrey. She had been away from Canada a long time. Politics changed.

'There's a school of thought that believes that white writers have ripped off native myths and stories for so many years that that material should be the preserve of indigenous writers alone now.'

'Oh,' said Audrey again.

'Yes, well, she's a little cantankerous, but quite brilliant, and as an anthropologist she does valuable – if currently unconventional – work. I think you'd like her.'

So, without knowing the topic of research the academic was pursuing, Audrey wrote back and said she'd be willing to help.

That Saturday afternoon Shereen came round to Audrey's flat. They did not live far apart, considering the sprawling distances of London, and this was part of what drew them together. Shereen propped up her umbrella in the hallway. 'You would think it hadn't rained for months,' she said. It had rained every day that week. She took off her coat and sat down while Audrey made tea.

'This is a nice flat.'

'It's okay,' said Audrey. 'I can afford it.' The flat was one of four in a large Victorian terraced house. 'The conversion's a little bit shoddy.' Audrey looked around. She liked her flat, simply because it was hers. 'I'm fond of it, even though it's got no soundproofing and when the people upstairs walk across the room the whole house shakes.'

Shereen was forthright with her questions. It was as though she had decided that they were going to be friends and that there were certain things they needed to know about each other. They had begun the process of excavating their pasts, scraping gently, blowing sand away. Audrey found her approach charming, her lawyer-ish exposition of the facts of her own life, her precisely worded queries about Audrey's. Much easier than with Jack.

Shereen told Audrey she was born in Calcutta into a Brahmin family of successful print-works owners. From the beginning, her mother, Lakshmi, 'had been determined that her only daughter's life would be as different from her own as possible', she said, smiling. 'There was a vogue for Western names amongst Bengalis at the time, but my mother insisted on going one step further and gave me a Persian name.' At sixteen, Shereen was sent to an expensive girls' school in London. Lakshmi held a faith in British education that was unshakeable, rooted in novels and plays, if not reality. Her husband did not object; he indulged his wife and daughter and had two sons to keep him busy.

The prospect of living in London filled Shereen with glee. Lakshmi bought a house in south Hampstead and enrolled her daughter in school. Mother and daughter lived together, Lakshmi doing all the cooking for the first time in her life, endless rounds of meals with the expatriate Indian community. Back in Calcutta that summer, Shereen planned her next onslaught on the city. Her father was ill and Lakshmi, after much hesitation, decided to send the girl back on her own – she would follow once he was better. She arranged for cousins to move into the house.

The cousins did not materialize and for those months Shereen lived on her own in London, sweet seventeen. 'This was my real Western baptism,' she told Audrey. It was the 1970s and the house jumped with punk and Bob Marley, her friends in the kitchen dyeing their clothes black in Lakshmi's washing machine. After two months, Shereen swept the debris under the carpet, Lakshmi returned, and their lives continued as before.

'I made the transition from Calcutta to London as though I had taken a bus from one street to the next,' she said. 'I held my breath and slipped into the stream like a fish, like a mermaid. Some people are good at jumping cultures; Lakshmi gave me faith in myself.' The chosen school was famous for the diversity of its students and Shereen fitted right in. '"I am an English girl now," I used to think sometimes, in my bed, at night. Of course, I was not.'

Shereen's academic career went from strength to strength – law school, articles in a big company in the City, a place in a lucrative high street firm, a partnership. Her mother saw how at home her daughter had become in England, at home in a way she herself would never be. She said she missed the light on the Hooghly, the sun on the wet reds, oranges, and yellows of the women's saris as they made ritual ablutions on Shivaratri. Lakshmi returned to Calcutta, leaving Shereen to stay. Their paths diverged, and the next time Shereen went to India she felt anglicized and Western, cut off from her family. She hurried back to England, shaking the dust of India from her feet.

Since then the family's fortunes had faded, the printing business had suffered closures, lay-offs. The last time Shereen visited Calcutta her mother had had a change of heart. '"It's time for you to come home," Lakshmi said to me. "It's time for you to marry, settle down. We can arrange something nice – someone nice – for you Shereen."' I was so surprised by this suggestion that I dismissed it out of hand.' Shereen thought her mother must be tired, feeling sentimental for some reason. Going back to Calcutta had never occurred to her as a possibility. After all these years London was her home. Shereen repeated the sentence as though to reassure herself. 'London is my home.'

'My mother thinks she has to keep me Bengali,' she continued. 'She doesn't realize that despite the veneer,' her gesture encompassed her hair, her short dress, her shoes with their neat Cuban heels, 'there isn't anything else I could possibly be.'

Later in the afternoon, Audrey mixed drinks, Whisky

Sours. She liked highballs, they reminded her of the cocktail parties her parents used to give in the sixties, glacé cherries or green pimento olives in the drinks, her mother's hors d'œuvres, smoked oysters on toothpicks, and pieces of celery filled with Cheese Whizz, the height of sophistication.

Shereen's loquacity provided Audrey with a strange release after Jack's evasive silences. 'When I left Canada,' she said, 'I thought things would be better – different – in London. I wanted to get away from my family, from people who thought they knew who I was.'

'To grow up,' said Shereen, nodding.

'To be anonymous. In the city. I wanted to live somewhere where I wouldn't know my neighbours.' This was the wisdom that Audrey was accustomed to displaying when asked why she had come to London, and as she said the words this time she thought of Jack, of urbanity and the hidden past, and wondered for a moment if, in fact, she still wanted these things.

Shereen asked about Audrey's own family, and Audrey gave her the facts, only child, working father, housewife mother, the mountains of her early childhood, the move to Vancouver Island – 'the North American trajectory – west. But I confounded them. I left. Went east, as far east as I could get.'

'And your parents?'

'Parent. My mother's dead.' Audrey had a facial movement that accompanied these words; without thinking she lowered her eyes, made her lips thin and moved her head backwards, as though knocking back tears. This silenced further questions on the subject. She had never actually told anyone how her mother had died, although she repeated the story over and over to herself, an irreligious hymn of disbelief. He drove into her. He ran her down. He was meant to be picking her up. 'I'm not really involved with my father any more,' she said, 'he's sort of out of the picture.'

'So tell me more about Jack,' Shereen said tactfully. 'What does he want?'

'Jack?'

'How's it going?'

'Well, I like him. He's nice to me. What's there to say?' Audrey shrugged and smiled. 'It's an affair, it's wonderful. Sex. Food. Wine. Conversation. There's nothing out of the ordinary about that.'

Shereen nodded. 'I've always wondered if he—'

The doorbell rang, Shereen stopped speaking. The winter afternoon had grown very dark and it was still pouring. Jack stood on the threshold, soaked by the walk from his car. 'Come in,' Audrey said. 'My God, you poor thing.'

Jack followed Audrey into her flat. 'I was just passing by and I thought I'd drop in, thought perhaps we could start the evening a little early.' He put one hand on her hip, she turned to kiss his slick cheek. A knot of anticipation formed in her stomach. She had been looking forward to seeing him.

In the kitchen Audrey made introductions. Jack was without a coat and his sweater was saturated. He took it off and Audrey went to hang it in the bathroom and fetch a towel. 'Here,' she said, giving him her drink, 'have mine.'

Jack sat beside the radiator and slowly dried his hair. His shirt was also wet, it stuck to his body. His skin looked soft and clean, his dripping hair even blacker than when dry. His trousers were soaked and they clung to him as well. Both women stared. There was a moment of silence. Audrey wished Shereen would leave so that Jack could take off all his clothes. But Shereen continued to sip her drink and look at Jack, amused. 'Do you always make such spectacular entrances?' she asked.

He laughed, enjoying their attention.

★

David lived in a cottage on the beach further out along the coast where Audrey grew up, further out along through the drowning rain. It was easy to find the entrance to the gravel road to his cottage – trees, collapsing wooden fence, no houses visible, an old 'No Trespassing' sign, postboxes. Down the lane to his house there were no lights, at night all was darkness. The cottage faced across the strait, nothing between the windowpane and, in the distance, the foggy mountains of the Olympic Peninsula, the northernmost tip of Washington State. On clear nights they could see the lights of Port Angeles, hidden most of the time by clouds and smoke from the sawmills still functioning over there. Audrey had always resented the fact that the sea view from Victoria was of the US – American mountains weren't good enough for her, Canadian mountains were higher, better.

The cottage was small, sunk into the mossy sands. Inside it smelt damp, slightly salty, the faint whiff of a large wet dog somewhere. It was bigger than it looked from the outside; there was the sitting room, the bedroom, the little kitchen, the bathroom with its old claw-foot tub. The first thing Audrey noticed was that there was no television. This seemed extraordinary, somehow ennobling. David said he worried that having a TV might stop him writing. He never showed Audrey and Jane anything he had written even though they gave him their work all the time. Showing his writing, actually letting them read it – they saw the manuscript piled up beside his typewriter every time they came to visit – would have broken the unwritten rules. He was the teacher, Audrey and Jane were the students. A simple relationship.

He was a good teacher too, in his way, even though Audrey came to realize that he hated teaching, he felt it wasted his time, he had only ever wanted to do it temporarily, before making a success as a novelist. Despite this, or perhaps because of it, he managed to instil in some of his students a desire to write as well as to read. Not just Audrey and Jane, but other students as well, unlikely people. If David liked you he could make reading feel worthwhile. Audrey had never had any trouble being interested in schoolwork, she was always able to do well. But Jane was different and Audrey could see, even then, the effect his casual enthusiasm had on her.

Audrey could not remember how, why, or when the relationships between them all began to change. She and Jane became closer, that definitely came first. And they started to talk about David. They had schoolgirl crushes on him, although they would never have thought of themselves as schoolgirls. She could remember thinking he was very sexy, with his cowboy boots, tousled hair, and blue blue eyes. He had a clean-shaven, almost boyish face and a large, sloping smile that could make girls squirm in their seats. He smelt very male close up, cigarettes, some kind of macho aftershave, like he lived on a diet of bacon and eggs. They knew he was divorced, which made them sad, and he seem impossibly old and experienced. He was thirty.

Audrey and Jane discussed everything about him, taking his body to bits one inch at a time. They had favourite clothes that he would wear; Jane would pass Audrey a note in homeroom where they went to register every day before classes – it might say 'The Jeans!' or 'Brown Corduroy, Jesus!' They imagined what he would look like without those trousers, or at least Audrey tried to, never having seen a man naked. Some days they would get over-excited, passing notes in a frenzy. They would sneak outside between classes, walk down to the far end of the playing field to smoke cigarettes and laugh to the point of hyper-ventilation, repeating things that he had said. Jane and Audrey called him David when they thought they might be overheard, as though using his first name was a secret code. Their lives possessed great drama.

It was through schoolwork that they got to know him a little better, a little differently than other teachers. They were in his story-writing and poetry class; that was why he began recommending books to them. It was like every reactionary parent's nightmare come true, little Audrey and Jane read Kurt Vonnegut, the next day they wake up debauched. First they laughed about him and then it became more serious. And eventually they ended up at his cottage late at night. He invited them when they lingered in his room after class one day, talking, flirting. He made it sound as though he invited students over all the time. They went as soon as they could arrange it.

After that Audrey and Jane really did have a secret, something that separated them from the rest of their classmates. They had been to a teacher's house, at night. They had seen him being human, out from behind the desk. They had talked to him without the mediation of the school's authority. They had turned the tables on what these relationships were meant to be. It was very exciting. Because of David, Audrey read Camus, Sartre, de Beauvoir, Kerouac, Joyce, Dostoevsky, Kafka, Eliot, Pound, even Gertrude Stein; she began to devour books whole, three at a time. *The Great Gatsby*, the green light at the end of the pier; *The Good Soldier* and its taut portrait of adult despair. David read poems out loud to them in front of the fire. Leonard Cohen, Sylvia Plath, Dylan Thomas, all the great sadsacks. Jane and Audrey were both dead keen on that kind of thing. In fact, Audrey thinks now from the safety of London, we are lucky we didn't top ourselves in some tragic act of female adolescent self-immolation. Jane sacrificed herself to David instead. And I left, I put six thousand miles between them and me.

In school David held himself aloof. He had to. It was their big secret, the three of them. No one else knew what was going on, although they speculated, especially Audrey's old friends, the ones she'd hung out with before Jane.

To them it must have seemed very odd. Audrey underwent a kind of metamorphosis, from the straight, bookish girl they had always known to this new girl, occasionally drunk, even stoned, in class. Half a pint of rum in a bottle of Coke down at the far end of the playing field, a joint rolled by somebody's brother. Once or twice her old girlfriends came right out and asked Audrey what was going on, but she would just smile. At last she had what she had always wanted, a bit of mystery.

★

'How do you know her?' Jack asked Audrey once Shereen had departed. They'd finished their cocktails, his hair was dry.

'We met at that party. You know, the same one where you and I met.'

'I didn't see her there.'

'Well, she was.'

Jack's clothes had dried as well, stiff against the radiator. 'She's lovely, isn't she?' he said.

He's just making an observation. Audrey adjusted her skirt. The bitch inside me. She almost laughed.

Later that night when Audrey unbuttoned Jack's shirt they found his skin stained blue, the dye in the cotton had run in the rain. Audrey drew a bath while Jack continued to undress. He left his clothes in a pile on her bedroom floor. She watched as he came towards her; it felt like a long time since she had seen a naked man walk through her flat. She stared at the lines his hipbones made, his thighs, the tiny black curls of his pubic hair as it climbed up towards his navel. She could almost feel her expectations rise with her heart rate.

After he eased himself into the water Audrey soaped his shoulders, the dye fading without disappearing altogether, a thin sheen of blue on the steady brown, darkening his pores. His wet skin felt like rubber beneath her fingers. He slid deeper into the water. 'Cheap shirt,' Jack murmured, his eyes closed, 'shouldn't have bought it.'

While he soaked Audrey went into the bedroom and picked up his clothes. She couldn't find his underwear and then realized he had not been wearing any. She pulled herself up short, surprised by a sudden recognition of her longing for contact. They had been meeting regularly, Audrey was enjoying herself but, even so, she saw clearly her willingness to allow Jack to set the pace, make the decisions about how and on what terms they might proceed. Was she that lonely? What did she want from him? Love? Company? Audrey realized she didn't know. Did that matter?

We have things in common, she reassured herself. We like the same restaurants. We do not have gardens, we do not want gardens. We live far away from our families. We do not keep pets. We watch TV movies late at night, sleep heavily, and do not talk much in the mornings. We aren't married to other people, have never been. We have great sex. A silent incantation. See, Audrey said to herself in the mirror, this was obviously meant to be.

Jack tried to pull her into the bath with him. She resisted for a while, then let herself slide.

The next morning Audrey woke up feeling displaced. Jack left early – what was it about him that unsettled her so? She pulled up the covers and wished for a moment that she had a mother to ring. Audrey thought about her mum, and then she thought about her dad. Her father had been away on business while she was growing up. He worked for the government and travelled a lot. He bought Audrey dolls to compensate. After one trip he brought home a very big doll with blonde curly hair; it was called 'Chatty Kathy' – pull the string dangling from the small of her back and she would talk. 'Feed me,' she'd say, 'I love you,' 'Clean me,' all the most important things. Audrey took care of Kathy but Kathy's voicebox would often break and she would fall silent. And then Daddy would take her away with him, from the small town in the Rockies where they lived at the time, to the Vancouver Dolls' Hospital. And a week later they would return, hand in hand, Audrey's father and Kathy, her chatter restored. When Audrey was sick with childhood things – measles, mumps, chicken-pox, flu – she used to ask her father to take her away with him, to the Dolls' Hospital. But she always had to stay home with her mother, and she envied Kathy's journeys with her father, and sometimes broke the string intentionally.

Audrey and her father had never talked, it never occurred to either of them, Audrey in her bedroom with her records and toys, her father in pursuit of his living. One small only child late in life did not make him a family man. And now it was too late.

Sometimes when Audrey talked to Jack, she felt herself falter, lost for words, as though the string had reached the end of its run and was wound up tight around the base of her spine once again.

Audrey's first requests from Professor Cronin in Toronto were straightforward, turn-of-the-century biographies of Hudson's Bay Company officials, memoirs of British men – Scottish merchants, Cornish adventurers, men of the Church – who had travelled to Canada during the seventeenth, eighteenth and nineteenth centuries. Published diaries of politicians involved in imperial policy, copies of which the professor's own library had not managed to secure. Audrey ferreted out the book numbers in the old, leather-bound catalogues, did searches on the computer, and was able to find most of what Prof. Cronin was after. The subject matter was familiar to her from her time at the University of British Columbia. She'd spent enough hours in the British Library since then to not forever associate research with that time, but it was the subject-matter, so resolutely Canadian, that brought back memories. She wondered what would have happened if she had had better teaching, a professor like Shula Cronin maybe, perhaps then she would have stayed to finish her degree.

She filled in white request slips, returning several days later to see what had surfaced, bubbled up from the bottom of the library's oozy pond. She photocopied tables of contents for Prof. Cronin, and, where she was sure of what was needed, copied the material itself, wondering if the academic fully comprehended the expense of this method of research. Audrey made good use of her time, ordering books relevant to her own work as well, researching two or three subjects at once. At the end of a couple of weeks, she stuffed an envelope full and posted it off to Toronto.

Toronto. Audrey had an English friend who had moved there years ago, and she had been to visit him twice. She had thought it ironic, at the time, going to Canada to visit an English friend, not knowing any Canadians in the city. The first visit was for work, she had commissions for a couple of interviews and a travel piece. It was March and her ears froze, making her homesick for childhood winters, re-membering soft falls of snow and muffled quiet as she battled against the wind on Queen Street. But she had liked the city, with its trams, cafés, and marketplaces, and had returned a couple of years later. She spent that week on the back of her friend Toby's bicycle – it was summer, they had gone from outdoor swimming pool to outdoor swim-ming pool, knocking back beer to combat the heat. At that time of year, Toronto lived in the streets, and she enjoyed it, despite the fetid lake that sat at the city's feet, signs posted, 'Danger, No swimming.' Toby was happy there, already he seemed more Canadian than English. But

47

Audrey was not tempted – the city was too small and she still desired the smoky metropolis of London, colossal and embracing.

The entrance to the British Library is guarded, like the gateway to heaven, entry barred to all those except the chosen. A friend who worked for a publisher had written Audrey a letter on headed notepaper saying she was one of their authors needing access to the library for her research and Audrey had been given a pass. Still, nine years on, she expected to be rumbled every time she went in, expected to be spotted as a fraud. But she wasn't, and no one seemed to begrudge her the hours she spent leafing through mouldy novels and obscure filmographies, ordering up from the stacks whatever took her fancy. The domed Reading Room with its whispered echoes, turning pages, the coughing and snoring occupants of the green leather seats: they'd been building a new library for years but it was a Sisyphean task and would never be completed. Audrey loved the library, it was full of stories, those within the texts, those being written there and then, and the stories of the readers themselves. The library at UBC had been a modern, efficient affair, Audrey had loved it too, but not enough to stay. In the Reading Room she felt she could settle. Sometimes she wandered around trying to see what books other people had ordered: young Asian man with a pile of Genet in translation, elderly white woman surrounded by Sanskrit texts. On the first day that Audrey went in to find books for Professor Cronin, she had been out too late with Gina the night before. She laid her head down on the cool desktop, closed her eyes, and fell asleep. Soon her mind filled with stories, transmitted through the wood of the desk, up the legs, along the carpet, a mingling of old and new, well-told and undiscovered.

The day was hot and airless. As they rode through the forest James thought he could hear the pitch in the pine trees slow-dripping. Needles snapped underfoot. He was accompanied by half a dozen men, all armed with muskets. Sweat slid down his back and was trapped by the corded waistband of his heavy company-issue trousers. The smell of the horses was powerful, the trek through the bush endless.

James was still a young clerk at Fort St James, newly wed to Amelia, when Chief Factor William Connolly travelled back east on company business, leaving his son-in-law in charge of the post. This was the first time James had been placed in a position of such absolute authority, and his colleagues mocked the seriousness with which he undertook his obligations. 'Nothing ever happens on Stuart Lake,' a clerk said, laughing, when James forced a second pelt count one afternoon. 'We always get our numbers right.'

Not long after Connolly left the post, bad news reached the stockades. A messenger arrived on horseback from the nearest post, Fort George. James met him in his father-in-law's office.

'Two men have been murdered.' The man was breathless.

James asked his questions slowly. 'Where?'

'Near Fort George.'

'Who?'

'Warner and Campbell.'

James had met both the clerks on several occasions and knew one of them quite well, Robert Warner. 'What happened?'

'Robert's been having . . .' The man searched for better words. 'He has been having a . . . liaison with one of the Carrier women.'

'Yes?' This was not uncommon, even though Warner had already taken a Cree woman as his wife.

'The Carrier, Tzoelhnolle, considered the woman his own,' the young man explained. 'Tzoelhnolle sought out

Warner and,' again the messenger began to struggle for words, 'and in . . . the ensuing fight . . . killed both Warner and Campbell – Campbell had tried to intervene.'

'Of course,' said James.

'Their bodies were abandoned on the ground outside the stockade,' the messenger said. 'We didn't know. That night, the corpses were torn apart and eaten by dogs. We discovered their remains the next day.' He swallowed hard and straightened.

There had been no Indian wars in that part of the country. Trading tribes and the Hudson's Bay Company had reached a high, if officially unacknowledged, level of inter-dependency. The Carrier: so named by the white traders because, when widowed, women carried their husbands' ashes in small satchels on their backs for several years before burial. Over the years their lives had become completely intertwined, through marriage as well as trade.

James was appalled by the news. He knew Tzoelhnolle as well as Warner, in fact he had spent a considerable amount of time with the Carrier trader. But there was nothing he could do to help – he had no men to send to Fort George. He could only sit and wait for further news.

The murderer surfaced several days later at an Indian camp on Stuart Lake. James set out to look for him. He had to be seen to act swiftly.

As they moved through the trees, the HBC party was spotted by Indian scouts. News of their approach sped ahead to the camp. Tzoelhnolle's brother rushed to the tipi where his sibling lay sleeping. He took hold of his shoulders and shook him awake. 'You must go, you must flee,' he insisted. 'There is still time to escape to the coast.' Panicked, the young Carrier scrambled to find a hiding place in the tent, his courage sapped by the dreams he had had, dreams of the dead men's faces.

James and his colleagues surged through the camp.

They could sense Tzoelhnolle was still there, even though his brother claimed he had vanished. They discovered him in his tent, under a pile of beaver skin, betrayed by a slim bare foot. James's assistant threw off the beaver pelts, and in that moment, James reached out a hand to the Carrier, marking the irony that Tzoelhnolle could not be protected by their trade staple, the very reason the HBC was in this place. Cornered, and mistaking the offered hand for a threat, the Carrier sprang forward and lashed out, stabbing James in the neck with an arrow, screaming words the white men did not recognize. James stepped back, clutching his throat, and his men moved around him. The Indian fought hard, but was soon overwhelmed.

Earlier, tramping to the camp, James had felt his nerves turn to sludge at the bottom of his stomach. Now, leading his men home with their captive, he tried to gather courage, summoning up Crown and Kingdom and Company, notions that he recognized were nothing more than abstractions out there among the trees, but notions he was forced to rely on none the less. He fingered the wound in his neck which was superficial yet painful, and looked on Tzoelhnolle. He could not quite believe what had taken place in his father-in-law's absence.

James knew that his authority, the authority of the HBC in the region, was slight, and the indigenous people's superiority – in numbers, knowledge, skill, time – was substantial. If relations turned hostile, the fort would be vulnerable. But two men had died, and justice must be pursued. In the summary and efficient manner habitual to the HBC, James sentenced Tzoelhnolle to hang.

A book trolley rattled past Audrey's chair, forcing her awake. She shook her head and looked down at what she had been reading, a dry history of the Hudson's Bay Company. She tried to remember what she had been dreaming an instant earlier, but could only catch vague echoes, like implanted memories. James Douglas. The Carrier. The trees.

3

Diary entry, James Douglas

Jack and Audrey went out to a movie, walking to the nearest cinema. They held hands, swinging along the pavement quickly. The rain stopped and the air felt warmer than earlier in the day. After the film, they went out to eat.

'Do you ever think about leaving?' asked Jack. Behind him the waiters came and went but he himself was still.

'London?'

Jack nodded.

'Yes, I think about it,' Audrey said, wondering if she had ordered the right thing. 'Once or twice a week, sometimes every day, whenever anything frustrates me. But I know I won't go. I imagine I'll be stuck here for ever.'

Jack leaned back in his chair. 'Why?'

'There's nowhere else for me to go. Where could I work? All my contacts are here.'

'You have a good track record, portfolio, and you're freelance, you could work anywhere.'

'I don't know. Can't go to New York, I'd need a green card.' She paused and looked at Jack who was looking at her. His gaze made her shift in her seat. 'I don't even think about the rest of Britain, Glasgow, Manchester, some little village somewhere – I'd be too out of place, too completely foreign. British Columbia – forget it. It's beautiful, but . . .' She did not want to go back. She paused again and felt a small panic that she worked to keep off her face. 'I don't speak any other languages . . . I've made my migration. Why? Are you thinking about leaving?'

Jack shook his head, leaning to one side to allow the waiter to put a plate down in front of him. The diners' tables were too close together. The music was loud and they were surrounded by people with voices that grated and brayed. 'No. I realized a while back that I'm as at home here as I am anywhere.'

Audrey was relieved they agreed, but she didn't want to show it. 'You're even more out of place than me here, in a way.'

Jack picked up his fork. He liked to eat and he liked to eat quickly. He was able to get a lot of food onto his fork and into his mouth while remaining composed. It was like going out to eat with a tidy animal, chops licked. Sometimes Audrey thought he was going to finish before she had even started. He chewed. She waited.

'Novelty value,' he said. 'I like it here, there's a certain – fluidity. I'm too lazy to go anywhere else. Ten years is a long time to have stayed in one place.'

That night in his flat Jack pulled all the covers off the bed – they had sex there, on the naked sheets. Audrey closed her eyes, gripped the sheet with both hands, and turned her head to one side, to stop herself from dying, swooning, going too fast. When she opened her eyes she realized she could see their bodies reflected in the mirror on the door of the wardrobe. She watched while they did what they did, and that made it all the more exciting.

She left before breakfast the next morning. Sunday stretched, endlessly. Audrey had never liked Sundays. As a child she had been taken to church, as a teenager she had thrown off religion and argued with her parents, her mother especially, her father lurking in the hallway. She refused to go and stayed in bed, feeling too guilty to enjoy the victory. Now Sundays made her feel restless. She went to buy the papers, some food, milk from the miserly shop on the corner, the Pakistani woman who ran it as short-tempered as always. She had been robbed so many times she hated all her customers. The shop smelt of Alsatian, but Audrey had never seen the dog. Perhaps it had been stolen as well. Once home, she thought about doing some work, but did not. The telephone rang in the early afternoon before she had had enough time to get completely bored.

It was Gina. Audrey could hear her child in the background; Charlotte was a bossy two-year-old who liked to press the buttons on the telephone while her mummy talked. It would be one of those conversations punctuated by Charlotte cutting them off.

When she was a baby Charlotte always used to cry whenever Audrey tried to pick her up. 'Does she always make strange?' Audrey had asked.

'What?' Gina crinkled her brow, smiling.

'Does she always cry when strangers hold her?'

'No. Make strange. What a weird expression.'

'I guess it's Canadian,' Audrey said, handing over the sobbing Charlotte. 'My mother used to say when I was a baby I did it all the time.'

On the phone Gina said, 'How's the big affair?'

'Fine. How's the big marriage and family?'

Gina ignored her question. 'Listen, you remember Deb Atkins, the woman who used to work in my office? You've met around here a couple of times.'

Deb Atkins, Audrey thought, short and blonde with big tits. She had once come to a party dressed in a French maid's outfit.

'Well, apparently she had a fling with your Jack. Last year.'

'Oh.' Audrey thought she did not want to hear this. Somehow the memory of the French maid's outfit made it worse.

'Yes, he took her out to the cinema and afterwards they

55

had sex in his car on the Edgware Road!' Gina laughed sharply. 'Isn't that hilarious?'

'Why are you telling me this?' Audrey thought about the Edgware Road. It carries a lot of traffic. Not the best place for vehicular sex.

'You want to know.' Gina paused. 'That was it, they didn't go out again.'

'Why not?'

'Deb said she felt too embarrassed. It sounds kind of sordid to me.'

Audrey felt flattened. 'Thanks for telling me, Gina.'

'I just thought you would want to know.'

'Thanks.' Audrey hung up the phone and went into her bedroom. People are malicious on Sundays, she thought, misplaced religious zeal. Gina must be as bored as me. She flopped down on the unmade bed, it smelt of Jack. Deb Atkins.

After a while Audrey got up again. She went to put on a record. Something melancholy, something that would remind her of the past. Leonard Cohen, his voice unmistakable, deep, sombre and hilarious. She played this record once a year, when she was feeling really lousy. Audrey thought of her friend from high school, Jane.

> I lit a thin green candle
> to make you jealous of me
> but the room just filled up with mosquitoes
> they heard that my body was free

Leonard Cohen always made her think of her teenaged self, of Jane and David. They used to listen to him together and even then, long before his most recent comeback, Cohen's best records were old. Audrey sat down to work. British Columbia, she thought, Leonard Cohen, BC. Not just my past, it was ancient history.

★

Audrey's parents spent most of their lives in the interior of the province. 'The Interior' is what locals call the vast hinterland that lies east of the coastal mountains, as if the wilderness of British Columbia is a kind of gynaecological nightmare. The Robbins moved around a lot before they had their child, from small town to small town. There were only two highways then, five hundred miles east to west, one thousand north to south, the shape of an upside-down and drooping T. The towns scattered along these routes were founded in the late nineteenth and early twentieth century by people with high expectations of forestry and mining, of timber and gold, of the money that could be made in a new country. Names like Hope and Trail or Natal and Kimberley. But the industries died or changed shape, leaving behind dozens of abandoned little communities, Yahk, Spuzzum, Bralorne, Fernie. Some of the towns her parents had lived in no longer existed.

Audrey's father worked for the province and her parents shifted between postings, making friends, having pot-luck suppers, playing bridge along the way. By the time she was born – they were in their forties and had given up on the idea of having children – they had slowed down a little. They did not move again until she was eleven.

Audrey was born in Colindale, in the Rockies, near the Alberta border: mining and logging, the sawmill like a huge burnt badminton shuttlecock, glowing red in the dark. Her memories of early childhood are a collection of postcards, hoar frost in winter, hot sun in summer, tobogganing and skiing, swimming in deep, black lakes. Then they moved to the Metchosin Road on Vancouver Island where snow was rare, where the summers were cooler, the winters wet, skies low, endless heavy rain. Audrey felt she was being deprived of her Canadian childhood. What is the point of winter if it doesn't snow? The mild coastal climate of the island was a tremendous relief for her parents after all those years of layer upon layer of clothes, snowsuits and idiot mittens, shovelling driveways, scraping the frost off windscreens, plugging the car engine into the power point at night, going to work through white-out blizzards, Audrey's mother driving, her father walking with his arms stretched out in front of the car, trying to find his way along the road, swinging a flashlight. But Audrey felt cheated by the move, as well as traumatized by having to make new friends. She was determined never to feel at home.

The west coast is a lush and green place, everything grows quickly, the earth made soft and pliant by rain. One winter before they moved west the Robbins visited friends in Vancouver – Audrey slept in their spare bedroom in the basement. On the bookshelf there was a large plaster cast of a hand that frightened her until she covered it with her sweater. In the morning when she opened the curtains the window overhead was smeared with huge, black slugs. Roofs rot, cars rust from the damp and salty air. Sometimes in February and March it is so wet you feel you are drowning, like you have to get away just to breathe.

*

The sex was good. Jack had a way about him, an ease with his own body, a regard for hers. He did not hold himself back, the nights they spent together Audrey had only to turn towards him and he would be there, pressed up hard, ready to take big bites. He did what she asked, and sometimes she didn't have to speak. She worried that her body might not please him, but it did, and she let it happen. It happened.

Audrey was surprised by how quickly Jack Campbell became part of her life, how important he turned out to be, his body, the things he had to say. Again and again she felt as though she was embarrassing herself, that the ease with which she made the necessary compromises – did Jack make compromises? – was almost indecent. Was she that eager for the things he could give her? It was not cool, she felt she was not behaving coolly and to behave coolly had always seemed the best possible course, especially when dealing with Jack Campbell, a man so very cool-headed himself. To withhold and be withheld. But Audrey was hot, sometimes when Jack was near her vision blurred, as though a heat-haze had risen off the tarmac suddenly. She was unnerved by this. Jack was not the sort of man to encourage and enjoy such ardour. He remained level, charming – cool – and Audrey took to burying her remorseless enthusiasm in work.

But there were moments, long intervals during the day, when she couldn't make herself work. She would find herself staring out of the window, thinking about sex, Jack's body, her response. How it moved her, how it took her beyond herself, how, that having taken place between them, she could not imagine staying cool. Somehow Jack did. Audrey could not.

And yet, gradually, Audrey began to learn more about her lover. He did not like talking about himself, did not like displaying his past. But he claimed he was interested in Audrey's past, and he encouraged her to tell stories, he liked to be entertained. She could make him laugh. And, as though in a kind of elaborate, camouflaged exchange, he too revealed himself.

Slowly, Audrey amassed some facts: Jack Harding grew up in New York, Harlem. His father owned three apartment buildings, his mother had been a dancer, and, like Audrey, Jack was an only child; private school on the Upper West Side. Father's three buildings became six, then nine, then he moved into property speculation in a big way and died of a heart attack at the age of fifty when Jack was fifteen. 'My mother came from the south,' he said, gesturing vaguely. 'Widowed at forty-five.' It took a while but, Jack told Audrey, his mother 'pulled herself together'. Louise Campbell became a member of a fund-raising committee for the Museum of Modern Art and, over the years, a well-established minor collector in her own right.

'She's done a lot for young black painters in New York,' he said. 'I like having her come to stay.' Louise and her jewellery, Louise and her cashmere. 'When she arrives the first thing she does is clean the bathroom, "So I can have things my way while I'm here," she says.'

Audrey's parents had not been to visit. Her mother had spoken of the possibility with enthusiasm, they'd never seen Europe, but Audrey had not been encouraging, the places she lived were never big enough for them to stay. Her father retired while she was at university, and if they had had plans to travel to Europe, they were thwarted. At the time Audrey could not imagine having to reconcile her life in London with a visit from her parents. And now her father could not, would not, would never travel.

'When Louise is in town I can tell myself that I have a real purpose in life,' Jack said. 'I'm here for my mother to visit, I think as I clean the bathroom so that it will be nice for her to clean when she arrives.'

Audrey sipped her wine. Jack kept talking, on the subject of his mother he was clearly inspired. 'Louise was very excited when I was accepted by the Slade. A London art school – now that was glamorous, even though she was frightened about what might happen to me when I went away.'

'Frightened of what?'

'Just being away – away from my family, my friends, from what we knew. There were few black students at the college, no black staff, except the cleaners, but it was okay. I did fine but I wasn't the brightest, not the one that everyone felt excited about. They thought I would do well, maybe very well if I worked hard enough. Louise was so pleased.'

Jack stretched and then massaged the back of his neck. 'I realized I had no real talent for painting during the final-year show. In a collective show any real originality is immediately obvious – my work was not like that. And besides, I never really liked getting dirty, all that oil, charcoal and turpentine. So I stopped painting when I got my degree. I haven't painted since.'

Jack talked without looking at Audrey, leaving her unable to comment or ask questions. She held her breath for a moment; he spoke as though he intended to say these things once and once only, and at the end there would be a test.

'So I went into television,' he concluded, making it sound like a *fait accompli*. 'Television saved me.' They laughed then, even though they both knew he was serious.

He stopped talking and pulled Audrey onto his lap. He had said enough, or so it appeared. She held his face in her hands and kissed his lips gently. She was not a small woman, but his arms felt large enough. She kissed him again.

Audrey had never understood what ailed her own father. He did not like to discuss it, nor had her mother. As far as they were concerned it was a nameless, causeless, cureless condition. Something had gone wrong, something no words, no amount of medical jargon, could reach. Each time Audrey went home to visit – she went twice in the five years before her mother died – her father was that much further away, that much more beyond her reach, his focus narrowed to getting through each day, his eyes following his wife around the room. Audrey thought he behaved as though he were not her father, as though he had never had a child at all. She was an unexplained visitor, they had not been introduced. And then her mother died.

Back at Fort St James, Amelia waited for her husband to return with his search party. She listened to the other wives

61

and their whisperings about the murderer, Tzoelhnolle, and the dead man, Robert Warner. For the women at the post events of this nature were difficult to bear, their loyalties tested to the extreme. In trading life the nascent conflicts between Indians and Europeans could be negotiated, lived with, made productive, seductive even. But when conflict was fully born, both sides were torn, the Indian side most cruelly. A Carrier woman, not long at the fort, her new husband a lowly Scottish clerk prone to incomprehensible homesickness for Musselburgh, felt the news too keenly. Amelia tried to calm her, to assure her of her husband's good faith. But the woman thought only of the plight of the young Carrier, mirror, as it might, her own fate, if relations between white and native were to break down. Tzoelhnolle, was her cousin, on her mother's side, and once Amelia learned this she gave up her attempts at persuasion. The young woman fled the post when they heard of the returning party and their captive.

Late that day, the summer sun still high in the sky at ten p.m., James evoked all the sundry powers invested in him. A crude scaffold had been hurriedly built outside the gates of the fort – there were no drums, no final prayers, no crowing crowd of onlookers. Tzoelhnolle kept his face stony, tears seeping from the ridges around his eyes, and the women hid themselves away. The Musselburgh man – not yet knowing he was wifeless – drew the noose around the Carrier's neck, and James gave the order. Tzoelhnolle kicked once and was dead, urine and blood spilling onto the ground. One young clerk vomited suddenly.

James released his men who filed into the fort heavily; he had not the heart to order the body buried straight away. It was brought down as the sun set, and left to lie in the cool breeze, the same soft, living, northern breeze that James felt on his own skin.

In a fearful symmetry with the earlier murders, the body of Tzoelhnolle was stolen by wolves in the night. The animals left a bloody and incriminating trail between the woods and the fort. James steadied himself for what might come next. Who has the power here? he wondered.

Kwah, the Carrier Chief, was renowned throughout the Stuart Lake region, having established close links with the tiny numbers of Europeans then scattered throughout New Caledonia. Simon Fraser, the early navigator of the interior, had traded with Kwah for food. Now it was under Kwah's leadership that native people caught and sun-dried the thirty to forty thousand salmon needed for trade currency at the inland posts. James knew that Kwah was a powerful and valued ally and trading partner, and here in the north the HBC were dependent upon him for food. He had learned soon after his arrival that Kwah was to be treated deferentially, to be given special gifts and credit.

The Carrier swore vengeance for the death of Tzoelhnolle and the destruction of his body. At Fort St James news of this reaction was not unexpected. A posse of Carrier, led by Kwah, arrived at the post, young men, Tzoelhnolle's friends and family, heated up, steaming with anger. Kwah entered the fort unobstructed, making his way to the main house, where his party was greeted by James. He knew the Chief well, but only in the shared peace of the fur trade; he had no idea how Kwah would behave now.

The old man, for even then he was more than seventy years of age, raised his musket and ordered that James be seized. James was not armed; he advanced alone and unaided towards the great Chief. All the young Carrier raised their weapons, waiting for their orders. James could hardly breathe. 'Two of our men are dead,' he said, 'and only one of yours.' But the Carrier chief spat on the floor.

Just then, Amelia came in from the private quarters where she had been hiding with the other women. Amelia felt less afraid, and less torn, than her companions – the Carrier were not her mother's people. Seeing the drama before her, she ran to her husband's defence, grabbing a knife and lunging at the intruders, like Pocahontas rushing to defend the Englishman John Smith two hundred years before. Her screams broke the silence and forced Kwah's men back. But her advance was short-lived and, much to her fury, a Carrier took hold of her plait. She was disarmed and pushed to one side.

Amidst a great welter of shouting and stamping, the advance on James began again. Tloeng, Kwah's nephew and presumptive heir, pointed a poniard to James's breast. He shouted, 'Shall I strike?' and again, 'Shall I strike? Say the word and I will stab him.' Others called out instructions, all in their own tongue. The HBC men stood as though fixed.

The other women, following Amelia from their chambers, implored the Chief to have pity on James Douglas. There were one or two Carrier still among them, and Kwah's men shouted their fury at these women, their sisters and cousins. Amelia broke away from the Carrier who held her and ran upstairs. She began to throw offerings of tobacco, rum, pieces of clothing into the midst of the crowd. The other women joined her, handing down appeasement to the men, blankets, cooking pots, food. Then Kwah, with a gesture that rendered the entire room silent once more, signified his acceptance of the gifts as a compensation for Tzoelhnolle's death. He bade his followers gather the goods and leave the fort peacefully.

It was over. James couldn't have been more relieved.

News of this confrontation between the Carrier and James Douglas of the Hudson's Bay Company went straight onto the bush telegraph that strung the inland trading posts together. Almost before the incident was over it was being retold with gory embellishments, twisted to suit the concerns of the teller – James Douglas, murderous and inexorable, seeking revenge, James Douglas, fair-minded, keeping the peace. Yet the veracity of each element of the tale was continually disputed: ruthless Indians, brave Douglas; brutal Douglas, righteous Indians. James himself knew the truth was lost, and shut his ears to the story and its embroidery.

'When can I see you again?' Audrey asked Jack. It was early the next morning, they were still in bed, and she was thinking about all the work waiting for her at home. She had a deadline to make by the end of that day, an eight-hundred-word article on new post-operative breast cancer treatments, for a women's page.

Jack moaned. 'Not until the end of the week.' He pressed his body against hers. 'I'm going away.'

'Where?'

'Just to Paris. Got a deal with a French TV company – we're going to make a programme about Martinique.' Jack made nature programmes, but he wasn't really interested in the wild, what lies beyond conference rooms and restaurant tables. Other people worried about that. He said all nature documentaries were basically the same these days anyway: see the lovely animals in their natural habitat, aren't they wonderful, isn't it a shame that they're about to be made extinct. 'Too fucking depressing!' He did a little dance on the cold floor.

Audrey followed him to the bathroom; she raised her voice above the hissing water. 'You love to work all the time – you love to go away.' She wasn't sure whether she was making an accusation or an observation.

He pulled the shower curtain to one side. Water hit Audrey's feet. 'Yup, it's true. Does knowing that make you feel any better?'

'I just envy you, I guess. Paris. Martinique.'

'No you don't. You like what you do. You wouldn't be you without what you do, without all your projects and ideas.'

'My little projects. Don't be patronizing.'

'Patronizing?'

'I can't help the way I work.'

'What the fuck are you talking about?'

Audrey climbed into the shower. Jack grunted as she pressed him against the tiles. The water was warm on her back. 'Let's go away somewhere together,' she said.

'Can't.' His voice was squashed, submerged. 'Once I get back, Louise is arriving.'

'What?' Audrey moved away, the shower curtain adhering to her skin.

'My mother's coming to visit. Didn't I tell you? Next week.'

'What will you do with her?' Audrey could not imagine.

'She's easy to entertain. You'll meet her. You'll like her. Everyone likes Louise.' Jack turned off the water.

Back in the bedroom Audrey lay down, wrapped in a towel. She looked at the flowers in the next room. Jack always had flowers in his apartment, white flowers. Everything was always neat. 'I'll have to invite you both for dinner.'

'Hmm?' said Jack, towelling his head. He stood in the bathroom, barefoot, the door open. He was completely naked. His legs looked long and strong.

'Dinner. You and your mother will have to come for dinner.'

'Good idea.'

'I'll invite someone else as well, take the pressure off. Shereen.'

'Great,' said Jack. 'Want some breakfast?'

'No,' said Audrey. 'Come back to bed.'

Later, when Audrey got home, the red light flashing on her answerphone, several sheets of shiny thermal paper curled up beneath the fax machine, she was overwhelmed by laziness, didn't want to work at all. She pulled the duvet off her bed, dropped onto the settee in front of the television, and lay there in an indolent stupor for the rest of the morning.

★

After his first invitation, Audrey and Jane started visiting David on Friday nights instead of driving into town to drink. Audrey would borrow her mother's car – she put a lot of miles on that automobile – go pick up Jane, who had usually managed to get some beer from an older brother or sister, and they would drive to David's cottage on the beach. He would be waiting, a fire burning, a record playing. They would settle in with the dog – she was called Suzanne, after the Cohen song – at their feet and start to talk. Audrey felt as though they could tell David anything, every thought either of them had ever had in their short lives. They didn't talk about school, or friends, or other teachers; they talked about Life and what they would do when they could finally start Living It. They were getting to know David, getting to see what he was really like, an adult, a man. They thought he must have a girlfriend, they were panting with curiosity, but they didn't ask direct questions. Instead they listened very carefully to every word he said, searching for clues, storing it all up for later analysis. They drank beer straight from the bottle, smoked cigarettes, and had a wonderful time.

Later, when all three were drunk, things would get a bit more desperate. They became sentimental, morose. Jane and Audrey sang along with the stereo. Suzanne barked as though to accompany them and David told her to shut up but the dog kept barking and they started to laugh and were unable to stop. Later still, Audrey grew tense. She paced around the cottage, back and forth between the kitchen and the front door, stepping over David's stacks of books and papers. He has a real life, she thought, and I don't. When will I escape? She ranted a bit, talked loudly, sometimes

67

stepping outside for a few gulps of salty, sober air in between experimental screams. And then she would come back inside to find Jane and David on the sofa, their bodies an inch or two closer together than before.

During the week they played it cool, nothing visible passing between the threesome. They knew that if the school had got wind of what was happening it would deal with them severely, David would lose his job, or, at the very least, have to leave the school and move elsewhere. Jane and Audrey were both under the legal minimum age for drinking; any fool could have figured out that their visits would end with Audrey drunk and driving Jane home.

But, apart from their Friday-night rendezvous, life and school continued. Audrey gradually lost touch with her old friends even though they continued to sit in the same classrooms day after day. She had next to nothing in common with Jane's friends, she still had an aura of the swot, a straightness that was distasteful to them. Kids who did well in school were known as 'brains'. 'She's a brain,' they would say. It was not a compliment. On other nights, Saturdays, sometimes during the week, Audrey and Jane would head downtown on their own to drink.

Jane's old boyfriend had disappeared, Audrey never felt certain where he had gone. She and Jane did not talk about him. Odd, given their eagerness to share everything. They had been lovers, Audrey knew that much. Jane said she liked sex but she didn't talk about the actual act, the mechanics, what it was like. Audrey thought this omission must have been due to her own inexperience, she would have only questions, no wisdom in response. Too much probing might seem voyeuristic.

★

Dear Audrey Robbins,

Thank you for the material you sent last week. Enclosed is a list of various chapters I'd like you to copy, as well as a new list of books and articles for which I'd like you to look. There was no invoice with the material you sent me: please do send an invoice this time.

You may wonder why I don't use the National Library in Ottawa to get these books. I find the librarians there most unhelpful; I believe they operate some kind of blacklist and that my name is on it. This doesn't concern you. I rely very heavily on the National Archive for much of my research – I've dealt with the archivists there for many years and find them generally more able to treat me and my work appropriately. As for the indigenous peoples of this country, they've been dealt with so badly for so long, it's little wonder that their priorities are so stern now. But I will continue to insist that notions of racial purity are a nonsense in a land with a history such as ours.

But I digress. I hope these lists give you the information you need. Good luck in the library. I was last in London as a student in the late 1950s; I'm sure the city cannot have changed much since then.

Yours sincerely,
Prof. Shula Cronin

The letter arrived and Audrey read it, then read it again. She hadn't a clue what Prof. Cronin was talking about. A blacklist in Ottawa? Racial purity? Audrey hadn't given the professor's requests much thought, it hadn't occurred to her that some of the books might be available in Canada. Shula Cronin sounded a little paranoid. She'd have a better look at the books this time, maybe that would help make sense of the letter.

*

Audrey bought everything for the meal with Jack and his mother in an Italian delicatessen in Soho on the way home from the library; she wasn't taking any chances with her own cooking. She made a salad, prepared starters. Shereen arrived early.

'Are you nervous?'

'No. Yes.'

'Well, don't be. I'm very good with parents.'

'Not just any ordinary parent.'

'Oh, all parents are the same. We'll tell her how wonderful her son is and she'll love us.'

'Have you heard from your mother?' Audrey asked. Shereen had been getting weekly letters from Calcutta, a recent innovation on Lakshmi's behalf. The missives arrived after long delays in the post, full of newspaper clippings and photographs. Lakshmi seemed to be trying to prove to Shereen that Calcutta was an interesting place, a city where exciting things were happening.

'The problem with Calcutta is that it's too interesting,' said Shereen. 'Life here is calm and sane in comparison. She is taking the wrong tack.' She sipped her drink. 'Does your father ever tell you it's time for you to come home?'

'No – he gave up on me years ago.'

'I don't know what I'd do if my mother died and I was still single – I'd have to go home and care for my father then. Was that ever an issue for you?'

Audrey shifted on her feet, flushed. She had always liked Shereen's forthrightness – here was a good example of it. She did not turn around from where she was working. 'No.'

'For years my mother thought getting married was the last thing I should do. Now she's obsessed with it. A nice Bengali boy from Calcutta. A proper Hindu wedding.'

'I wonder why?' Audrey was attempting to dispose of the packaging from the food she had bought, hoping that

70

Jack's mother might think she had cooked it all herself from her own recipes.

'My mother is becoming more traditional in her old age, I don't know. She's afraid I'll be barren and old and unhappy.'

'Listen, Shereen,' said Audrey, waving her wooden spoon, 'next time you go to Calcutta, I'll come with you. I'll have a quiet talk with your mother. I'll tell her you are a big powerful lawyer here in London, that everyone admires you and wishes they had your life' – Shereen guffawed – 'and that it's all down to her. And what a wonderful daughter you are.' Audrey paused.

'The same kind of thing that we'll say to Louise about her son?'

'That's right.'

'So I won't be barren and old and unhappy, will I?'

'Oh yes, I love India,' Louise was saying. 'I've been several times. But never to Calcutta.'

'Well, be sure to let me know when you do go,' said Shereen. 'My mother loves to meet people from abroad. She'll take you to see the sights herself.' Shereen smiled.

'It's my favourite thing – travel,' said Louise. 'I come from a very poor background –' Audrey felt her gaze '– and poverty does not frighten me. But I love to come to London and meet Jack's new girlfriends.' She turned and smiled at her son. Audrey saw her teeth were square and very white. 'They've been from all over the world, haven't they, Jack?'

Audrey forced herself to stay seated. This was the first she had heard about Jack's United Nations tribe of girlies. All evening she had felt nothing but anxiety. She kept finding herself staring at Louise, her mouth slack. Jack's mother looked very young – she wore her hair straightened and had not one fleck of grey. Her trouser suit was neat and expensive, in no way motherly. She was terrifying. Audrey coveted her pearls, and her sang-froid.

Jack placed his arm along the back of Audrey's chair. He leaned over while his mother talked to Shereen. 'Delicious,' he said, licking his lips lasciviously. Audrey's smile was strained. Louise, sleekly groomed, politely friendly, made her feel ugly and inept, pale and messy. She was relieved that Shereen was there to help carry the conversation and, at the same time, annoyed that Jack's mother was so interested in Shereen. Sometimes Louise seemed under the impression that Shereen was, in fact, the new girlfriend. Maybe she would prefer it that way; maybe she disapproved of Audrey. Audrey tried to dispel her thoughts. She turned to Jack. He had not said much all evening, just pulled out his mother's chair when she went to sit at the table. This gesture amazed Audrey. She waited for the evening to end.

Later that night Audrey sat up in bed, volume 'C' of an encyclopaedia balanced on her knees. Jack had taken Louise home; Shereen had left after helping with the clearing up. Audrey was wide awake. She had bought this 1942 edition of the *Encyclopaedia Britannica* at a second-hand bookshop near the library a few years back; she had purchased two volumes a week, it had taken nearly three months to buy the whole thing. It was totally outdated, full of countries that no longer existed, facts that were no longer true. Britain still had an empire. Audrey turned the pages and looked at the pictures until she reached 'Canada, Dominion of'. The immigration drain – before World War Two Canada lost as many people to the US as it allowed in from elsewhere, people drawn to the bright lights down south like children to sweeties. As she read the entry one of her hands fell asleep, circulation cut off by the weight of the book. Canada, thought Audrey, too heavy, too big, too few people. No wonder I feel lost when I go there.

That night, when she fell asleep, she dreamt she was back in high school. Her adult self, her London self, back in the Vancouver Island classroom. Sitting chemistry exams.

Swot that she was, Audrey was never good at sciences. Knowing she would fail. Caring – but unable to do anything. There was David, walking past the door of the classroom. Followed by Jane, who looked through the door without seeing Audrey. There was David again, walking in the opposite direction. Followed by Jane.

In the morning Audrey woke up full of her past, as though she had up-chucked in the night and behind her lips her mouth was brimming. She swallowed hard, bile, she was alone, there was no one to tell the dream to. Why had this part of her past suddenly become so present? And the James Douglas story, bubbling up inside her, threatening to overflow.

She wondered if David Dumont was still a schoolteacher. She imagined he must be. Even then she felt he would never finish that manuscript. She could be wrong, of course, she knew that, he might be a famous and successful novelist working under a pseudonym: Stephen King. But Audrey imagined he was still teaching high school somewhere, a little bitter, resenting his students as he got older and they stayed the same age. She wondered if he had continued to 'befriend' his students. Perhaps she and Jane weren't the first. Maybe a whole string of girls came to his door clutching Jean-Paul Sartre to their high and round teenaged breasts.

Audrey's ex-friend Louise approached her after class one day. 'Have you and Jane been going to Mr Dumont's place?' she asked.

'Where did you hear that?' She hoped her tone was noticeably scornful.

'Just around. Have you?'

Audrey smiled at Debbie. They had once been good friends. 'No,' she said, 'don't believe everything you hear.'

Jane was also being quizzed. She lied like Audrey and then, together afterwards, they felt smug and privileged. Yet they did worry that people might find out somehow,

73

that the visits would have to end. But nobody seemed sure
the rumours were true, people asked but then were
reassured by the replies, as if the triangle of Jane, Audrey
and David was just too improbable to believe.

So they kept returning. Friday nights. And David kept
inviting them. Inside, long, dark evenings in front of his
fire. Outside, the rain making slip against the waves. They
were in it together, those three.

★

Some say it was Kwah who saved James's life that day,
persuading the angry relatives of the dead man that an
explanation and an apology were sufficient. Amelia knew
that the Carrier would accept gifts as compensation, she
knew how to make amends. Yet in his official report,
James's father-in-law, Chief Factor Connolly – who returned from back east several weeks after the incident –
blamed Kwah for the turmoil. Despite James's objections,
the Carrier Chief was banned from the post for several
months. The situation was dangerous – it was a showdown
between two groups of people who had dealt, fairly
peacefully, with each other for years. Now that balance was
tipping.

It was the tradition in New Caledonia for New Year
celebrations to take place at HBC trading posts. That year,
months after the incident with Kwah, Connolly arranged
for much to be made of the event. On New Year's Eve, the
local Carrier were invited to the post and presented with
sweetener gifts, this year more elaborate and valuable than
before. A party ensued, Hudson's Bay Company rum
flowed, cannons and muskets were fired at midnight. Once
Kwah and all the Carrier were suitably drunk, Connolly
gave a signal and the women and children were ushered
away. Then the HBC men set about the Carrier; a great
brawl consumed the crowd, as though a dark wave had

passed overhead. James stood in the door and watched while, in the distance, the native men were bloodied and bruised. He himself felt the lesson bitterly. In the subtle battle between white and indigenous he saw who the winner would be.

4

My Dear Sir,
Without knowing where this may meet you, whether at Norway House enjoying hymeneal sweets, or doing the graceful among the trans-atlantic fair, it begins its travels certain of finding you in some corner of this nether world; though people on the eve of marriage often fancy themselves a mile or two above it. Whatever Poets may imagine, the wedding day is assuredly the happiest day of life, and it is a thousand pities it should ever be clouded by intrusive reflections on the increasing cares of life, such thoughts however force themselves upon the mind, and temper the job of seeing one's firstborn enter upon the stage of life. There is a strange revolution, in the manners of the country; Indian wives were at one time the vogue, the half-breed supplanted these, and now we have the lovely tender exotic torn from its parent bed, to pine and languish in the desert. What a debt of gratitude you incur, through such heroic devotion, which a lifetime of the tenderest attentions can hardly repay . . .

James Douglas in a letter to James Hargrave, fellow HBC official, on the occasion of Hargrave's wedding to Letitia Mactavish, whom he planned to bring from Scotland to the fur country

Audrey was on her way to a meeting with a features editor, Carmen Bosnay, for whom she had worked for a number of years. Audrey had been writing for Carmen when she came across a story involving the treatment of black adolescent patients in one of London's mental hospitals. She spent a week interviewing drugged-up teenagers; they shuffled along the corridor in blue pyjamas to see her in the visiting room. The article, so lengthy and bleak it was almost a gothic novel, had been stalled by the magazine's libel lawyers, then substantially rewritten by Carmen herself. When the piece was finally published an internal inquiry took place at the hospital, and one orderly was sacked; otherwise, things continued pretty much as before. Audrey tried to get a follow-up commission, but Carmen didn't fancy pursuing a campaign for disturbed young people, the story didn't have much market appeal, and, with its accusations of institutional racism, was potentially libellous. She attempted to sell it elsewhere but there was no interest in the general press and, very quickly, Audrey lost her contacts in the hospital. But she continued to write for Carmen Bosnay, who was very thin and looked as though she styled her hair with a blender every morning.

The day of the meeting, Audrey felt stiff and bruised from sex, light-headed, as though Jack's hands were still on her body. He had stayed the night before; they had gone out for a meal and he had eaten off Audrey's plate without asking. She took it as a good sign. At her place they watched television, then went to bed early. This was when they got along best, in bed. Jack made love like he ate, greedily, and she liked it.

This morning he took ages to get dressed and leave her flat, even though he knew she was in a hurry. Now she was running late. King's Cross Station was closed – a bomb-scare, who was it who was planting bombs these days?, or perhaps a strike – thousands of disoriented commuters thronged the pavement. It was impossible to get on any of the buses, they were too full. Audrey attempted to wave down a taxi but ended up walking to Covent Garden. London heaved with irritation.

Once she arrived the meeting went well. Carmen liked Audrey's proposals and commissioned two think-piece features, one on therapists and false memory syndrome, the other on new forms of cohabitation. Afterwards Audrey found a sandwich bar where she could have coffee. She sat down with a newspaper, notepads and files spilling out of her bag. She felt relieved but not very optimistic – now she would have to write the articles. A moment of fatigue.

She mulled over the meeting. Carmen Bosnay had been friendly enough. In the tightly knit little glossy media world Carmen was famous for being single – single, vampish and rapacious. Audrey shuffled her papers. There was a fine line between being admired for staying single, the swinging city girl, and being a pitied and pathetic, lonely thing. She sat up straight and told herself off for lacking confidence. It was tiring, life, living. Audrey sighed and got on with it.

'Have you heard this thing,' Shereen said one evening after the two of them had been to a movie, 'about getting married if you live in New York? That a woman over thirty is more likely to be struck by lightning than she is to get married?' They were in a gay bar in Soho, it was chic and expensive and the men ignored them. Soho had become a gathering place for men wearing smart suits, sharp haircuts, and elegant, well-polished spectacles, the molly houses of Clerkenwell moved up west. They were gorgeous and they knew it.

'Where did you hear that?' Audrey asked, laughing.

'It's true! I don't know where I read it.'

'Somebody's mother invented that story just to keep us

in line.' Audrey had not seen much of Jack during the two weeks that his mother had been in London but that hadn't mattered. Jack and his mother had done art, restaurants, shopping. Now Louise was gone they were back to normal, going out a couple of evenings during the week, work allowing, spending Saturdays together.

'No, it's true. New York, London, wherever, there aren't any straight men. Haven't you noticed? You found one, the needle in the haystack, but look at all the wonderful, brilliant, single women you know. Look at me!'

'You have had plenty of boyfriends, Shereen.'

'Have *had*, past tense. What's happened to them? They've all scarpered. I'm not fussy – but are they around, availing themselves of me? No.'

It was a familiar theme in Shereen's conversation, one that Audrey enjoyed. She thought her friend incredibly attractive. It is strange that she is single, thought Audrey, that she is, and I'm not.

'What are we doing in a bar like this then?'

Shereen scowled. 'Since when would you want to meet a man in a bar – no thanks.'

'Maybe you should try one of those dating agencies.'

'A dating agency,' Shereen repeated. 'I've got my mother for that – she could find me a nice Bengali man, older preferably, traditional, with a bit of cash, who lives in London and won't mind a woman who is a little shop-worn.'

'You don't want that.'

'I don't? Arranged marriages can work extremely well.'

'I didn't realize you were lonely.'

'I'm not lonely, I just want, well, you know, sex.'

Home on the tube at midnight, standing room only, everybody smelling of cigarettes, booze and office sweat. Audrey read the evening newspaper, hanging on the strap, lurching forward when the train came to an abrupt stop between stations, where it stood for long minutes.

The door of her flat locked behind her, Audrey decided to do a bit of late-night furniture arranging. She moved the armchair to the opposite corner, by the window, and sat on it for a moment, but that wasn't quite right. She pulled the settee forward. A roll of paper fell out from behind. She got down on her hands and knees and smoothed it out on the floor, trying not to tear the corners. It was her mother's family tree. Audrey's father had given it to her when her mother died, she had not looked at it then, or since. Her grandparents were dead by the time she was born, all four of them. But here they were on this bit of paper, espaliered, names and dates dangling like grapes.

Her mother's English family was traceable through twelve generations. The tree gave date and place of birth and date and place of death, little hints of what each person had done, each branch of the family depleted by windfall, departures to southern Africa, India, the Caribbean, Australia, Canada. Most of the women – sisters, wives, and daughters – seemed to have stayed behind although there was one great-great-great-aunt born in Weymouth, died in Delhi. The migration that Audrey knew best was that of her mother's parents; they had emigrated to Canada just before the First World War. Her mother had told Audrey about them when she was little, her parents who had taken the train that led to the boat that left England for Montreal and then another train across Canada to British Columbia. They settled near Vancouver. Audrey remembered her mother's voice, she could hear her now. 'One year after they arrived, they re-packed their trunks, turned around, and returned to England. Like a kind of dance,' Audrey could see her mother do a little two-step, 'the continental drift.' The journey took weeks, the Rockies, the prairies, the St Lawrence Seaway, the passage across the Atlantic and, finally, home. Back to the familiar, tea and shops, far away from the wild tree-stump loneliness of British Columbia. But, once back in England – Norfolk, 1916 – there seemed to be no reason to stay in that water-logged land, so after another year they turned around again and travelled back to Canada. By now the war was gouging Europe, both lost brothers in the trenches in France. They arrived in Vancouver and stayed on the coast, never to return to Britain again.

It was her mother, her parents, their parents and all the other generations standing behind them that Audrey tried to conjure as she looked at the tree. She was a little drunk, but that didn't matter. Who were they? The non-commissioned officers in the British Army, their wives fanning themselves in the European Ladies' Enclosure, the 'Other Ranks' in India. Sailors in the West Indies, farm labourers in the fenlands, sugar beets, carrots and potatoes. What did it mean to have these people in her past, traces of them in her genes, her genealogy? What does it mean to be a product of that empire, of this migration? Audrey's grandparents moved to another country, Canada, cold, white, far-away. Their child, Audrey's mother, was firmly Canadian, English only for steamed Christmas pudding and trifle with sherry. Who had her mother been? Thinking of her made Audrey ache. She held herself, gripped her sides, as though she was in pain.

Audrey's father was a different story. He was from an old British Columbian family. Her mother had always said he was distantly related to Sir James Douglas, after whom Douglas Street downtown had been named, but when she was a child Audrey had never taken the claim too seriously. Her father had never made it himself. Seemed odd to be descended from a street, even if it was the main street. Her father's parents spent their lives in the interior of the province, small towns, unpaved roads, bear and moose wandering down the road, wolves on the outskirts of the newly created municipality.

And Audrey's own migration – what compelled her to leave British Columbia and travel to England, to London, a place that she had only seen before in books and music and film? London had been like a dream to her, an adolescent's dream of adult sophistication – books, music, film – complex pleasures – love. When she was with Jane and David she listened to Van Morrison and Leonard Cohen, but at home in her room, locked up at night, she played the Sex Pistols, the Damned, the Buzzcocks, on her little turntable. Teenage kicks and I want to be sedated. She leapt around her bedroom in the back of beyond like she had seen people jumping up and down on television, on the news, there were no music programmes. One of her ex-friends was obsessed with the Jam and displayed a Union Jack in her bedroom, longed for a Mini Cooper. It was impossible to be a punk in BC in the 1970s, but Audrey tried it out in front of her mirror.

The London she found when she finally got there was not the London she expected, it was not all Holland Park, Mayfair and Chelsea. She had missed punk, it was burnt out and dead, already National Heritage. What she found was a city of extremes, riches and poverty, grinding politics, dark winters, smoky pubs and draughty sitting rooms. The smell of diesel, buses, black taxis. Geography, and a clear sharp feeling of being alone. The whoosh of noise and dirt as the underground train enters the station. She used to think that the city was the only possible place she could live. Not just any city either, but London. Grimy London, city of her dreams. A perfect city in many ways, dark and private. A city with a history, not like where she came from. Even now when Shereen asked – everyone always asked, eventually – 'Why did you come here in the first place?', Audrey could not explain.

'I just came. I thought it might be somewhere I could feel I belonged.'

'And do you?'

'No. In a way.' She told her story about being descended from a street. Shereen laughed happily.

Amelia was pregnant for the first time the winter James left her behind at Fort St James to travel to his new posting at Fort Vancouver, south on the Columbia River. She would travel, with the baby, the following summer. James wrote twice a week, letters stacked up and waiting for a north-bound party to carry them, and held his breath at night when he thought of his wife and her labour. But the child – a girl, Amelia – perished at birth. She failed to breathe.

When Amelia and her mother, Suzanne, buried the baby in the tradition of the Cree none of the white men at the fort had the heart to object. Like most customs in this land, the native way made better sense than the European. After that severe loss – how she and James had celebrated when they realized she was pregnant – Amelia looked forward to leaving Stuart Lake. The news of the child's death was sent on ahead, but Amelia longed to mourn with James. When the day of departure came she stepped cautiously into the heavily laden bark canoe, kneeling tidily in the prow, her long skirts tucked beneath her knees, taking up the paddle as she waited for her father. On the bank the slender white trunks of the birch trees shone, silvery leaves turning white, black, white, black, in the breeze. In front of her the lake flowed smoothly.

'No, Amelia,' her father, William Connolly, objected. 'You must sit in the middle of the canoe. Thomas and I will paddle.'

Amelia began to object, she had looked forward to stretching her arms out over water, under sun.

'No. Move back.'

She closed her mouth and let no word escape. The restrictive corset, newly arrived from England, a gift from James, her breasts still weeping milk, she would be better off seated in the middle. She could take up a paddle if and when her help was needed on the river. Then there would be no choice.

As she rose to move, her bare feet stepping lightly over the frail skin of the canoe, she glanced back, beyond her father, to where her mother stood near the horses, beneath the trees. Their eyes met and Suzanne Pas de Nom uttered a few Cree words, a brief keen for her daughter's departure. Fort St James to Fort Vancouver, a great, serrated distance, perhaps one thousand miles by river, packhorse and portage; Amelia knew it might be years before she saw her mother again. She called to her, and forced a smile, and Suzanne raised her hand. Amelia knelt down in the canoe once more, impatient to leave paining farewells behind. Her father pushed the low vessel into the lake, jumping in, scarcely wetting his trousers.

Amelia bore the journey well, despite its arduous length, down jutting rapids, through deep and perilous canyons, bivouacking through the trees. Her father shot a deer which they cooked and fed off that night, carrying the leftover meat with the supplies. Amelia's memories of the journey would be forever tainted with the smell of charred, slightly high venison. But she had no complaints, despite continuous discomfort and fatigue. She faced her destination at all times: James. Her father's men admired her resolution. They reminded each other that she was half-Cree, and thus, half-wilderness herself.

Fort Vancouver sat on the broad high bank of the Columbia River where it swooped down from the north and began to turn towards the sea. The river could be traced, in all its windings, for a long distance through the newly cultivated flatland; beyond lay an interminable forest, melting into a blue haze, from which rose Mount Hood, capped with snow and ice. This was the vista that greeted Amelia Douglas on her arrival, that had once greeted James.

When the party landed James rushed out through the

excited crowd to meet his wife, and they embraced in full view of the company. Later, in the privacy of their quarters, James peeled Amelia's dress, stiff with river water and sweat, away from her shoulders. Her body bore no trace of her pregnancy, the journey had worn her small and thin once again. Amelia saw that James had changed too.

'There's grey on your head!' she teased him. 'You've grown too old for me.'

'You're muscled like a boy, and your fair skin . . .' – he ran his hands down her bare arms, then up their tender length to her chin – 'You are very brown,' he said, and she heard a tinge of regret, 'like an Indian.'

'Like my mother,' said Amelia, reaching for him, 'like a full-blooded Cree.' James held his wife close for a long while, the soursweet smell of her body familiar to him.

HBC department headquarters since 1828, Fort Vancouver was a much bigger and livelier post than Fort St James. There was a sawmill, a gristmill, blacksmiths, carpenters, coopers, tinners and bakers, all within the tall wooden stockades. The climate was much milder than that of the north and on the plantation, the land surrounding the fort, a farm had been established. Crops of vegetables and grain were harvested regularly, James said they were already producing enough flour to supply all HBC posts in New Caledonia. Even grapevines and apple trees were flourishing, and as James walked Amelia along the river-bank, pointing downstream towards where the large herd of wild Spanish cattle and horses grazed, she laughed and said she could never have imagined such abundance, accustomed as she was to the north. As he took her hand, the wind loosened her hair, and it flew around her face. He smiled as she struggled to recapture it; he knew that from a distance his great height made him look father to Amelia's small-framed child. But she was no child, despite appearances, and she pushed herself against him, her brown eyes staring hard into his.

'Amelia?'

She waited for him to continue. It was three days since they had been reunited and she still longed to hear his voice.

'Will we have another child?'

She gulped sharp breath at the memory of their lost baby. They had been over it, Amelia had told her husband exactly what happened, each stage of her painful and profitless labour. That was behind them now.

She smiled fiercely and drew James's face down to hers. 'Yes James,' she said, 'soon.'

Yet even at Fort Vancouver, southern and mild, there was hardship. The winter could be long, the wolves murdered the hogs and the fox took its prey from among the fowl belonging to the fort. Not long after Amelia arrived an epidemic swept through the local people, malaria carried by mosquitoes. Amelia ministered the dying without fear of transmission. She thought it her responsibility.

The post was only seventy-five miles from the nearest sea-port and there were ready supplies of hitherto unknown luxuries, imports from California, goods from all over the world traded by sailors. James bought Amelia gifts of jewellery and lace on his travels up and down the coast, once returning with a pair of silk stockings that Amelia unwrapped and held to her cheek, slowly stroking her skin. They were bound together in an easy physicality, and together they sought – and found – pleasure. She fell pregnant again, and they were exultant in the big iron-framed bedstead James had shipped from San Francisco. This time Amelia was hardy in her pregnancy, she grew strong as well as large. The child was a boy, they named him Alexander, and called him Alec.

James travelled a great deal on HBC business, trading and reconnaissance duties, often leaving his new family for weeks and weeks. He held posts of successive importance and, on his forays, could see the expanding importance of the region and its resources quite clearly. But he always returned home well pleased to see everyone, to embrace Amelia.

On one occasion James arrived at the fort during supper. The children greeted him riotously, rushing away from the table, climbing up his legs and into his arms. James laughed and picked up his son. 'Do you shout the most loudly?' he asked of his boy. Alec shouted 'Yes!' and raised his little arms high. James threw his son into the air. Alec went up, up, up, the boy crowed like a raven, he thought he might fly, up into the roof beams of Fort Vancouver. He peaked, his body curved, and down he came, the great distance into his father's outstretched arms. As he landed there was a terrible cracking, something snapped, his baby's back or his neck. He let out a sharp cry and James thought he was laughing until he felt the small body relax, slip away.

The boy broke, irretrievably, like a precious piece of china carried from the old world to the new. Alec died in his father's arms, aged three. James held his child roughly against his chest and wept. He cried out to the room, 'No!' and 'Why?' Amelia stood on the other side of the table, unable to move, her face trapped in a smile. Her stomach heaved as though she too was still laughing. Alec, their one child, Alec. Someone took the boy from James's arms. Later, he was laid to rest in a tiny coffin, lowered into an icy hole dug the previous autumn before the ground froze too solid for unexpected burials.

James could not be consoled. His grief was unimaginable, even in a country inured to death, remote and unforgiving. He spent the night wandering in and out of the fort, past the stockades and down to the river, through the mud and the snow and the cold blasted air that he knew had followed him from the north. Amelia rocked herself back and forth in their bedroom, in the great bed where Alec had been conceived; she turned away all offers of company, suddenly shy of the other women and children of the fort who had seen Alec die and now offered her sad looks and sorrow.

On the second day her husband crawled to her in the dead of night.

'How I loathe myself,' he whispered, his breath chill. 'How I loathe living, while he is dead.'

'Accept it, James,' Amelia said, her back straight, her face lifted, with that strange fatalism she had learned from her mother. 'Accept it. He is gone. Come to me.' And Amelia forgave her husband when he went to her in the night, and soon she was pregnant again. But these two dead children, first Amelia, then Alec, did not depart entirely, and stayed by James and Amelia always.

On Saturday night Audrey and Jack met Shereen and went out for a meal. In the restaurant Jack and Shereen got along like old friends.

'By the time I was born,' Shereen was saying, 'India was already independent and even in Calcutta things British had disappeared. If it hadn't been for my mother I could have been a proper Indian girl, a nationalist like my father, but she sent me to English school, she gave me novels by Kipling and Dickens and even Iris Murdoch for heaven's sake.'

'Why did your mother like all that stuff?' asked Audrey.

'Her father had given her English books when she was a child. My grandmother and aunties told me other stories, sang to me, but it was the books that interested me. There was this family rumour that my grandfather had been in love with an Englishwoman before he married my grandmother – I don't know if it's true, but he had a passion for Shakespeare.'

'Seems so bizarre,' said Jack, 'there you are in India, reading Shakespeare.'

'Well, there's nothing wrong with Shakespeare. But I was in my twenties before I read anything written by an Indian and that was only because I had a Bengali boyfriend from Bombay who shamed me into it.'

'A Bengali boyfriend from Bombay?' asked Audrey.

'Sounds like a song, doesn't it?' said Jack, smiling. He hummed a tune and continued to motor through his pasta. Audrey put her hand on his knee under the table.

'So tell me why you flirt so much with Shereen.'

'Flirt? Me?'

Audrey looked at Jack. They were lying in bed. Jack had lit candles, puffed pillows, poured drinks. Audrey had spoiled the mood.

'Well,' he said, spreading his hands innocently, 'you never know. I might need a lawyer one day.'

Audrey laughed.

'Actually, I'll tell you my secret. You know I make documentaries?' Audrey nodded as he put his hand on her stomach. 'Video diaries?' This was something new. 'Live-action video porno?' For a moment she believed him. 'As a matter of fact, I spent the afternoon editing my brand-new, ever-expanding collection of videos of you and I having sex. I'm off to Cannes next month to get a distribution deal.'

Audrey blushed. 'It's not true.'

Jack made an obscene lens-focusing motion with his hands and pointed to a blank corner of the room. 'Can't you see the camera?'

Audrey looked, feeling uneasy. 'There's no camera.' She folded her arms across her breasts. Jack rolled towards her, rested his chin on her shoulder, and began to bite her neck.

'Of course not,' he said, sliding his hands down her abdomen. 'What do you think I am, a pervert?'

'Yes,' said Audrey. Jack snagged her pubic hair with his finger. Music played on the stereo. Audrey shut her eyes tight.

When she was a teenager, Audrey used to love going over to her friend Jane's house. Her bedroom was right at the top of the stairs – up there they would shut the door and listen to records. Listening to records together, an alternative form of communication. Not punk; Jane loved Taj Mahal, Willie Nelson and Bob Marley. They would listen to Bob Marley all day. Audrey could picture her friend's face clearly, her smile. The thing about Jane was this quality she had – she was so wonderfully sexy somehow, without being vain. You just wanted to get her to smile at you, everyone felt that way. Audrey had seen David look at Jane like that. It was difficult not to envy her, to keep jealousy at bay.

And jealousy had other guises, had made other appearances in Audrey's life since then, slowing down her heart, twisting her gut. It was Jack; Gina was right, his flirtatiousness was difficult to bear. It was like dating a movie star, she thought, no gesture without a little self-consciousness, without an awareness of its impact. After the dinner at Gina's Audrey had abandoned trying to integrate Jack into her social life – they saw each other, and they saw Shereen, who had somehow come to belong to both of them. Jack had his own friends – Audrey had not met any of them.

Audrey considered talking to Gina about Jack – the details of the relationship were fine, it was the larger things that worried her – but her friend had been so keen to run him down in the first instance that Audrey thought she could not possibly be objective now. And when she saw Gina – on the rare occasions Gina could leave Charlotte with Bob and come out of an evening – the last thing she wanted to do was discuss relationships. Gina was a good-time girl, or at least she had been before nappies slowed her down, and when she went out she liked to go out and stay out and pretend she didn't have a home to go to. A trip to the cinema would lead to a visit to an after-hours club which would lead on to dancing somewhere else and, then, eventually, a drunken ride in a minicab, Gina hanging out of the window propositioning passers-by. When she wanted to, Gina could look great. In clubs men would sidle up to

Audrey, offer to buy her a drink, and then ask, 'Who's your friend?' Audrey was used to it, it made her laugh, but when they went out she had to be prepared, lipstick in place, hair just so. Lots of flirting, cigarettes and drama, Audrey keeping pace with her, but only just. Discussing Jack, or Bob for that matter, was not on the menu. And Audrey did not want to be told that there was more to the situation than her own paranoia; she was happiest blaming herself.

And anyway, she reasoned, it is good for Jack and me not to spend too much time together. We are not an old married couple. Think of all the unpleasant things I might discover about him. Like he is addicted to sport on TV, football, cricket, golf, athletics – what if he loves to watch car racing and wants to share his passion? What if he is obsessive about ironing, or picky about whether jam is scooped from the jar on a knife or with a spoon? What if, on the nights Audrey is not there to hear, he farts and snores? Think of all the hideous revelations she is avoiding. Think of all the things Jack might discover about her. No, it was better to keep the arrangement as it was, tidy, distant. Romantic, even. Preserve a little mystery in life. Keep herself veiled.

They didn't talk about her whiteness, his blackness. If Jack had thoughts on the subject – whether that might be the tender luminosity of the skin beneath her breasts or the politics of jungle fever, sleeping with the white devil – he did not mention it. And Audrey kept mum too, but it was around them, the immutable fact of the colour of their skin. It doesn't really exist, Audrey told herself, race is a concept somebody invented to keep us apart. If whiteness is a construct, blackness is too. She didn't worry about the contradictions inherent in what she was thinking, it was easy to block it all out with a kiss. It wasn't a problem. There was no problem. She liked it that way.

Audrey looked over the books and articles that Prof. Cronin had commissioned her to find. Turning the pages, she wondered what it was, exactly, that the professor was writing. The subject of each book was clear enough, but how did the texts relate to each other? Shula Cronin had asked her to dig deep into Hudson's Bay Company journals, records from the Colonial Office and the Royal Engineers. But she also had Audrey searching for material on Quebec, on hydro-electricity in that province, North American hydro-electric development in general, as well as early ethnographies of the indigenous people in Quebec, from the time of Champlain to the present day, Oka and beyond. If this was what Prof. Cronin wanted copied from the library in London, Audrey wondered what she had the archivists in Ottawa pursuing.

With her next parcel of papers she wrote a polite and diplomatic letter, enquiring about the book Cronin was writing, positing that the research might be more fruitful if she knew the professor's subject-matter more intimately. She remembered to include an invoice – the bill for photocopying was almost as substantial as the bill for Audrey's time.

The reply came swiftly, the letter landing on the doormat with a thud.

Dear Ms Robbins,

I did not hire a researcher to then be made to justify my project to that said researcher. It must be a prerogative of scholars everywhere to be allowed to conduct studies in privacy, without fear of outside judgement, without waiting for, or indeed, expecting, approval. Unfortunately I am unable to come to London myself: in 1976 I was involved in an aeronautical incident while travelling west to Prince Rupert. The plane went down – crash-landed – on a lake in BC. I survived, others did not. As a result, I no longer fly and, in this day and age, with the pressures of work, travelling by ship is not a viable alternative. There, you have had it from me. It is not something I like to write or, indeed, think about.

I'll say no more. Your cheque, in sterling, is enclosed, along with a new list of publications.

Yours,
Prof. Cronin

'Jack,' said Shereen, 'that was delicious.' They were having dinner in his flat. Earlier in the week he had mentioned he was inviting Shereen over. Audrey assumed that meant she was invited as well. It was only when she arrived and found them at a table crowded with photographs and half-empty plates that she thought perhaps she was not.

'These look really good to me,' said Shereen. Jack was showing her photographs of his own work, faded Polaroids of the paintings he had abandoned after art school. 'I don't see how you could just give up,' she continued. 'What do you think, Aud?'

Audrey picked up one of the photographs, looked at it and then looked down at Jack who smiled at her from where he was sitting.

He hasn't shown me his work.

Jack leaned back in his chair, lifting the front legs off the floor. 'The world didn't need my mediocre paintings.'

Shereen laughed, showing her teeth. 'Modesty doesn't suit you somehow. Let me see the rest,' she said, leaning towards him.

Jack reached down to the box under the table. Audrey had never even seen the box before. She didn't know what to do with herself, they were having a good time without her. She should not be there, she was not invited. As she walked into the kitchen she heard Jack say, 'Look at what I found, Shereen, look at this one. Now you have to admit that's garbage.' Shereen gave a little squeal.

Audrey sat propped up in bed and opened the encyclopaedia at random. It made for peculiar bedtime reading, the formal language, the dated statistics, the predetermined political view of the world, quite contrary to the novels she read ordinarily.

> The land surface of the earth is estimated to be about 52,500,000 square miles. Of this area the British Empire occupies nearly 16,000,000 square miles. By far the greater portion lies within the temperate zones and is suitable for white population . . .

She found it surprisingly difficult to put down – as well as difficult to prop up. She entertained herself with the contrast between nights in bed with the *Encyclopaedia Britannica*, nights in bed with Jack Campbell. Each had its own unwieldy pleasures. But the encyclopaedia could not stop Audrey's mind from returning to earlier that evening – Jack and Shereen. Audrey imagined what she would say to Jack when she next saw him. She would confront him, clear the air, give him a chance to come clean.

'Why did you leave so early?' Jack asked a few days later, sprawled on Audrey's settee. 'I thought you would stay the night.'

He arrived and Audrey's determination departed. She did not speak calmly, her voice soft and unthreatening, 'Jack, do you fancy Shereen? Because if you do, well, it's best to tell me now. It's okay.' None of that. He came through the door carrying flowers, he undid the top buttons of her shirt and kissed her neck. Her resolve fell away. Look at him now, she had been crazy to have such thoughts. She felt foolish and ridiculous, embarrassed by her own green and ragged doubting. 'I was tired,' she said, and left it at that.

They went to bed and Jack got on top of Audrey almost immediately. She pushed him and he rolled over, holding her on top of him. 'Let me fuck you,' he whispered, his dark eyes shining. 'Let me have my way with you.'

After that, several weeks passed. Shereen did not ring. Audrey had grown accustomed to speaking to her once or twice a week, seeing her with Jack, more often without. When they were on their own they got along well; Audrey's paranoia dissipated. But now Shereen did not ring and Audrey did not call her either.

Another month went by and Audrey worked hard, producing a couple of articles a week, haunting the library, carrying the mountains of newspapers she accumulated across the park to the recycling bins. When Jack wasn't working they went to movies, out for meals, for walks. She did not raise the subject of Shereen. And this silence rendered her less able to talk with Jack about other things. This is something I'm used to, she thought, this is the way it is with men. This is why women's magazines have such healthy sales. I talk to my friends, and they are mostly women, with friends talk comes easily. With Jack she kept perfectly calm, she hid what was there, she learned from his stillness, she made his intransigence her own. And she was not without her own reticence. She was equal to him in that. If you ignore a problem for long enough maybe it really does go away.

The encyclopaedia gave her clues, its confident authority rendered comic by the way the world had changed since it was published. It gave the facts, displaying alphabetically what it knew to be important, it laid the world bare, made everything explicable. It claimed to know the truth about history, even when speculating.

It is difficult to estimate the antiquity of man's settlement in America. It is probable that the ancestors of the Indians came by the north-western route across Bering Strait. Even at the present time the passage freezes so solidly that it is possible to walk from Asia to America.

And then Shereen did ring, one Sunday afternoon when

Audrey was pacing the flat, thinking over an article she was writing.

'I'm sorry Audrey, but I've been incredibly busy at work. And my mother has been driving me insane, she's been ringing me every other day.'

'Is something wrong?'

'No, she's just . . . I don't know. She's depressed. She's trying to persuade me to go home for a visit next month but I'm not able to get away. She is furious with me.'

'You're sure you can't go?'

'No way. I don't want to anyhow. Not just now.' She paused. 'And how's Jack?'

'He's fine.' Audrey made her voice sound firm.

'We should meet, just you and I. Okay Audrey?'

They embraced. Shereen had had her hair cut, it swung around her face prettily. Audrey felt struck with instant sorrow when she saw Shereen, they were friends, she wanted to stay that way. Bad faith between friends is a sour thing. They bought each other drinks and talked for a long time, relaxing. Shereen made Audrey laugh with her quick criticisms of other people. They talked about work, complaining.

'And so you're definitely not going to go visit your mother?' asked Audrey as they embarked on a new round of drinks.

'No. I've told her. I promised I'd try and go in the autumn. What about you? Any trips home planned?'

The question surprised Audrey. 'No, nothing planned.' She considered her explanation. 'When I used to go for visits I always ended up feeling stuck, like I didn't really grow up, like I hadn't spent the time working in London. I lost my sense of myself somehow. And once my mother died . . . My father doesn't see anyone.' She wasn't sure whether this was true. She looked at Shereen, she couldn't tell how much she really wanted to know. Their eyes met.

Something passed between them, Audrey smelt it. It was Jack, it was rivalry.

Shereen flicked her hair back. 'I feel like there's an identity waiting for me in Calcutta,' she spoke quickly, 'a whole other life I could just step into – London would disappear.'

'But of course it wouldn't.' Audrey relaxed back into her seat. At least she wouldn't have to talk about her father now. 'You've been here too long.'

'Sometimes I imagine what it would be like to go back,' said Shereen, 'to live that life in that way. The monsoons – how would I ever deal with the monsoons?' She paused, thinking. 'My shoes would get wet. And that would be the least of my troubles.'

And then later, after another drink, feeling brave, Audrey asked, 'So why haven't you rung?'

'You haven't rung either,' replied Shereen, immediately defensive. Audrey frowned. Shereen shrugged her shoulders and then rubbed her neck. 'Audrey,' she said. They looked at each other. 'Your boyfriend . . .'

'Yes?'

'He's too handsome for his own good.'

'I've heard that before,' Audrey said, turning away.

'No, he's too . . . you know how flirtatious I am.'

Audrey nodded, frowning still.

'I stopped ringing because I didn't want to see you, because I didn't want to see him, because he . . .'

'What?' said Audrey, exasperated. 'He made a pass at you?' Made a pass, a quaint expression, she thought, disconnecting herself from the conversation.

Shereen shook her head vigorously.

'You made a pass at him?'

Again she shook her head.

'What is it Shereen?'

'You're making this hard.'

'What are you trying to say?'

97

'Nothing happened, it's just . . . I was worried something would.'

'You were worried something would,' Audrey said, breath leaving her lungs.

'Yes. Jack's not exactly pushing you down the aisle, is he?'

Audrey didn't know what to say. She didn't want to be pushed down the aisle.

'I mean, he seems to be looking for something Audrey, and, well, I don't think that something is you.'

Audrey sat back in her seat, looking at Shereen. 'And you think it's you?'

'No, God, no,' said Shereen. 'There are things about him, his experience, that I don't think you can understand . . . or share . . . that I . . .' She paused. Audrey knew what Shereen was saying: it's a race thing. Audrey opened her mouth to speak, but Shereen beat her to it.

'It's just . . . I wouldn't trust him if I were you. I'm seeing him next week' – Audrey raised her eyebrows. 'Well, I wanted to get things out in the open. And I want to see him, I like him.' Shereen blushed.

Audrey looked away.

The next night in bed Audrey spoke slowly, her voice low, controlled. 'Jack, what do you think about fidelity?'

'Not a lot,' said Jack. Before she could reply he slid down under the covers and rested his cheek on her thigh. Before his tongue distracted her, Audrey realized she thought faithfulness was important, very important, obligatory, and it required – it would require – persistency.

★

When she was seventeen Audrey was nothing if not persistent. She kept on driving her mother's car down to

David's cottage with Jane. Together they pursued this relationship with their teacher. It made them feel mature, Audrey thought it was the first grown-up thing she had done. And the triangle deepened, growing heavier, it sank into the sand, Audrey, David and Jane.

David was good at all kinds of things; he was good at making Audrey laugh, at making her want to read all the books and listen to all the music in the world. He was good at making Jane smile, and he was adept at making her sad. Some nights, as Jane sat by the fire close to tears, Audrey paced the cottage. It was as though Jane knew something, what, Audrey could not guess. As though she saw what was going to happen. Audrey was going to leave. And she and David, well, she would be left behind.

And Audrey did leave her behind one night, finally. It took a long time to happen, but it did. Perhaps she was the one who was holding things up by being there, in the way. But probably not. They needed to be watched, they needed someone to see, a witness. And Audrey was that witness, she fulfilled the role well. She watched and, when it was time, she went away.

She left Jane behind in David's cottage. David had put the dog outside and while she got into the car Suzanne whined as though she wanted to leave as well. It was very late as the car went up the drive.

And somehow since then Audrey has always felt as though she did not leave that night, as though she was there in the room watching as they embraced. David took her in his arms – Jane! she was only seventeen – and then they walked into the bedroom. Audrey's eyes lift and she sees their shadows on the wall as their bodies meet, as they both sigh with all those months of longing. He kisses her, she kisses him. She wants him as much as he wants her. The fire crackles in the next room, Leonard Cohen goes around and around on the turntable. The dog scratches the door feebly, asking to be let in.

And then later as it begins to get light outside, Jane lies on her back facing the ceiling. David sleeps, one arm across her breasts. She lies on the bed and wonders what is happening. She thinks about having to go to school on Monday morning, having to see David in class. Audrey leaves as Jane begins to cry again, Audrey leaves as she thinks this will not make her happy. She leaves and then she is the one who is alone in the dark, driving.

At school on Monday Jane looked fine, she made a loud joke in Math class. At lunch they walked to the end of the playing field. 'Well?' Audrey said. Jane said nothing, looked grave. 'How did you get home?' she asked.

'He dropped me off at the top of the road. I walked back. No one saw us – everyone was asleep.'

'Have you seen him today?' David had become 'him', somehow saying his name was too frivolous, flirty.

'In the hallway. We didn't speak.' Jane's voice was distant, she looked out across the field, back in the direction of the school buildings, blue cigarette smoke twisting around her face.

Audrey felt shy when she saw David in the corridor that afternoon and then the next day in class. He hesitated whenever he looked in their direction, becoming a little clumsy. Audrey and Jane sat together but they didn't look at each other, couldn't think of anything to say. The secret was so big now, the weight was suffocating.

David invited them to his place as usual on Friday night. Audrey picked up Jane. They talked about other things on the way, about classmates and their arguments. It all seemed very childish, they had aged one hundred years. Jane held her body stiffly.

Audrey did not stay long that evening. They started out like they always had done. David tried hard to be entertaining, they talked about books. Jane said very little. David played records but no one sang along. Audrey had one beer, one only. Being with them was somehow sobering. 'Okay,' she said, 'I'm going.' She stood. She felt awkward, in the way, as though she was coming between them. Should she just assume that Jane would be staying? She looked from Jane to David. Neither of them spoke so she left. Audrey left them behind in the cottage on the beach.

★

So, fidelity is not the most important thing in the world. Relationships can withstand violation. Monogamy is not necessary, when there is more, when there is agreement. There are other kinds of loyalty, more ways to render a commitment.

Audrey scribbled these notes on a scrap of paper. She was not in the habit of fabricating reassurance for herself, it was not something at which she excelled. She sat back and read the lines out loud then added one further:

If you want to, you can make anything work.

Promises, vows, pacts. They had not made any of these. Audrey thought about her parents. When her mother died they had been married for forty years. Forty years of absolute faith, sleeping together in the same bed, night after night. Audrey thought gloomily that if she and Jack were married tomorrow – and they would not be – they probably hadn't enough years left to live to get to a fortieth anniversary. Her parents' marriage wasn't perfect, but at least it was long. Didn't that count for something?

Her schedule was busy over the next few days. She saw Jack on Friday night. They went to the movies and then home to bed, fucking each other hard, not talking. Jack was preoccupied – his production team was in Martinique and they were having difficulties, he was going to fly out some time soon. He didn't elaborate, Audrey didn't ask. She hadn't spoken to Shereen that week, hadn't seen anyone else either. Work was going well.

On her own at night, she kept returning to her encyclopaedia.

> Migrations, or the shiftings of peoples, have been universal
> on the earth in space and time . . . The movements of
> people which are sufficiently dramatic for the ordinary
> historian to record are often of less importance than the
> quiet, steady drift of a population from one area into
> another, as, for example, the emigration from Europe to
> America in modern times. Movements may result in a
> noticeable or even fatal depletion of a country, and the
> parent country may remain desolate or may be filled up in
> the course of time by an alien people.

Audrey felt as though she was searching for something,
wisdom the big brown books might impart. Some nights
she turned to the encyclopaedia and opened a volume at
random, as if its Second World War certainties might
explain things, might help assemble her thoughts into a
coherent shape. Inspired by her research for Shula Cronin,
she read and re-read the entries under Britain, England,
Empire, Quebec, Canada, British Columbia, but they
described strange places, nowhere she could recognize. She
turned the pages until Jack forced his way back into her
thoughts. Then she fell into an erotic slumber, full of
questions, unnamed desires.

Not long after James and Amelia departed Fort St James for
Fort Vancouver, Amelia's father retired from his post as
HBC Chief Factor, leaving the fur country, returning east.
William Connolly had had a long, respected career, and
owned a profit-share of the Company. He took his wife,
Suzanne Pas de Nom, back to Red River, where they had
been married *à la façon du pays* many years before. Once
there, Connolly suddenly announced to the world that his
marriage had never been real, never properly sanctified, a
country marriage, a bush marriage, of the forest not the

city. He repudiated his wife, Suzanne Pas de Nom, and his children, all of whom were adult by then, married, like Amelia, with children of their own. He placed Suzanne in the care of a convent. Then in Montreal he married a white woman, his cousin, Julia Woolrich. The custom of the land was not custom enough for William Connolly.

News travelled slowly from the east to the west, and Amelia received word of her father's faithlessness soon after the death of Alec. She could not travel to her mother, it was too far, they hadn't the resources or time. So, instead, Amelia worried, and speculated.

For both Amelia and James, Connolly's actions were horrifying. Connolly repudiated the very thing upon which they were building their lives, mixed blood, the very thing that ran through their veins. In the populated east, people approved of Connolly's actions, they thought he had done the right thing in leaving the Cree woman and marrying one of his own kind. One of their own kind was the very thing that Amelia and James could never be.

Amelia was twenty years old when Connolly repudiated her mother; she had been married to James for nearly four years. Her father had betrayed the woman Amelia loved above all others, and he betrayed the contract between native and white, he tipped the precarious balance maintained there on the edge, sending the rest of them through the ice. She despised her father for what he had done. He made a mockery of her life, of her own marriage.

And Suzanne Pas de Nom, *pas de nom*, without a name, in a convent after all those years of marriage to a white man. Amelia wondered, did the prayers of the nuns help compensate? Did the whirling incense of the chapel numb her sorrow and shame, she herself a convert from long past? Or did she stare at the lime-washed wall and whisper Cree words, thinking of her children, of Connolly, of Julia Woolrich, the eighteen-year-old white girl for whom he had abandoned her?

In the night, as she lay awake, Amelia resolved to forget her father. In the morning she told James her decision. He knew her resolution was like a thing of iron, and yet he was afraid for her. He had always been the one who had bricked up his past, built a wall between himself and Scotland and all that came before his boat landed in Quebec. He could not give her lessons in forgetting. She tried to erase her father – how could she erase him? – from her memory. Some nights she lay awake wondering if she could feel her own marriage breaking apart. Would she see it coming? Her mother had not. She looked at James and thought of the day when he, too, might walk away, leaving her to her half-remembered Cree ways.

James caught her look. They were lying in bed. A single candle burned. The smell of cedar, ever present, came to him suddenly. He could hear the river, heavy with early spring, in the distance.

'I will never leave you, Amelia.'

'No, James?' Amelia knew she could – she must – believe him. She did believe him although the air was full of betrayal, native and half-breed women and their children, their unspoken vulnerability. If James was to leave her she could not return to her mother, Suzanne Pas de Nom was taken away, destroyed when Connolly broke the bargain they made. Where would she go? Who would she be?

'No. I do love you,' he pressed.

And she turned to him, her parents banished. She tugged at the ties on his nightshirt, a ragged bit of cloth that he had brought with him from Lanarkshire and not yet been able to discard. She placed her hand against his bared chest and felt him breathe. James shuddered to think of Suzanne Connolly abandoned and spurned. He thought of his own mother. He pulled Amelia closer, burying his face in her black hair.

★

Sunday afternoon Jack dropped by unexpectedly. Audrey had left his flat early Saturday to go home to work; she was late with a deadline. She hadn't asked what he was doing that evening, Jack preferred to leave things that way. It was not unusual for him to stop by but today felt different. When Audrey opened the door and saw it was him she knew something had happened.

'Hi,' he said, tramping across her carpet in his well-polished boots, his leather jacket flapping. 'How's work?'

'Good, I—'

'Could I have a cup of coffee?'

'Sure,' said Audrey. She went into the kitchen. He followed her.

'Stay in last night?'

'Yes, I got quite a lot done.'

'Good, good,' he paused.

'What about you?' she asked.

'I went out with Shereen.'

'Oh?' said Audrey, plugging in the kettle. 'What did you do?' She tried to sound casual but she was paying close attention to what Jack was saying, memorizing every word, every gesture he made. She felt as though she was deciphering as he spoke, like he was using a foreign language.

'We slept together, Audrey.'

Audrey looked at her hands. She saw they were wrinkled, her skin dry. She walked past Jack into the sitting room, stopping in front of her desk. She looked down at her work, the messy piles of papers, the unsharpened pencils, the pens with their inky nibs. She had left her computer on. She turned it off.

Audrey thought back to the first time she met Shereen – at a party, the same night she first met Jack. And the second time, the second party, after she had spoken to Shereen on the telephone about the article – that was her second meeting with Jack as well. It was as though Jack and

Shereen had been proceeding in a line towards each other and Audrey had somehow got between them, intercepting their progress, getting stuck, in the way.

'I thought I should tell you as soon as I could.'

'Why didn't you ring me up while you were doing it?' She spoke without looking at him.

'Audrey.'

She turned away.

'I don't feel that things between us have to change.'

'No, of course not, no reason to change. You can have two women. Nothing unusual in that.' She looked away again. 'Did you use a condom?'

Jack folded his arms, angry.

Audrey walked out of the room, into her bedroom. She sat down and waited for Jack to leave.

PART TWO

Making strange

I don't know a single white who doesn't start salivating when the issue of interracial copulation is raised. As long as there's at least one taker, I'll have work in America.

Dany Laferrière,
Why Must a Black Writer Write About Sex?, 1994

5

Jack left Audrey's flat. She heard his heels echo on the stairs. She wiped her eyes, although she hadn't stopped crying, and tried to drink the coffee she had made for him, her breath jerky, her throat constricted. Gina had said he was a bounder. Gina told me about his affairs. Audrey thought about ringing Shereen and screaming at her, but did not. How could they treat me this way? She sat down at her desk. After a while she made herself work.

Later, Audrey looked up from her computer, out the window at the street. Five geese in a mazy formation flew noiselessly overhead, migrating between city parks.

She did not want a long dark night of the soul to descend upon her now. Jack was gone. When he closed the door she knew right away not to put up an undignified fight, ring him, demand to see him, bring him face to face with her dismay. She thought he would be adept at moving from one alliance to another, he would not have doubts or regrets. If it did not happen with Shereen he'd be off again. There was no point in pretending otherwise. Accept defeat gracefully. There had been no real battle. She had to get on, she had to keep going, she had to work to save herself. Keep everything under control. When someone leaves you it can lead to dark corners, to places you've never wanted to go. Audrey willed herself in the opposite direction, into a kind of solitary limbo, auto-pilot controls switched on. She had survived the departure of a lover before, she would survive it again. It was a straightforward exercise in self-control. She took comfort in this resolve and, at the same time, wondered how long it would last.

That night, before she went to bed, Audrey got out her stepladder and searched the corners of the bedroom ceiling for hidden video cameras. Behind the pictures, above the picture rail, along the skirting board. She looked under furniture, and, seeing the dust, had to get out the hoover as well, castigating herself for sluttishness.

Once in bed, she lay awake. There had been lots of clues, but she had chosen to ignore them, to live with them. Jack had made his feelings plain, she had no claim on him. And she had lost a friend as well. Lost – she was sure of that, there could be no resolution, a time would not come when she would say, 'Oh, it was bad then, but we're all good friends now,' smiling while other people looked on, warmed by her benevolence. Once again, Audrey felt disconnected from herself, from the events, as though it was happening to someone else, not her. Oh, it didn't matter, there were worse things in the world, her little love saga meant nothing.

★

Audrey knew that Jane and David kept seeing each other, although after the third time Audrey left Jane behind at the cottage, she herself stopped going. They did not talk about it, she just stopped, she did not want to go any more. It had become difficult for the three of them to spend time together. It was as though there was something large hovering over their heads. Audrey felt squashed. The tension between Jane and David was palpable, their desire. They both seemed depressed. Maybe it was the influence of all those Leonard Cohen records, but Audrey thought that people were supposed to be happy and carefree when they were in love, not dour and strange. It was as though from the very outset they felt they were ill-fated, that made it more romantic. And, of course, it was. Ill-fated. And romantic.

Once she stopped delivering Jane into David's arms it became more difficult to talk. Audrey was embarrassed by what was happening. She did not want to think about it too hard, she knew that might lead to admitting to disappointment that David had chosen Jane, not her. It did not bear thinking about. But Jane was always the one everyone felt was meant for this kind of thing, fated for love, fated for sadness. Audrey blamed Bob Dylan. She thinks now that if David had come anywhere near her at the time she would have deflected his advances. 'It's not me you want, it's Jane.'

So Jane no longer said what she was thinking. They kept up their old sinful ways, getting plastered on the weekends, going to parties where they ignored everyone else, making plans they already knew they would not carry out. A couple of times they met David downtown in their favourite divey bar, the Beaver. They used to serve beer by the gallon there, waiters would weave through the dark crowded room carrying trays laden with as many as a dozen jugs. British Columbia had very draconian liquor laws; the sale of alcohol was controlled by the state. In bars customers had to be seated at tables in order to be served. Walking with a drink in your hand was illegal. Audrey imagined these laws stemmed from the days of frontier saloon-bar brawls, when to stand up with a drink probably meant you were about to throw it at someone before beating them up. It was easy to imagine this happening in the Beaver. But Audrey did not go out to David's cottage any more. She had been excluded from that.

Without telling Jane, Audrey began to apply to universities.

★

On each new day, Audrey worked. Making herself a fresh cup of tea every time she finished a paragraph, she turned on the answering machine and unplugged the telephone.

She worked on articles in the morning, sought commissions in the afternoon, and went to the library or stayed at home and read in the evening. She found it easy to lose herself in activity. London was a city that inspired overwork. The work-ethic bred in the air, a protestant contagion. Audrey was susceptible to it.

Late at night she would stop reading and, before she went to bed, listen to the messages on her answering machine. There would be one or two calls from editors, perhaps a few words from Gina or another friend. Every two or three days there was a message from Shereen. 'Audrey?' she would repeat, 'Audrey?', as though expecting her to pick up the phone. 'It's Shereen. Ring me. I want to talk.' Audrey stood perfectly still while Shereen's voice played, staring at the blinking red light on the machine. Eventually Shereen said good-bye and Audrey let the stinging angles of her shoulders relax back into place.

She met Gina for a drink one night. This was a big step.

'I feel like I haven't seen you all year,' Gina said. She was dressed as though she expected to go to a club later, hair slicked down, make-up perfect, on form.

Audrey felt exhausted. 'How's Charlotte?'

'Not a baby any more. We might have another one.' She rolled her eyes at the thought. 'But what have *you* been doing? You never answer your phone.'

'Working.'

'You work like a slave, when do you have time to see Jack?'

'I don't.'

'Well, that's the perfect recipe for a healthy relationship,' Gina said.

'He dumped me.' The shock on Gina's face gave Audrey a mild thrill. 'He went off with a friend of mine.'

'Who?' said Gina, indignant.

'You don't know her.'

'The bloody bitch. The bastard. You poor thing.' She

scooted along the bench, put an arm around Audrey's shoulder and squeezed hard. 'Fuck. You poor fucking thing.' She squeezed again. 'Well, I always said . . .'

'You always said he was too good to be true.'

'And I was right.'

'I don't know,' said Audrey. 'I didn't give him all that much to hang on to in the first place.' She had negotiated this position for herself.

'That's right, blame yourself.'

'I'm not blaming anybody—'

'That's your problem, Audrey, you've become too English. Too self-contained, too restrained somehow. You should be having a fit.'

'Well, I am having a fit. In my own way.'

'By working too hard.'

'Work is interesting. I've got to make a living. I can't completely fall apart.'

'Oh come on. Drink up. Let's go dancing.'

Audrey stood against the wall in the dark club. Gina swung around on the dance floor by herself. Gina knew everybody. As she watched, Audrey thought, Gina's a good friend. Gina's my mate. She was the only one who asked questions about Audrey's parents, who had tried to get her to talk when her mother died. Audrey loved her for it, although she hadn't talked. Almost, but not quite.

Audrey dragged on her cigarette, leaned back – the wall of the club was covered with damp Styrofoam spray-painted black – and hunched forward again. It smelt in there, it really did, sweat, sex and toilets, she had to smoke just to breathe. Gina had taken something that made her even more hyper than she already was, but Audrey preferred to drown in drink.

A few days later, Audrey took off, like a Canada goose, she flew to Toronto. She needed a holiday, and a TV advert for

Air Canada had reminded her of her friend Toby. She packed her bag and left a light on in her sitting room for the burglars. She hadn't been out of London since before she met Jack.

In Toronto, the sky was a clear, reassuring blue and, at the airport, the tarmac melted under the sun. Audrey took a cab to Toby's apartment – he lived above a Ukrainian bookstore on Queen Street. He was away, but he had arranged for her to stay at his flat with his girlfriend. She rang the bell on the street and, moments later, a window overhead flew open. 'Who's that?' someone shouted.

Inside, Maisie Roscoe did not introduce herself. She had rag-doll hair the colour of a Coca-Cola tin and she wore a short black Lycra dress that was slashed between her breasts. She had bare legs, bare arms, an amazing tan. High-heeled mules hung off her feet and she wore kohl around her eyes, lots of dark and creamy lipstick. She was skinny and nearly six foot.

'Toby said you'd arrive today – what's your name again?'

Audrey offered to stay in a hotel.

'Oh no, this apartment is huge.' She spread her spindly arms wide to indicate its vastness. A ceiling fan turned, the curtains on the balcony doors moved gently.

'I won't be here that much – I'm working,' Audrey lied, feeling compelled to apologize, 'and I fly home in four days.'

'I love your accent,' Maisie said, 'it's just like Toby's.'

'Oh,' said Audrey, deflated.

Maisie showed Audrey her room, gave her a set of keys, and said she was off to work. She said she waitressed in a bar up the street, and invited Audrey to come along later to have a drink.

Maisie left, and Audrey fell onto the bed. She had never done this before, flown somewhere for no reason, by herself. Without Toby around she knew no one in Toronto. Except Shula Cronin, of course. She opened her satchel, pulled out the professor's letters. Staring blankly at the letterhead, she resolved to call tomorrow. Then she washed her face and went out for a woozy, post-air-cabin-pressure, walk.

It was just getting dark and outside, Toronto was lighting up. It felt strange to be in Canada, and yet not in BC. She was still three thousand miles away from her father, close, but safe. Canada was home, she thought, dousing herself in irony. She could come and live here if she wanted. This part of the city had not changed since her last trip, a slightly surreal combination of Central European bakeries and bars too groovy to breathe in. Audrey didn't feel at home on the grid-arm streets of Toronto, even with the seductive warm air on her face. On every street corner, the day crowd thinning, the evening scene thickening up, Audrey saw Jack, in the angle of a neck, a dark skin, a leather jacket, a briefcase. Her heart speeding up, slowing down. It was never him, how could it be? She hadn't told anyone in London where she was going. He would not have come after her.

She went into the bar where Maisie worked and had a beer and a cigarette with her on her break. Her hair looked even redder, blood red, in the blue lights of the bar; she kept saying she hoped her dealer would come in. When Audrey headed back onto the street, the night was black and much cooler. She walked back to the apartment quickly, her head spinning with alcohol and jet-lag. Maisie made her feel old.

The next day, after a deep and syrupy sleep, Audrey rang the university. She felt a little trepidation, given the bizarre and stern letters Shula Cronin had written. But she was in a strange city and felt compelled to make contact with at least one other of its inhabitants. And, she was curious about the academic.

'Professor Cronin speaking.'

Audrey identified herself, but met with a blank. 'London. The British Library.'

A shocked silence. 'Is there a problem?'

'No, Professor Cronin, no problem. It's just that I'm in Toronto for a few days and I wondered if we might meet.'

A little reluctantly, or so it seemed, Shula Cronin agreed to see Audrey the next day.

They met in a neighbourhood called the Annexe, a better class of groovy bar and bookshop than Queen Street. Audrey waited anxiously in a café – she had spent the morning shopping and had bought books and some clothes. She watched Shula Cronin enter the café, let her peer around at the other diners for a few moments. She knew it was her immediately, although she did not look like Audrey had imagined. The older woman's hair was a short, grey crop, she wore rimless spectacles on a gold chain. Her arms were boldly bare, as unfashionably tanned as Maisie's. She had on open sandals and faded blue jeans and a tight T-shirt that showed off her breasts, showcased her breasts, in fact. Audrey remembered suddenly that Carol Lumbank had mentioned something about breast cancer. And, just as suddenly, she remembered Shula Cronin had said in her last letter that she had once been in a plane crash. At the time, when the letter first arrived, Audrey hadn't thought about it, a plane crash fitted right in with the spiky cussedness of the rest of the letters. Of course she had been in a plane crash, she was obviously a woman to whom things happened. But now that she was there, in the flesh, standing a few tables away, all Audrey could think about was – a plane crash, you survived, how absolutely extraordinary.

Shaking herself from this reverie, Audrey waved. The professor walked towards her, launching into a stream of self-conscious worrying even before she sat down.

'Why are you here? Is it – is there something wrong? Have you got family here?'

'No, I—'

'You sound very English. You've been away too long. Is Toronto your home? Where are you staying?'

In stops and starts, Audrey answered her questions, although Shula Cronin never seemed satisfied with her replies. She pulled a sheaf of papers – the latest fruits of her research – from her bag and handed them across the table.

'Oh thank you. Very good. You're from BC? How interesting. You know, so am I. I come from Prince Rupert, but of course I haven't lived there for years. I did all my primary fieldwork there in the early days. All that rain. On a good day, when it's just drizzling, everyone remarks on what wonderful weather they are having, just like in Ireland. Have you been there? To Prince Rupert, I mean. And the Charlottes – Haida Gwaii? Do you get to BC often? Where's your family? Have you children yourself?'

Audrey tried to keep up, giving one-word answers, nods and shakes of her head. They ordered salads and cappuccinos. Eventually Shula Cronin began to slow down.

'You must forgive me – I – get a little nervous. A little excited.'

'That's okay.'

'Why are you here? It's unexpected, is it not?'

'Yes, I just wanted a break. To get away.'

'You really do sound very English – not completely English, but very much so.'

'I do?' Audrey felt a little dismayed, like she had when Maisie claimed she sounded just like Toby. Foreign in Canada, and a poncey accent to boot.

'Don't worry. I won't report you.' She smiled.

'Professor Cronin—'

'Oh, don't call me that. Shula.'

'Shula. I – I hope you don't mind me asking – well, I know that you do mind, actually, but I'm going to ask anyway, now that we've met, face to face.' Audrey paused, hoping Shula would smile encouragingly. She did not. Audrey figured she could get away with one personal question, either about the book and the research, or about the plane crash. She paused, trying to decide. What was it like? Did it happen before you knew it, or were there long moments of freefall? Did you see the ground rush to meet you? It was a lake, wasn't it? The water. Did you think you were dead? Did those little lights down the aisle come on? Audrey was not afraid of flying, she never thought twice before getting on an aeroplane, but the idea of being in a crash was truly awe-inspiring. She was dying to ask about it. She took a deep breath. Her heart was pounding. 'What *is* your new book about?' That was that.

'You heard what happened with the last book?' Shula's look was piercing.

'Yes, I did.' The problem with her residential background.

'Have you read it?'

'No—'

'That's it. People judge it, but they haven't read it.'

'I haven't judged it.'

'No, not you dear, I don't suppose you have. Well, this time I'm really going to give them something to talk about.' She smiled broadly and looked happy for the first time since they met. Audrey waited. 'I'm writing a book about Québecois nationalism – about the separatist movement, its historical roots, its present-day hypocrisies. I was going to call it "Quebec: Who Gives a Fuck?" but I think that's a little strong.' She laughed.

Audrey laughed too, more out of surprise. 'A little strong, yes. What's it called now?'

'Oh I don't know yet,' she waved her hand dismissively. 'I'm tired of listening to politicians and other academics bang on about it, it's time to have my say.'

'What's your thesis?'

She peered at Audrey, as though sizing her up. 'Those nationalists – at their most extreme – believe in racial purity. They think the Québecois are a race. They do – believe me. I am going to write a book that shows how those people, that race, from Samuel de Champlain onward, are descended from mixed blood – the blood of the English as well as the French, the Algonquin, Huron, Iroquois, Mohawk . . . the blood of the French empire – West Indian, Vietnamese, Haitian . . . and that their notion of racial purity is as backward and ill-informed as that of the Ku Klux Klan.' Shula stopped speaking, and looked triumphant.

Audrey cleared her throat and wondered if she dare to speak. 'So, that's still a big issue here then?'

'Yes,' said Shula, 'yes it is. And you cannot believe how boring and low the level of debate is, for the most part.'

'Are you sure this is – wise?'

'No. It isn't wise. But there are certain things that need to be said – it's not their land, how can it be, if it belongs to anyone it belongs to the indigenous people. That's true of the whole of Canada. Same goes for the water, the right to sell hydro-power to the Americans. It's all a lie. Modernity is too mixed up – no one is pure. Purity is a disguise.'

They had their lunch, and they talked on, and Shula became more motherly and benevolent when she realized that the younger woman was not going to attack her views. Audrey was happy to admit that she did not know much about the situation, she had lived away too long, Victoria was far from Montreal, London further still, she didn't really have an opinion about Québecois national sovereignty. This seemed to free up Shula, and she talked unguardedly. She gave Audrey a list of recommended reading which Audrey obediently noted down and promised to pursue.

'So tell me about your education.'

'My education?' Audrey wasn't sure what she meant.

'Yes, what kind of degrees do you have – where did you study? Did you study journalism?'

'No, I . . . I don't have a degree.'

'No degree?' Shula said, adjusting her glasses where they swung against her chest.

'I dropped out. UBC.' Audrey lifted her hands apologetically. What could she say to an academic? 'I was doing a degree in History.' She decided to wing it. 'I got very interested in the history of BC – post-white settlement, that is. The fur trade. James and Amelia Douglas, that kind of thing. There's a family connection – my father is supposed to be related to Douglas in some way.' Audrey shrugged, feeling vaguely embarrassed by this claim.

'Our family histories often have relevance to our futures, don't you think? It's not something people pay much attention to these days. Do you regret not finishing?'

'No. Never gave it a second thought. Well – I left for personal reasons.' Audrey could feel herself blushing. 'But it's funny, I do think about James and Amelia – the Douglases. They've begun to inhabit my dreams somehow.' Shula looked interested, so Audrey went on talking. 'It's funny – ' she kept saying it was funny, when, of course, it was not – 'I've been having a hard time lately, and it's as though my past is coming back to me, pressing in on me.'

'I find that as one gets older, this happens.'

'Yes, but, I thought it happened when you were really old, in your eighties,' Audrey laughed.

'I think that reinhabiting the past is part of being adult. Only the very young and the very lucky have nothing following them.'

'Yes,' said Audrey, 'you're right.'

When they parted ways, Shula Cronin kissed Audrey on the cheek. Out on the pavement, Audrey turned and watched her walk away.

That night, even before she went to sleep, she knew she would dream about James and Amelia, technicolour dreams, as though she'd been there, as though she knew how they would feel and think.

At Fort Vancouver James and Amelia wed a second time.

With the rapid development of the settlement came an increase of white settlers, with population came greater concern for European custom and habit. James saw it was a slow process, an accretion, and he felt reassured; New Caledonia would never catch up with Britain when it came to double standards and complex social mores. Herbert Beaver, an HBC chaplain – everyone in the fur trade had to struggle to keep a straight face when introduced to the Reverend Beaver – arrived at the fort with his English wife, Jane. There were still very few white women in the far west, Jane Beaver one of the first. She and her husband made no effort to conceal their disapproval of 'country marriages', no matter how faithful. Officially proscribed, these marriages went unrecorded in Hudson's Bay Company journals, but the Beavers had travelled widely west of Red River and were alarmed at the numerousness of these alliances. On arriving at Fort Vancouver, they snubbed Amelia Douglas when James introduced her as his wife.

Herbert Beaver took James to one side. 'Among the white race, marriage is sacred,' the cleric said, his eyes narrow and square-sided.

James nodded his head in sonorous agreement. After a moment, brief but telling, he realized that the Reverend was implying his own marriage was not. Struck dumb, he allowed the man to slip away. He leaned against the wall, the splintered wood poking through the rough cloth of his shirt. He looked for Amelia, but could not find her.

Later, in the corridor outside his office, James overheard Jane Beaver lecturing a young HBC clerk. Her voice rang out. 'Indian wives,' her tone was harsh, 'and their half-breed offspring, are little calculated to improve the manners of society.' The Beavers had gone on the warpath.

James sank into melancholy. He examined his life, his actions. At first he could see no true difference between his marriage and any other. His wedding vows were embedded in his heart, and he dismissed the words of the chaplain as the chatter of a new arrival, slightly bowed by the fresh, open world of the west. After so many years in the bush he had grown accustomed to keeping faith at his own pace without the Church to guide him, and, besides, the English Church had never been his own. Herbert and Jane Beaver, with their eastern ways and morals, Jane and her bonnet and stays, Reverend Beaver with the bible he never seemed to close, were impossibly formal and fey, and Jane Beaver so cold and rude to Amelia, this alone was enough to provoke James. But still they went on, harping on their one-note melody.

'What is it about?' Amelia asked James in their private rooms.

'Our marriage, Amelia – the Reverend does not consider it . . . proprietous.'

Amelia laughed.

'It's not . . . gentlemanly.' He searched for words to explain and, as he did, he understood he was made uncomfortable by the steady nudging of the Beavers. They were like their namesakes, gnawing away at the trunk of a tree, weakening it at its base. He liked to do things by the book, he could not abide duplicity, nor moral turpitude, and shuddered to find himself accused of these vices. His thoughts went directly to his father's behaviour, and the fact of his own illegitimacy. He was the only man on the entire vast continent who knew his father's story, yet he could not bear to think of himself repeating it, living it, even if no one would recognize it as such.

'But we've always been together,' Amelia replied plainly.

'There are people who do things differently from us, away from our world here. In Montreal, London . . . and Red River,' he said, reminding her of her mother.

'But we are far from those places.'

'Not so far, Amelia, and we will be brought closer yet.'

The Beavers' complaints and objections became increasingly bitter and damning and shrill. In the small enclosure of the fort, there was no escape. Amelia took the reminder of her mother's fate to heart; James kept his thoughts of his own mother to himself. Without having to discuss it much further, they consented to a Church of England wedding. More than a decade after their original union on Stuart Lake, they stood up together in the small chapel, newly built of red cedar, wearing their best clothes, James a waistcoat, Amelia in a bonnet at the insistence of Mrs Beaver. They drank HBC rum with the company. Afterwards they took pleasure in the idea that they were newly wed.

The Reverend Herbert Beaver and his wife did not last long at Fort Vancouver, soon retreating back east to the Red River Settlement, where European manners – and wives – were fast becoming the norm. A year later James heard that when Jane Beaver was asked what she thought of the Wild West, and of being one of the first white women to see it, she complained of the mosquitoes, and the half-breeds.

But even after ten years, and the great changes of their times, James and Amelia were captured by each other and the shifts and stirrings of their marriage. Amelia, with her small sturdy body, gave of herself to James in a way that continually charmed and hypnotized him; she found something in him, some indefinable trait he could not and was not called upon to show any other person. They dipped together and this is what they shared, their marriage consecrated not once, but twice, in the custom of the land, and then in the custom of the colony. They felt a double bond, and this gave them succour through the multiple births and deaths of their babies. Amelia Douglas bore fourteen babies in twenty-five years, and more than half of them dead: Amelia in infancy, Alexander – named for James's brother – in the air, John – named for James's father

– all dead in the first five years of their union. Maria and Cecilia, twins, Cecilia the sole surviver, named for James's sister. Ellen, dead, and then a string of children who lived – Jane, Agnes and Alice. And then Margaret, aged two, and Rebecca – named for James's mother's mother – dead, one after the other. They never got used to burying their babies, but when James and Amelia and the four living children were to finally depart from Fort Vancouver, they left behind a row of gravestones that marked a terrible passage. By then James could have grown shy of touching Amelia for fear of inflicting on her another confinement that would end in pain – but Amelia took solace in her husband's embrace, in their mutual passion. She always believed that her children would live. There was no other way.

At home, James and Amelia watched eagles, caught salmon, told warm stories to the children on cold winter nights. Then, in 1849, James was appointed Chief Factor to the HBC post on Vancouver Island, a site he had reconnoitred himself six years previously.

And so to Fort Victoria, and two more late children, James and Martha, the last twenty years younger than the eldest living. James called Vancouver Island his 'Eden'. There he embarked on his rapid progress to head of state. Their reformation was remarkable, Atlantic crossings and Cree myths, transporting them to a middle age of expansion and security.

The next night Maisie held an impromptu party in the flat after closing hours. Audrey was asleep, but she was soon woken up. She got dressed and put on some make-up. In the large main room of the apartment music was stonking, low bass loud rhythm, and twenty people were dancing very slowly, Maisie slowest of all. There was a bag of cocaine on the kitchen table and no one noticed when Audrey sat down in front of it. It had been a while, but she remembered what to do. These few days in Toronto – she was flying back to London in the morning – had not really done the trick. She turned her chair around to watch people dance. Maisie smiled and waved in slow-motion. The thud of the bass both agitated and soothed Audrey. Maybe when she got back to London Jack would have changed his mind.

Maybe not.

Audrey returned home to find her answering machine flashing lights like a police car. Five messages from Shereen – one for every day she'd been away – and five messages from her parents' old friend, Dorothy Jones. It took a few moments to connect the name to the person. Dorothy Jones whose hip was broken when Audrey's father ploughed down the women outside the Chinese restaurant. Dorothy Jones, whose family did not sue.

'Audrey, this is Dorothy Jones, friend of the family. Please call me on 604–968–5222.'

'Audrey, Mrs Jones again. We need you to call right away. Just in case you didn't get it last time, my number is 604–968–5222.'

'Audrey, Dorothy. Perhaps you are away, dear. Please call as soon as possible.'

'Dorothy Jones. Audrey. Your father has passed away. There was no pain. Please get in touch as soon as you come in.'

'Audrey. Dorothy Jones. Are you there?'

Audrey listened to the messages, fast-forwarding over Shereen. Then she replayed the tape, stopping after the words, 'There was no pain'. She picked up the phone and, without thinking, dialled her parents' old number. She put down the receiver, took a deep breath. 'There was no pain'; was this her absolution? She rang Dorothy Jones. Mrs Jones said that her father had 'found peace at last'. Audrey counted the days backwards – her father had died the day she flew to Toronto.

'He is at rest now, with your mother.'

Audrey was unable to reply.

'The funeral is going ahead, dear, we didn't know where you were. But if you come now, you'll make it in time. You should come home, sort out his affairs. And if you could phone your father's lawyer, that would be good too. He wasn't uncomfortable, dear, the doctor saw to that.'

'How's your hip?' The voice that came out of Audrey's mouth was not recognizable.

'Well, I'm golfing again, Audrey, thank God.'

'That's good. I'll be there soon. Wait for me.' Audrey put the phone down. She had been in Canada when her father died, but on the wrong side of it. It was a large and non-negotiable failure. Before her mother died she used to plan what she would do if anything happened to her parents. She had a litany she'd repeat while lying awake at night: I will use my credit card, I will ring the airlines and get the next flight to Vancouver or Seattle, they make allowances for this kind of emergency, I can be there in fourteen hours, at the most twenty-four, in this day and age it hardly matters if you live six thousand miles away.

Of course, things went wrong for her father more gradually than that, and Audrey's mother was never one for late-night phone calls even when her husband was in serious difficulty. She'd always wait a few days, until things were better, then she would call and inform Audrey of what she'd missed. And things always did get better, they always had.

When she was a teenager in British Columbia Audrey used to think that everyone was basically the same. She thought the people around her all came from white Anglo-Saxon stock, or maybe German at a pinch. There were always Chinese kids in her school, even in the interior, Japanese, people from the Asian sub-continent, and of course native people, the indigenous people, particularly on the coast. But they – who? her family? her teachers? – thought of BC as a white place, a white British place somehow. Her parents' friends were all white, and that seemed ordinary. They held differing political opinions, of course; when Audrey was young her parents had leaned to the left. She remembered that Dorothy Jones always had very firm politics, firm to the point of rigidity. Audrey could remember a conversation where Mrs Jones said she believed in hanging the poor. Even when Mr Jones, her husband, was dying, blind and raging from alcoholism and diabetes, nothing made Dorothy Jones uncertain. When Audrey was fourteen – serious about her schoolwork, the glass in her spectacles thickening every year – Dorothy Jones had looked at her across the dinner table one evening and announced, 'Boys don't make passes at girls who wear glasses.' Audrey, mortified, had asked and been allowed to leave the table. As she rose, Mrs Jones, a wide and jolly smile on her face, held up the now empty bottle of wine and exclaimed, 'Another dead Indian!' Audrey's father leapt up to get more of his home-made blackberry wine from the refrigerator, and Audrey had felt a sore and burning loathing as she left the room.

They'd been great patriots, Audrey's parents. She remembered how her mother had loved the glamorous Pierre Trudeau and his vision of a bilingual Canada, two nations, one flag, whatever that meant. Two nations, as Shula said, what about First Nations? But still, Audrey could remember lighting up with anti-American passion at certain times, over certain things, like the idea that Canada was somehow less interesting than the States. On trips south when she was a kid they would meet Americans who hardly knew where Canada was even though they lived less than fifty miles from the border. This seemed unforgivably stupid at the time. Now Audrey sees it as part of the American way, that epic self-absorption almost endearing, a whole nation of Jacks maybe.

Audrey had come to London to get away from all that –

never-ending, always the same. Trips to the US, ice hockey on TV, old family friends, their opinions. Boys and girls wearing red-and-black-checked lumberjack shirts, driving souped-up cars, still listening to Supertramp, Fleetwood Mac, and the Sweet. David and Jane. Her parents.

At the funeral she met a bunch of old men who had spent the last five years playing cards with her father. Apparently, he had played a mean hand of cribbage. The sun shone and it was a blue, blue, clear day with little breezes off the ocean. Everything went smoothly – Audrey's parents had planned their funerals years before, bought the plots, picked the coffins, paid for the gravestones, written the inscriptions. There was nothing for Audrey to do, except shake hands with ancient men, be patted on the arm by ancient women, and watch her father laid to rest in the ground next to her mother. She had difficulty recognizing people, Mr McGrath, Mrs Reisner, they'd all aged so. In their eyes she thought she saw reproach for all those visits she hadn't made, but she blinked and turned away. She wore a black dress that in London had looked as though it would do, but in Victoria, at the graveside, felt too short, too low-cut, too tight. Her mascara dripped and ran all over her face, black tracks of emotion and shame. Her father, dead. She had not seen him since her mother died. She didn't know what his room at the home had looked like, what pictures he might have hung on the wall next to his bed, whether he slept well, what he ate, whether he learned to live again after the death of his wife. Audrey couldn't ask anyone these questions now, not even Dorothy Jones. It was too late.

There was no money, she hadn't expected there to be. Audrey signed forms and paid the solicitor for his time. She went to the home and collected her father's belongings from reception – one shoebox and one carrier bag. She did not look at their contents but deposited both at a charity shop before driving the rental car to the beach. She hadn't been to Victoria for a long time, but the ocean was still in the same place.

★

Eventually, amazingly, time crept forward towards graduation. Audrey and Jane were going to finish high school. They were supposed to be convinced that their lives would never be as good, or fun, or happy, again. For those people for whom high school had not been good, or fun, or happy, graduation was little more than a year-long build-up to vast depression and hangover. Audrey knew she would not have a date for the party, but she was not concerned. She would go with Jane – how could Jane have a date, if her date was not to be David? Her mother was making her a dress, she hardly ever wore dresses, but on this she had been forced to concede. Jane wasn't getting a new outfit, but that didn't matter, Jane would look sexy and cool anyway. It was all too gruesome.

But gruesome is as gruesome does and they made their plans – they'd have a stash of beer in the boot of Audrey's mother's car, and they'd arrange a rendezvous with David after midnight at the big party, it would look unplanned, they could spend the time together, just the three of them in the midst of all that revelry. Audrey knew, she was absolutely convinced, that high school was not going to have been the best time of her life, there was no question, but Jane suddenly looked less certain.

And then, Monday before the Friday Graduation Ceremony – an arena had been rented, a local rock band hired, decorations were being made – Jane passed Audrey a note in homeroom, something neither of them had done in ages. She was pale, her hair lank, her shoulders almost bowed.

Audrey kept her hands in her lap, below the desk, unfolding the note so that no one else could read it.

129

Frank is home.

Frank, Jane's old boyfriend, the basketball hero, the one who'd gone off to South America or somewhere, had come home. Audrey folded the note into neat halves, quarters. She looked at Jane, who returned her gaze. She felt a surge of panic. What would happen? To their friendship? To David? To their plans for Grad? She was desperate to talk to her friend.

But now that Jane's life had complications of adult proportions, she became even more elusive. Every time Audrey tried to speak to her that morning, she slipped away. At lunch Audrey stood outside the front door waiting for Jane to come out, but when she did she said, 'Frank is waiting,' and walked towards the parking lot. Audrey recognized Frank's car, the black Camaro he must have stored in his parents' garage for the year. That night she phoned her house, but Jane's mother said she had gone out. The rest of the week, taken up with preparations for Grad, exams and papers already finished, out of the way, Jane did not come to school.

Audrey's mother finished the dress. In it, Audrey looked like a giant angel's-food cake. The dress had creampuff sleeves and a high waist, and the pale material she had liked so much in the fabric department of the Hudson's Bay department store was the colour of toothpaste. When Audrey tried it on for the first time she cried in front of the mirror. Her mother looked on, bewildered.

Friday morning Audrey was decorating the arena with the team of volunteers she had joined at the last minute, determined to find some way to cope with the event. She was on her hands and knees stapling pink toilet paper in flower-like shapes onto an enormous banner that read 'Good Luck To Our Class'. She looked up, and Jane was standing there. She was wearing her faded and torn jeans and a tight white T-shirt that had a small tear above her navel. Her hair was tied back starkly and she was wearing dark glasses and smoking an extra-long cigarette. When Audrey looked at her she felt a familiar surge of lust and longing.

They walked outside into the sun. Jane offered a cigarette, and Audrey took it.

'Frank is taking me to Grad. He came back specially.'

'He did?'

'Yeah.'

Audrey couldn't think of anything to say. She had guessed this would happen. 'Are you happy?'

'Do I look happy?' Jane raised her sunglasses. Her eyes were scarcely open, the circles beneath them swollen and dark. Her cheeks were hollow, her lips thinned and cracked. Audrey saw that the skin under her nose was reddened and raw from crying.

'I haven't got a date,' Audrey said, her voice weak. Now it seemed important.

Jane let her sunglasses drop back into place. 'You can come with us. Frank won't mind. As long as I let him fuck me, he doesn't care about anything.'

Audrey blinked, and tried not to step forward. She wanted to ask questions, about Frank, about David, about everything, but Jane's dark glasses, angled towards her, stopped her. She could see herself reflected in the lenses, odd-cornered, distorted. Frank was tall and blond and very athletic, not the kind of guy to whom Audrey had ever been able to speak. Frank was old Jane, Jane before she and Audrey had become friends, Jane before Leonard Cohen and David. Audrey wished she could vanish and find herself living in another place.

Graduation happened. Her parents came and waved to her up on the podium. After the formal dance, which was a complete ordeal – Audrey danced with David once, which somehow made it worse, Jane was there with Frank and a big gang of her old friends – she drove her mother's car to the beach party. She sat in the sand and leaned against a log, twelve bottles of beer and a mickey of tequila lined up in front of her. She watched the flames of the fire flicker in the brown glass. Every once in a while she thought she heard Jane's voice, high-pitched and laughing too loudly, and later, she thought she could see Jane and some other people dancing in the water, splashing and falling over each other into the waves. From a car stereo Pink Floyd and Alice Cooper bombasted forth. There was no sign of David, no teacher would have dared show their face. A group of grads roared off in a pick-up truck to paint the date and their school's name on the overpass of the highway. Audrey hadn't changed clothes, and her big dress slowly filled with sand, so that when she tried to stand she was unable.

On Monday morning a letter arrived offering Audrey a partial scholarship at UBC, in Vancouver. Without consulting anyone, she wrote back and accepted.

*

Audrey could remember being very, very happy. Inconsolably happy, happiness with tears. On the steps of the British Museum, swinging around, arms wide – this city is mine! Mine. Out on the pitch of the cricket ground at the Oval – she and a friend, drunk, somehow got inside, onto the grass in the middle of the night. They danced around each other, choking, spluttering with laughter, her friend shouting the name of her favourite cricketer, 'Viv Richards, Viv Richards'. On their knees, kissing the earth. A walk along the Thames, down the steps at Vauxhall to kick blackened tin cans along the muddy bank, stranded by the tide. In the Underground even, stale piss, filthy tiles, little black mice scurrying under the rails – this was it, it was London. It was her first city-love, and a love affair so true and strong she felt the city embrace her, she clutched it to her breast. She breathed it in like it was Eden.

But this had changed now; she hadn't noticed when it

began to alter. Prior to Jack, one, two, three years ago, maybe more. Perhaps it paralleled the fate of the city itself, the twists and turns of politics, boom and recession, Livingstone and Thatcher, a gradual descent into ungoverned chaos. London had suffered a loss of identity and, with it, Audrey suffered a loss too.

But it wasn't true, Audrey thought, a city as old as London could never lose itself. It had always been dirty and luxurious, empty warehouse, teeming palace, this was not new. Change was cyclical, it had to be. For many years London has no governing body, then it gets one, elections, controversy, then it's gone again, abolished. Hospitals are private, for a while they are all public, then, gradually, they go private again. Beggars crowd the streets, the homeless, the sick and the wretched. Then they are gone, swept up and barrelled into jobs and secure places. Now they are back again, Audrey meets them in doorways and at train stations. Bombing campaigns start, finish, start again from a new direction. The Thames flowed under the bridges, the clouds moved overhead. It was no better, no worse, than any other time, and London had not really changed.

And, therefore, she reasoned, neither have I. She could not leave, she didn't want to. She was part of it.

6

*You would be delighted with a morning peep of the
varied and highly tinted foliage at James Bay. The
splendour of its rich and gorgeous hues, reflecting the
bright rays of the morning sun, are beautiful beyond
description . . . The air is fragrant with the sweets
exhaled by the wild rose, now blooming in countless
abundance. It is indeed delightful to wander about,
amidst the beauty and wild luxuriance of nature – so far
surpassing in grace the utmost efforts of art . . . The
sweet little robin is pouring out his heart in melody,
making the welkin ring with his morning song of praise
and thanksgiving.*

James Douglas in a letter to his daughter, Martha, 1873

And so Audrey flew back to London from Canada for the second time in two weeks. She hadn't remained in Victoria long after the funeral, she saw no reason to hang around. She was staying in a motel, in a room right next to the ice machine. At night as she lay in bed, trying to sleep, she would hear people filling their ice buckets, giggling. They'd be having parties in their rooms, later they'd rev up their cars. Dorothy Jones had offered to put her up, but Audrey couldn't face that. Her father's death left her feeling cold, very cold, ice-chilled. She hadn't intended to punish him by staying away for so long; she had only done as he had asked, it hadn't been difficult, not really. In London it was easy to forget where she came from, what she might owe to people elsewhere. After the death of her mother, her father was a little old man, and she could no longer recognize him. He wasn't the same man who had come home from business trips with dollies and new pyjamas under his arm. He wasn't the same man who had stood straight-backed in photographs, a whole head and shoulders taller than her mum. He wasn't the same man. But now that he was dead she knew that, in fact, it was him, he was her father. In the years since her mother's death he had made no demands. Audrey telephoned him at Christmas, and on his birthday, sometimes unable to get through. She wrote fairly often, and twice a year sent packets of clippings of articles she had published that she thought might interest him. But he did not reply to her letters. When they spoke he said his handwriting had deteriorated too much. 'It's got so bad,' he said, 'even I can't read it.' On the telephone his powers of speech were diminished as well. He had always been an absent father, and now, Audrey thought, he had disappeared for real. His absence was permanent.

Every year, on the anniversary of her mother's death, Audrey spent the day in bed, under the covers, deep down in a well of blankets, a pillow pulled, lid-like, over the top. This was her mourning. The past year Jack had come round without warning, used the key she had lent him to let himself in, and, when he discovered her lumped form in the bed, pulled out the covers from the bottom of the mattress and climbed into the stuffy hole with her. He'd found her tearstained, her lips puffy, her nose wet, and he had fucked her gently, her body cradled into his. Then he had made her lunch before he left to go to work. It was a better day than other years. Audrey had tried not to think about what her father might be doing.

But now he was dead, and Jack had left, and she was taking the ferry to Vancouver where she would board a flight back to London. It was raining hard, fog moved over the waves, low cloud blowing across the strait. She sat in the forward lounge and looked out the window.

There she was, by the railing, Jane. Audrey felt strapped to her chair. Jane was out there, pregnant, getting drenched, oblivious to the rain. She's out there, thought Audrey, like the last time I saw her. I must do something. I must speak to her. I must make her understand that we can be friends. Audrey pulled herself out of her seat, lurching into a standing position. Just then the rain seemed to increase, water streamed down the window like a dense curtain of beads. Jane turned and began to walk towards the window, her face obscured by the hood of her anorak. She came slowly forward. Audrey placed both hands on the glass, as though she could stop the rain, and draw Jane near to her. Jane moved under the protection of the gangway. She lifted her jacket away from her face. And Audrey saw that she wasn't Jane at all, but another woman, a young woman, about the age Jane would have been when Audrey last saw her.

She wasn't Jane.

Weeks passed, neither quickly nor slowly, time carried with it no freight. Audrey did not ring Jack and Jack did not call her. It was as though they had not spent any time at all in the same bed. It was as though they had never met.

Audrey did not return Shereen's phone calls, although Shereen continued to leave plaintive messages. She lay awake at night and pictured them together. She imagined them having sex, she imagined their bodies, creamy brown skin-tones poured together, producing a love-slick. She rose every morning and began to work immediately.

Audrey thought London a good place to be lonely. Everyone was alone. At the bus-stop, the library, the pub down the street, the queue at the post office, the cinema in the afternoon, here no one spoke, there were no couples, no mates, no words between strangers. Everyone was waiting. Audrey wondered what they waited for. To leave, to go elsewhere? Did life begin somewhere else, around the next corner? Would Audrey recognize the turning when and if it came? And physically, the city streets, the monuments, the very buildings themselves – how could there be such a lonely place? The lowering sky, the babble of unknown languages, everywhere people unable to make themselves understood. Sometimes Audrey went out to sit in the park on blustery afternoons, to watch the sky. Children played alone on the swings, not even the children spoke to each other.

Audrey slipped into slovenliness. She stopped cleaning her flat. The newspapers and magazines she bought every day piled up around the bed. She began filing her work on the floor, in the kitchen. She wore the same loose-fitting trousers and baggy shirt day after day. She took no exercise and ate little. She stopped rewinding the tape on her answering machine and began storing cassettes full of Shereen's voice repeating 'Audrey? Audrey?'

When she had to leave the flat for work it was easy enough to slap on a presentable face, her good suit, smart shoes, briefcase. Pulling the door shut, she could leave her misery behind for a few hours, sitting there, surrounded by paper.

One evening, feeling cold and stiff from crouching over her desk for too long, Audrey stopped working and went to run a bath. On the way to get a towel she stood in front of the small portrait of Sir James Douglas which her mother had sent her years before, when she was at university in Vancouver. 'Our relative!' she'd written on the back. Audrey kept it propped up on her dresser, dusted it from time to time, and never looked at it. In the portrait, an early photograph, Douglas is wearing a uniform. He is very tall and imposing. Behind his right foot there is a shadow of another foot, as though he shifted while the shutter of the camera was open. On his left is a false mantelpiece, a photographer's prop. His right arm is balanced on the back of a tall chair. He is frowning at the camera as though wary of what it might reveal. Audrey imagines his voice, deep, Scottish, capable of boom. Who was this man, lost to a previous century? And Lady Amelia, his wife? She looked at Douglas's face once again. He would have spoken softly to Amelia and when they were alone Audrey imagines she might have sat on James's knee. He might have held her close.

And so, to Fort Victoria, Vancouver Island. A city conjuring itself from the mud: one Hudson's Bay blanket for every forty cedar pickets cut. A view from the hill of mountains and sea – hummingbirds, wild blackberries in the heat of late summer, buckets full of clams and oysters. How James and Amelia loved this place. In the mornings when James awoke with the mute breeze on his face he thought himself back in his mother's house. He had arrived in Quebec at the age of sixteen and some days he felt as though he had been crawling through the country ever since, across endless prairie, through rough mountain passes, sluiced by countless rivers, washed up onto a thousand lake shores, until now, finally, he had reached the end of the trap-line and emerged into sunlight and fresh salt air. He gulped it down; he entered into it. It was his.

And Amelia too – the island was a better place to raise children, the soil more yielding. Now she could give up digging graves and cultivate niceties instead of crop-bound survival. Soon she would travel by carriage, not horseback, not canoe. A banquet at her Victoria house was kitchens away from a winter diet of powdered salmon at Fort St James.

James planted his foot in the seasonal mud and saw the expansion of Empire before him. In London, Earl Grey was in the Colonial Office; he had the Cape, Australia, New Zealand, the West Indies, British Guiana, India, the Maritimes, Upper Canada, Lower Canada and all the other latitudes and climes to worry about. New Caledonia and Vancouver Island were very far away. Mail took one year to arrive from London and, later, with the advent of the cross-Panama connection, three to four months. The Colonial Office relied on James Douglas to follow orders; they responded slowly to his endless letters and reports. London supported him – they sent the Royal Engineers to help build roads – but London ignored him at the same time, and he used their ignorance to his advantage. He was appointed Governor of Vancouver Island and, later, the mainland territory of New Caledonia as well.

This was what James had been waiting for – this appointment and nothing less. If he had crawled through mud, he had been propelled by his own ambition. He'd been a patient man, paying homage where homage was due. Now he had real authority. It was like a board game, the new territory free of markers and rules. James was a canny player.

Victoria was as different from Fort Vancouver as that place had been from Fort St James. When James and Amelia arrived, the settlement had a population of '435 white souls'. Under his governorship the site moved from scrubby fort to budding metropolis, cobbled streets, government buildings, department stores. Great houses were built, one for James and his family. If it was possible for the place to become more British, James determined it to do so.

Amelia influenced James in his negotiations with the coastal tribes and the peoples of the interior, she retained her loyalty to the Indians no matter how her life differed from theirs now. James was barracked by journalists on the recently established newspaper, the *British Colonist*, for Indian policies they considered too liberal. South of the border, aboriginal peoples were being bounty-hunted and gunned down *en masse*; they were dying in New Caledonia too, but more slowly. James's general policy was to give people the land they requested. Because they were not farmers, the indigenous peoples did not value land in the manner of the settlers and never demanded much more than ten acres. James took the land away, but he did it politely, amassing a great deal of it himself.

In the bath, Audrey tried to submerge all of her body, from the neck down, but this was not possible. Her knees jutted up from the water like volcanic islands, her breasts bobbed like flotsam, and her shoulders, which ached, got cold. Jack had not rung; he was not going to ring.

*

After Graduation, school ran down into summer quickly. It was difficult to imagine not ever going back. On the last day she went alone to say good-bye to David. The corridors felt unnaturally empty, echoey, a cleaning crew had moved in to work on the floors. David was seated at his desk. All the windows of his classroom were open, and outside the playing field glistened green and newly mown. Audrey propped herself on top of a desk opposite his.

'Have you had an education?' David asked, smiling.

She smiled back. 'I have.'

'You're smart, Audrey, you'll do well.'

'I'm going to go to UBC – they've given me some money.'

'That's great news. Congratulations.' David stood, walked around his desk, and held out his hand. His grasp was warm. Audrey tried to remember if she had ever touched him before.

'What about you?' she asked.

'Me?' He shook his head, his eyes widening. They were both not talking about Jane. 'I'll be here next year. And the next, I suppose.' He let go of her hand and sat on his desk. 'But this is not goodbye. I want you to come to see me.'

Audrey wondered if he meant here, or at his cottage. She nodded. 'I should go now.'

'Okay,' he said. 'But I know we'll keep in touch.' He paused. Audrey thought he was going to say something about Jane. She hoped he would not. 'See you,' he said.

'See you,' Audrey replied, and she left the school. Jane wasn't there. Audrey had seen her only once during the last week. She had been emptying the contents of her locker into a gym bag.

'I never really expected to graduate,' she said.

'You didn't?'

'No. I always thought I'd be one of those people who drop out in Grade Ten and are never seen again.'

'It's a big achievement,' Audrey said, without meaning it. The gap between them seemed much wider suddenly.

'Yeah,' said Jane, 'that's what they say.'

'Call me.'

'Okay. I will.'

Audrey got a job downtown at Juliet's – an Italian restaurant, pizza and steaks, run by Greeks – and began to save money for university. Her parents had a bank account they had opened when she was born – her education fund, they said. But even with that, her savings, and the scholarship, she would still have to find a part-time job in Vancouver. Jane had not managed to get a job after graduating. As far as Audrey could tell, she spent all day in her room in her parents' house, smoking and listening to records, and every night out with Frank.

Audrey made good money at Juliet's. Even in Victoria, a small city perched on the tip of an island on the edge of the Pacific, the west beyond the west, there were enough people to fill the restaurants late into the night. The cooks were thick, brainless boys with large tattooed forearms who complained violently when the manager hired wait- resses they considered overweight or unattractive. 'God, not another fat slut,' they would say, whining, grinding their molars. 'You're bringing us down, Mr Kostas, come on.' They didn't seem to think Audrey was a fat slut, although knowing this didn't make her feel attractive. The cooks were always getting each other's girlfriends pregnant but, even so, they were usually good for a laugh. They kept everyone awake during the quiet spells before midnight with their practical jokes and farting competitions.

The summer sped by. Audrey worked all the shifts she could get, sometimes as many as seven twelve-hour days per week. She could double her wages with tips. Most days she would start at three and work the six o'clock dinner rush. A second rush would begin around eleven and last until well after two a.m. Her favourite customers were older single women who drank and smoked, often ex-waitresses themselves. They were the ones who expected the best service, and they were also the biggest tippers.

George Kostas, the manager, was all right, mildly fresh, but he spent most of his time in his office and was usually gone by seven or eight. The other waitresses were friendly and helpful when she made mistakes, not yet into the groove, the waitress swing. The table staff were all female, a Juliet's thing, the only man working in the front of the restaurant was the much put-upon bus-boy who appeared from time to time. The uniform was especially tacky, floor-length black skirts and white blouses.

Audrey liked working, she found waitressing strangely rewarding. There was something about being able to cope with a crowd, with people and their different demands, being efficient and getting the timing right for each table, that was very satisfying. Bringing people food and making sure that they were happy – it was enjoyable even though her feet ached.

At the beginning of August, Audrey spent the evening on her own with Jane. Before then she had gone to the movies with her and Frank once, but Frank had made it clear he did not think it an ideal arrangement. Jane and Audrey met in the early evening in a dark piano bar they used to frequent. They started off drinking expensive and powerful cocktails, Long Island Iced Tea, 'all the white alcohol,' the bartender said, vodka, gin, white rum, tequila, with a dash of Coke, 'to make it taste like tea.' Jane was paying, she said Frank had given her some money. They settled in for a session, and talked about nothing.

'Have you seen David?' Audrey finally asked, late in the evening. His name felt strange to her, she wondered if perhaps she should revert to calling him Mr Dumont, despite the fact they had graduated.

'Yeah.' Jane turned to the guy who was sitting on the arm of her chair. Lonesome men in the bar kept hitting on them, it was difficult to get any peace. 'Leave us alone,' Jane said. There was a large rubber plant behind where they sat. She pulled one of the big leaves down in front of their faces. Audrey felt like they had crawled into a tent. 'His girlfriend is back around again.'

'Really?'

'Good timing, eh? What do they call it? Synchronicity.' She laughed and looked angry. 'She was around the whole time.'

'What do you mean?'

'She lives in Langford, just down the road. She's a doctor.'

'A doctor?' Audrey had never met a female doctor.

'A doctor. She's two years older than him.'

'Older?' Audrey was amazed. 'Does she know about you?'

'No. But, lucky me, I know all about her.' Jane let go of the rubber plant and the broad leaf bounced above them, tapping Audrey on the head. They began to laugh and couldn't stop. They had another cocktail and when Audrey stood up to leave, the room swayed, the rubber plant reached for her, pushed her away. They were too drunk to go home so Audrey drove to Dallas Road. They parked the car and scrambled down onto the beach. Across the strait the lights of Port Angeles flickered. The moon was low and the water was perfect and still before they ran, fully clothed, into it. Audrey fell backwards into the sea, screaming. Her eyes were open as she sank below the surface; her mouth, throat, and nose filled with cold salty water and, before she rose up coughing and choking, she saw the bright watery moon overhead and felt the sodden weight of the distance between herself and the real, breathing world out there.

*

Then there was the day that Audrey found herself weeping in the supermarket. She had gone shopping because there was nothing in her kitchen, nothing in her fridge, and she realized she had not eaten a proper meal in weeks. It was all very well to be working hard but there was no need to punish herself as well, she reasoned, although punishment was what some twisted part of her craved. She left her desk and walked to the shops.

And yet it was the supermarket that broke her down. She did not know why, nothing had ever happened to her in a supermarket, it was not a place she and Jack used to frequent, at home her mother had always done the shopping. She was not sentimental about fresh peaches out of season or breakfast cereal, she had no foodie rituals, she liked to eat but the activity was not especially important to her, shopping for food even less. She liked restaurants primarily because they were full of other people. Unlike Gina, she did not need to feed her friends. I cook for you, I know you, was not an equation she had ever made. Perhaps it was her sudden proximity to the frozen food display, all that cold air bearing down on her, that did it, made her feel her solitude. Audrey began to cry and as she shuffled along with her trolley, her one-pound coin shoved into its handle

144

mechanism, her groceries stacked neatly, tears ran down her face and she did not try to stop them. She had no tissue nor handkerchief and the salty spill stung her cheeks. She thought of Jack and she thought of home, and she wondered where that might be. Was home a person, someone other than herself? Was home family? If so, Audrey thought, she would never find it, never feel it now, and for a moment, just a brief moment, there in the supermarket, she wanted everything to change. To stop. To leave. To not be the same. And she kept on crying and continued on her single way, up one aisle, down the next.

The electronic beep, beep of the check-out never failed to mesmerize her. She bought a lottery ticket – she had not stopped buying lottery tickets – and went out to the car park, to the taxi rank. At this supermarket all the mini-cabs were driven by Eritreans. They had formed a cartel. They knew Audrey by sight and helped lift her shopping into the boot. Today, she thought, as she settled into the back seat, we will have conversation.

She cleared her throat and caught the driver's eye in the rear-view mirror. 'How are you?'

'Oh, fed up.' He smiled toothily.

Audrey crumpled. 'Why's that?'

The driver put his arm along the back of the passenger seat and turned to look at her. 'I'm driving this bloody taxi.'

Audrey did not know her neighbours, the other occupants of the flats in her building. She knew their names, their occupations, but not much beyond that. Meeting them occasionally in the street, in the stairwell, she'd say hello, then continue on her way. The woman who lived directly below was a therapist. Her name was Karen. She saw people – clients or patients or whatever they were called – at home in the room directly below Audrey's sitting room, beneath Audrey's desk. In the afternoon Audrey could hear their voices, the rise and fall of the client, the low murmur of the therapist.

One day, rackety at three p.m., waiting for the phone to ring, Audrey heard the familiar drone begin. She went into the kitchen and fetched a glass tumbler. She placed it upside-down on the floor beneath her desk. She lay down, propped herself up on one elbow, and put her ear to the glass.

At first all she heard was the murmur, slightly amplified. But then the client's voice rose, and Audrey heard words, actual speech. The speaker was a woman. She was talking about being dumped by her boyfriend. She sounded angry. She mentioned her mother, and then her father. Audrey lay perfectly still, afraid to move in case, down below, they guessed what she was doing. The client's voice went quiet and, a few moments later, rose again. 'He's a bastard, a fucking bastard, to make me feel this way.' Audrey could hear at least half of what the client said, but none of the therapist's replies. It was like listening to someone try to give themselves therapy.

All afternoon Audrey lay on the floor with her ear to the tumbler. That client left, another arrived. It was like lying in bed, half-asleep, listening to the radio, a new dramatic monologue every fifty minutes, talking heads. Except it was real people and their problems, real problems, their angst. Audrey found it soothing.

And then she began to give things away. There was too much stuff in her flat. She got up from her desk one day and went into her bedroom and stood in front of the wardrobe. There were a lot of clothes she hadn't worn for years, clothes she had bought and never worn. She began pulling old dresses, trousers, and skirts off hangers and stuffing them into plastic bags. She went through her chest of drawers ruthlessly, underwear, socks, stockings. She took two suitcases out from where they had been stored, under the bed, she could get rid of these without even opening them. She called a taxi, took everything to Oxfam, then walked home and went back to work.

Gina rang. 'Okay girl,' she said, 'what is happening to you? People are talking. We're worried.'

Audrey murmured, she didn't feel like arguing. She tried to keep using the keyboard, hoping Gina would not hear.

'Stop working for a minute, I want to talk to you,' Gina demanded.

Audrey sat on her hands, balancing the phone on her shoulder. 'Okay,' she said.

'Right. Today is Friday. Bob is babysitting. We've been invited to a party at Jaime's – you know him, the Chilean, unless you've forgotten there is a world outside your flat. Everyone is expecting us to be there. I'll come around to your place after eight o'clock. I want to borrow that pink dress.'

'It's gone.'

'What do you mean?'

'I got rid of it.' Audrey paused. 'I'm cleaning my flat.'

Gina arrived with a bag full of make-up. 'I have to borrow something. All my clothes feel like mummy clothes to me; I don't own anything groovy any more.'

'Take your pick, if you can find anything,' Audrey waved in the direction of her bedroom.

'Pour me a drink.'

The party was in Ladbroke Grove, west London. Audrey knew almost everyone there. No one asked about Jack. She wondered if they had all been warned, but then decided that no one was interested in what was going on in her life anyway. She stood by the table where the drinks were kept, clutching a bottle of beer, and watched Gina dancing in the middle of the room.

At Gina's insistence they had dressed up. Audrey was

wearing her favourite dress, earrings, lots of lipstick and jewellery. I look like an idiot, she repeated to herself. I look like a drag queen. She emptied her fourth beer and opened another. Gina jumped in her direction and stopped, a little breathless. She smelt, rather deliciously, of sweat, her skin slicked and shiny.

'Give me that,' she said, holding out her hand for the bottle of beer. Audrey blinked, swaying slightly. 'How many have you had?'

'You can't drag me to a party and then disapprove when I get drunk.'

'I'm not disapproving, I just want to catch up.' Gina smiled. 'Let's go sit down.'

They sank into a sofa and gossiped about the people they knew at the party. 'You've got to do something,' Gina said eventually.

'What do you mean?' Audrey replied, thinking I don't want to hear this.

'Stop moping. He was a wanker. He dumped you. So fucking what. He didn't deserve you.'

Audrey couldn't bring herself to smile or speak. She waved her bottle around instead.

'And that Shereen – well, does she call herself your friend?'

'Not any more, I guess,' Audrey said. 'It's not her fault.'

'"It's not her fault" – of course it's bloody her fault, it's both their faults. It's your fucking fault too, for going out with him in the first place.'

Audrey contemplated pouring her beer over Gina but decided she would rather drink it. 'I don't care. They can go fuck themselves – or each other for all I care.'

Gina seemed satisfied with that. 'So what are you doing with yourself?'

'I'm working hard.'

'And where have you been? Your answering machine is always on.'

'I went to Toronto.'

'What?' Gina crossed her arms. 'Thanks for telling me – Audrey, sometimes I wonder – what kind of a friend are you? You never tell me anything!'

Audrey was taken aback. 'And then my father—' she began, but Gina wasn't listening.

'Go and get me another beer,' she demanded. 'And then you will tell me everything.'

Audrey nodded, obedient, and walked towards the far end of the room. It was dark, someone had turned all the lights off and the music was very loud. She made her way, brushing against people, trying not to stagger. She had almost told Gina – should she tell her? The death of her father, the departure of Jack, she thought the first should make the second seem insignificant, but it did not. It all felt uniformly lousy. She slithered through the crowd.

Jack and Shereen were standing beside the drinks table. Audrey saw them in the orange haze that floated through the window from the streetlamps. They were in each other's arms, they were kissing, Jack bent over, Shereen reaching up to meet him. Audrey watched. They look ridiculous, she thought, they're the wrong size for each other. They kept kissing and kissing as though they would never stop. I've been orphaned, she wanted to shout, I am all alone in this place. But her mouth wouldn't open, her vocal cords wouldn't work. She turned and walked back through the dark room. Gina had fallen asleep. She sat down and leaned against her. Her body felt warm. Audrey closed her eyes.

They woke early the next morning. Jaime, their host, was still wide awake, clearing up the debris, dancing while he worked, the music down low. He called taxis for them. 'I feel disgusting,' Gina confessed.

'I feel all right,' said Audrey and, despite her hangover, she did. 'I saw Jack and Shereen kissing,' she added calmly.

Gina and Jaime looked at her. 'No you didn't,' said Gina. 'They weren't here,' added Jaime. 'I didn't invite them.'

Audrey had cleaned out her wardrobe, cut away all excess; she cleaned her flat with the same stoic energy. When she was not working, she was perched outside on her window-sill, polishing the glass with vinegar and old news-papers, determined not to look down and grow dizzy. She walked over to the high street one afternoon and the greengrocer flirted with her. She was shocked, mortified even. He was sixty years old and wore bits of lettuce in his hair, his fingers stained green by cabbages and sweet, rotting sugar snap peas. His wife stood behind him serving someone else, but Audrey found herself thinking, gosh, maybe *he* might keep me company. She shook her head to dispel this vision and went next door to buy a newspaper. The newsagent's was vibrating with music. Usually the shopkeeper played Hindi soundtracks, bhangra, occasion-ally rap. But today an ancient Leonard Cohen song was making the empty milk bottles shake.

Nodding to the guy at the till by the door, Audrey wandered through the shop. At the back, a white rasta was leaning on the fridge cabinet, next to the soft drinks, nodding his head in time to the music. 'Yes, and Jane came by with a lock of your hair, she said that you gave it to her, that night that you planned to go clear . . .' Audrey looked up, wondering if the sound was coming from a radio, and saw a battered tape deck on top of the fridge, the cogs of the cassette player churning around. The rasta stood as though in a trance, half-smiling to himself. Audrey thought of speaking to him, but did not.

She continued to go to the library for Shula Cronin. As well as that she had several old commissions outstanding, one for an article on a criminal appeal taking place that week. She did not often write about crime or the courts, it was difficult to get work in that area without specializing, and she wanted to do this piece well. Dragging herself up and away from her computer, into her suit, shoes, brief-case, she took the tube to the High Court in the Strand. Outside, a small group was protesting the innocence of the three men about whose appeal Audrey had been asked to write. Television news crews hovered. Several uniformed police officers. Seeing all this activity gave Audrey a start. She remembered when she used to get excited about journalism.

The applicants for the appeal were three young men known as the M25 Three. They had been convicted of aggravated assault, murder and robbery. The police claimed these men were members of a gang that had driven around the M25, the motorway around London, and committed a series of violent burglaries during one long night. A number of the surviving victims of the crimes had said in their original statements that either one or two of the three-member gang were white. All three convicted were black. One of the convicted, Raphael Rowe, had a white parent. The QC for the Crown referred to this man as a half-caste, quoting the West Indian slang, 'redskin'. The QC claimed that Rowe was 'the rogue white man' whom the victims stated they had seen. Rogue white man, thought Audrey, like a rogue gene that causes congenital deformity. The young man – in a suit, looking serious and tense – had dreadlocks, neatly tied back with a piece of string, oddly appropriate in a room full of old white men wearing curly yellowing wigs. Audrey imagined that all his life Raphael Rowe had been black, despite his white parent. In school, to his friends, to the police, to the newspapers, to the prison officers inside, he was a black man. The facet of the case seemed stark, the insecurity of the convictions indisputable – there was the question of three white men who had 'co-operated' with the police and been given a twenty-five-thousand-pound reward – but in court that day the three judges were fixated on Rowe's rogue white parent. The appeal was quashed. Raphael Rowe was a white man for one day.

Audrey took notes, went home, and wrote the article that evening.

The following afternoon, while she was making coffee, the phone rang. She picked it up.

'Audrey? Is that you?'

She nodded without speaking.

'It's me, Shereen.'

Still Audrey did not speak.

'Oh God, I've been trying to get you for so long. I didn't expect you to return my calls. But I want to talk.'

Audrey said nothing.

'Listen, don't hang up. I'm sorry. I tried to warn you . . . I – I can't believe what happened, I felt like shit about it. But, it just felt, I don't know, inevitable somehow. I didn't mean for it to happen, but it did. Something took place between Jack and me. There's nothing wrong with that. But Audrey, I feel bad about what happened between us. It's making things sour for me.'

Audrey pulled the receiver away from her ear and looked at it.

'Jack, he . . . sometimes I think he'll leave me as easily as he left you. It's almost sinister. But I'm happy somehow, I don't know.' Shereen paused and then said, passionately, 'How are you?'

Audrey held the cool plastic of the receiver against her face. She cleared her throat.

'Audrey?' said Shereen.

She hung up. She put the phone down without having said anything at all.

She continued making coffee. The phone rang again. She picked it up.

'Don't hang up! We've got to talk. I've never done anything like this before. I talked to Jack's mother Louise about it – she said that this is what Jack does, leave women – but that she thinks Jack is really in love with me. Audrey, you always said you thought he'd leave you. I want us to be able to get through this, I'd like to remain friends.'

Audrey put the receiver on the kitchen counter. She turned on the coffee grinder. Shereen was shouting, her voice tinny down the phone line. Audrey put the coffee into the filter paper. Shereen went on talking. She poured water over the grounds. The smell persuaded her; she hung up the phone again. She pulled the jack – Jack! – out of the wall and did not put on the answering machine. Her collection of cassettes of Shereen's voice was large enough already. She was growing tired of it.

Later Audrey plugged the phone back in and rang Gina. 'Hey Genie,' she said, 'let's go out to a nightclub this weekend. Somewhere really wild, I don't know, where all the men are gay and we can dance around our handbags and forget everything.'

At her desk, Audrey paused, shivering involuntarily. She sipped her tea, and began to type again.

And then one day he did call. Jack rang early in the morning, before Audrey had drunk her first cup of coffee. She was still lying in bed, dozing.

'I'm coming over,' he announced.

'Why?' said Audrey.

'Shereen wants us to sort things out. She wants us all to be friends.'

'I don't want to be friends.'

'Neither do I. But I'm coming over anyway.'

Audrey stayed in bed. Later she heard Jack's boots on the stairs. He knocked on the door heavily, the noise echoing around the flat. She got up and put on her dressing-gown, gulped the glass of last night's water beside her bed.

Audrey opened the door. There was Jack, looking the

same, smelling the same, as ever. She stepped to one side and allowed him in. He walked into the sitting room. She followed.

Jack stood in the middle of the room, surveying Audrey's chaotic desk. 'This place looks different,' he said. 'It's a mess.' He turned to face her. She thought of objecting, she had cleaned it recently after all. Instead, she nodded, rubbing her eyes with the back of one hand. Her dressing-gown fell open slightly. She pulled it together, tightened the belt, then dropped her arms in an effort to appear relaxed.

'How's your mother?' she asked, for want of anything else to say. She put her hands in her pockets.

'Fine.' Audrey's dressing-gown loosened and slipped open again. Jack's gaze travelled from her face downward. She decided not to pull it together this time. She stood, not speaking, feeling the hard, cold, floor slightly sticky beneath her bare feet. Jack cleared his throat. He looked around the room and began to walk towards her bedroom. 'You've got rid of lots of things,' he said. Audrey nodded, brushing past him. I am doing this, she thought, we are doing this, it is all right. She sat down on the bed. Jack hesitated, looking at Audrey and away. Then he walked towards her. She leaned back at the same time as he knelt in front of her; she closed her eyes as he pushed his face between her legs.

They fucked on Audrey's bed, Jack kept all his clothes on, hardly pausing as he undid his trousers. Audrey kept her hands in fists at her sides and her face turned away. She did not touch him, they did not kiss. They fucked each other, and they did it violently. He came with a muffled grunt, a moment before Audrey. Then he was standing, doing up his fly, and leaving. Audrey turned over onto her stomach and waited for the door to close behind him. Instead of crying, she laughed.

PART THREE

Lovely tender exotic

*In the evening we all went to a ball
given for the officers of the* Plumper. *We
met all the young ladies of Vancouver
Island, they only number about thirty and
are not very great beauties, however, I
enjoyed myself very much, not having had
a dance for such a long time. Most of the
young ladies are half-breeds and have
quite as many of the propensities of the
savage as of the civilized being. Two of
the Miss Douglas' the Governor's daughters
. . . had just had some hoops sent out to
them and it was most amusing to see their
attempt to appear at ease in their new
costume.*

Extract from the diary of an officer
on the HMS *Plumper*, August 1858

7

When Audrey first came to London she was amazed by how black the city could be. This was something she had not considered when she thought of London, dreamy at seventeen. But it pleased her: she came from a place where on the surface everyone seemed pretty much the same and she craved difference, she craved change. When asked where she came from she would say behind a tree somewhere in British Columbia, and this might have been true for all she knew about London, about Britain, at the time. *Monty Python*, Christopher Robin, *Fawlty Towers*, the Sex Pistols, Shakespeare, *Brideshead Revisited, Upstairs, Downstairs*: now as she thinks of these things she laughs and wonders, was that what drew me here? In London she recognized nothing but monuments from photographs and street names from song lyrics, which felt like a lot at the time. She arrived in the city expecting to find herself inside the beating heart of everything, but instead found there were large parts of city life that she couldn't find a way into. There were tensions and divisions. She opened her mouth to speak and was transfixed by her own difference. It was like discovering that she had been adopted.

But learning that some things in London could not be hers, would never be hers, did not deter Audrey, did not depress her. She was an optimist, after all, she was young, she was a Canadian – that said it, right there. She was her nationality. Wasn't everybody? Who is English, who is British, she wondered, of all the people I see in these streets, who is foreign, and what does it mean?

But, it didn't matter, Audrey was a girl, and girls could

have a good time these days, young women could do what they wanted. And Audrey wanted to be a journalist, she worked hard, she wrote a lot, she turned herself into an idea factory. Everything she did or saw became a feature article, everything anyone said had the potential to become 1500 words in a women's magazine. Some people complained that Britain was a small country, cramped, dark, too full. But Audrey didn't feel that way. In London she found large-ness, largesse, in London she discovered the world. The city seemed enormous, uncharted, and in some ways, unnavigable, a place of real mystery. She launched herself upon its wide sea, swam the depth, and found something that belonged to her, something that made her feel she belonged.

Audrey recalled a conversation with Jack. 'I don't belong anywhere,' Jack had said. 'Nowhere is home.' He meant this positively, he believed it was a good, post-modern, contemporary way to feel.

Audrey shivered. She recognized his words, she had probably said them herself at one time, but now they made her feel dread. 'Here,' she whispered, 'here is home.' She meant their bodies, their minds, their hearts.

'I'm not at home in myself either,' Jack said.

Audrey's vision of belonging to Jack – home is us, you and me in each other's arms – dissipated. 'Home is not all it's cranked up to be,' she said, more loudly this time. 'London is a place for unbelonging, for unbelongers like you and me.'

It's all lies, Audrey thought. None of the stories we tell about ourselves, none of the stories we tell of others, are true, are the real truth. Everything hovers somewhere between fabrication and fact. Everyone hovers somewhere between belonging and homelessness.

So now Audrey was the other woman, there was no getting away from that. Jack established a routine with her, like a parent whipping a new baby into shape. Shereen got Fridays and Saturdays, and Mondays and Wednesdays as well, Audrey got Tuesdays, Thursdays – almost the weekend – and the occasional Sunday. Audrey didn't ask if there had been someone else before, when she got the major share of the week. She felt she had even less of a right to ask personal questions of Jack now. She remembered he once said he didn't like things to be complicated. She wondered what on earth he had meant; this new arrangement was the essence of complicated.

There were two questions, however, that she felt she must ask. One evening, she cleared her throat. 'Has Shereen,' he was watching the news on TV, 'Jack, has Shereen been tested for HIV?' He turned towards her quickly, as though angry, but when he looked at her he nodded. Her second question – one more, she thought, one more while he's paying attention to me – 'Does Shereen know you are here?'

Jack leaned back on the settee and stretched. He was fully dressed but she knew his stomach was a hollow curve that led down to his pubic hair. He shook his head, no, and pulled her face forward, kissing her as if to soften his answer, to stop further questions. But Audrey had nothing left to ask.

On their nights together they did things exactly the same as before, except they had more sex. Jack would come to her flat at the end of the day and they'd fuck before going out. They'd eat somewhere fashionable, Jack favoured places that had new English cooking; 'I could eat Sticky Toffee Pudding for ever,' he claimed. In those restaurants the tables were usually small so it was easy for Jack to get his hand up her skirt, for Audrey to slip off her shoe and place her foot between his legs. They'd eat without talking, except to make comments about the menu, the food. Then they'd go back to Audrey's flat and have sex again. Exhausting, piercing, soulless and soulful; they were defining each other afresh, through fucking. And that was it, in the morning he'd be gone again. He'd rise especially early, six or half past, shower, and slip away. Audrey would lie in bed, half-awake, wishing she was someone else.

*

September came, and Audrey departed for university. Her mother helped her pack; they had decided she could take whatever she could fit into the car, but in the end she took just one suitcase full of clothes, her records and record player. She left everything else behind in the room where she had grown up, the shelves in the cupboard stuffed with games, teddy bears, and dolls, Chatty Kathy still there, way at the back, no longer functioning. Her father was unable to come to Vancouver, he was working, so Audrey and her mother made their own way onto the ferry by themselves.

At university she lived in the halls of residence, had a room on her own, and a food pass for meals in the canteen. She quickly fell into the rhythm of classes and parties that is university life. Her major was History, she wasn't sure why, it felt like a decent compromise, somewhere between English and Philosophy. She made a couple of friends, and they'd take the bus downtown into the city on weekend evenings. UBC sits on a point, ringed by heavily wooded endowment lands and, beyond the trees, the ocean. The campus has an isolated, rustic feel, even though the student body is large. Audrey spent a lot of this first year just trying to figure out where she was, in the curriculum, in the department, on the campus, on a map of the city. She found that it rains even more in Vancouver than Victoria, twice as much in fact, but that the rain was conducive to study, cosy fug in the library. She kept up with her courses, worked one shift per week in the student union bar to help pay for her books and social life, and became a little promiscuous. Nothing out of the ordinary.

Boys were easy to meet at university, easy to find, easy to misplace. They caught her eye, she caught theirs. It was exciting, Audrey felt licensed, unleashed. She went along to the student clinic and got a prescription for the pill, then lost her virginity to a boy from Kamloops. She sat behind him in one of her classes. He had very fine, downy blond hair on the back of his neck, his eyes were blue and he spoke in a slow drawl. They got together in the student union bar, in a big gang of first years, all of whom had dropped acid at the beginning of the evening. They played Janis Joplin records and everyone danced, psychedelic and electrified, pretending it was the sixties, away from home at last, windmilling arms, laughing. Later, people began to pair off and Audrey and the boy from Kamloops went back to his room. He put Wreckless Eric on his turntable, they took off their clothes, got onto his bed, and did it. Afterwards, Audrey felt relieved. At last she had done it.

They stayed friendly, but didn't sleep together again. Audrey kept expecting to meet somebody she really liked, and was surprised when she did not. At UBC there were boys from all over Canada, from the US as well, but none of them were what she wanted, and none of them wanted her either.

When she went home at Christmas, she felt as though her parents had become strangers. She had forgotten her mother's cooking, plain and filling, everything chopped into very small pieces, she had forgotten her father's habit of sitting with his feet propped up in front of the television screen. She had forgotten how the house smelt, pine air freshener, her mother's perfume, and the absolute silence at night. Christmas Day was awkward, lonely, and Boxing Day was even worse, as they trooped *en famille* around to the neighbours. Audrey rang Jane, but Jane's mother said she had moved in with Frank. She took down the new number but left it on the table beside her old bed, her narrow old bed with its worn and soft floral sheets, until the day before she was due to leave.

'It's me,' she said loudly when Jane answered the phone.

'You! I've been waiting for you to call. How are you? What's it like?'

'It's okay, it's hard work, I have to write lots of essays all the time. You'd hate it.'

'I'd hate it, I know. I'd hate it. I wasn't cut out for university,' she said reassuringly.

Jane had moved in with her boyfriend Frank in October, she now had a car and a waitressing job. She suggested taking Audrey out for a drink, and Audrey agreed. She felt guilty when she told her parents, their last evening together before she went back to Vancouver, but the thought of doing the dishes with her mother and watching the television with her father yet again felt like too much to bear.

They went to a local bar. They were both beyond the legal minimum age for drinking, finally. Jane looked the same – it had only been four months, but everything else felt altered to Audrey. She expected Jane to have changed.

'What's it like, living with Frank?'

'It's okay. It's great. It's nice. I do his laundry,' Jane laughed.

'Really?' This seemed at once grown-up and depressing.

'We can do what we want whenever we want. That's interesting.'

'Interesting?'

'You know – we can make lots of noise. We can have sex in the shower.' Jane smiled and Audrey nodded.

'You can do anything you want.'

'We have competitions to see who can last the longest before coming.'

'You do?'

'Don't look so amazed – that's what couples do, isn't it?'

'Don't ask me.'

They bantered on for a while and Audrey found herself thinking that Jane really did look happy. Maybe Frank wasn't such a bad thing.

'I've seen David once,' Jane said, unprompted. 'He came into the restaurant, by chance. I served him.' She laughed again. 'That was embarrassing. He waited around until my shift ended, then we went and had coffee.'

'Yeah?'

'That's it. He seemed all right.'

'Didn't you – didn't you want to—'

'I live with Frank now, Audrey. That's over.' Jane's voice was firm, almost scolding.

'But aren't you – weren't you—' Audrey couldn't bring herself to ask if Jane had been in love with David, it seemed too stupid, ridiculous, immature. 'Don't you miss him?' Audrey realized at that moment that she herself did, she missed David and Jane, the three of them together.

'It's better this way, me and Frank. I've known him a long time. David would always have had to be a secret. At least for a couple of years anyway.'

'Did you tell Frank about him?'

'Are you kidding?'

They talked for a little while longer, but Audrey felt deflated. Hadn't it been amazing, their affair? Could it be over, just like that? She suddenly thought that she and Jane had nothing in common, nothing at all, as though they had never been friends. Audrey had gone back to being a swot, Jane back to being one of the cool ones, one of the ones who got away.

She drove Audrey home, they made fulsome farewells, and Jane promised to come to Vancouver, and Audrey caught in herself a dread of this potential visit. As she was getting out of the car, her friend spoke once again.

'I do miss him. I do want to see him. All the time.'

Audrey bent down to look into the front seat.

'But when Frank came back, what could I do? I didn't know what to do. And David didn't say a word. He didn't say anything, Audrey. He didn't help me.'

When Audrey went into the house her parents were watching the television, it wasn't late. She had a cup of tea with her mother in the kitchen.

'I don't like to see you working so hard – you should give up the bar job, and concentrate on school,' her mother said.

'I like to work.'

'Well, you shouldn't have to. We didn't go to university, but we know what it's like, trying to make ends meet. We want you to take this.' She handed Audrey a cheque. 'Promise me you'll quit.'

Audrey took the money and gave her mother a hug, moved by this gesture. Her eyes filled with tears and she embraced her mother again. I'm not a very good daughter, she wanted to say, not a very good daughter, but a daughter none the less.

She knew she would not give up the job. There was something about university that made her feel trapped, squashed between the pages of a heavy book like an insect; working gave her an edge, made her feel like she studied because she wanted to study, when she could be doing this other thing, making her way in the world.

She went back to Vancouver, the halls of residence with their thin walls and endless rounds of strip poker and two-for-one drinking competitions. For some students, every hour was happy hour, but Audrey opened her books and sank down into her seat and was drawn into a new world, the old world. In her reading on the history of British Columbia, New Caledonia as it was then called, she came across James and Amelia Douglas, and she was struck by their story.

★

164

One evening, all of Victorian society emerged from its houses and made its way to the Governor's Ball, held in honour of a visiting ship, HMS *Plumper*. The new town hall had been decorated with bunting, evergreen boughs, and flags, and flowers overflowed on the tables. There was a band composed of local musicians – three fiddlers and a pianist who sat stiff-backed in front of the first piano to arrive in the colony. Governor Douglas was dressed in his finest frock-coat, trousers pressed so taut they might snap, and Amelia, by his side, wearing imported silk gloves and a velvet dress. They took their place among the company – HBC officials, merchants, naval captains and army officers, all the young women of the town, the young wives and their blushing husbands. Their own daughters were there, Cecilia married already to John Sebastian Helmcken, Jane affianced to Alexander Grant Dallas, Alice, Agnes, and little Martha dressed up and smiling. Even young James, who was ten, looked handsome, although he was too shy to dance.

The others danced, all of them, they had been practising around the dining room for weeks. Amelia removed her hat and danced with her husband, who then danced with each of his daughters before handing them on to younger men. At midnight supper was served and there was punch, and rum, and gin. Alice escaped from her mother's side to a table where she sat and flirted with three officers from the visiting ship. After supper, the dancing recommenced. When the Douglases returned home at four a.m., they found the soles of their shoes worn through in patches.

Wealth commanded respect in the colony and the fact that he was the largest landowner on Vancouver Island did much for James's fragile prestige. As the island boomed, Americans began to arrive to start businesses and settle with their families, a type of immigration which James favoured. Many of these Americans were Southerners and they brought with them their ideas about colour bars and just how much black blood was acceptable in a proper human being. Other settlers began to arrive in increasing numbers and the quiet snowy world created by the fur trade, the pragmatic marriage between the Hudson's Bay Company and the indigenous people, began to fragment – an estrangement took place. It was no longer acceptable to take native brides. James received a letter from a distressed colleague who wrote, 'This influx of white faces has cast a still deeper shade over the faces of our Brunettes in the eyes of many.' It was well known that Amelia was a 'half-breed', not whispered but shouted in the streets. Rumours about James's own background began to circulate.

In London whenever Audrey spotted people she knew and hadn't seen for a while she almost always felt compelled to cross the street and look the other way, not wanting to be seen or spoken to. She'd go for long stretches in the city without running into anyone she knew, then when she did all she wanted to do was hide. She often felt ashamed by this impulse – how could I be so antisocial, how could I have become so unfriendly? It was as though in London there just wasn't time to speak to people, not enough room somehow, not enough space on the street or in the day, and who knows what they might say? Audrey discussed this with Gina – they ran into each other on the tube; they had not spoken for weeks. Gina admitted that she was feeling guilty about not having rung and that when she had seen Audrey across the carriage her first impulse had been to turn the other way. But their eyes had already met by then, it was too late. They both laughed and felt appalled.

As soon as Audrey began to speak, she knew she had a problem with Gina, there was no way she could tell her she was seeing Jack again. Perhaps that was why she hadn't rung, she couldn't face telling lies. Or not mentioning the truth. Gina would be outraged by the new arrangement, she would accuse Jack of taking advantage, of treating

Audrey like a whore. This was a nonsense, Audrey knew it, she was meeting Jack half-way. It wasn't like he and Shereen were married. Being the other woman had its advantages: less responsibility, more free time. She no longer had to agonize over whether or not he loved her. He didn't, that was that. For Gina, Jack was a bounder, and he'd bounced off out of bounds, and she was glad. Audrey suspected that her other friends would be more approving of the new racial combination, preferring Shereen the Indian with Jack the African-American to Jack the black American with Audrey the white Canadian, but Audrey couldn't see where the cultural advantage might lie.

Audrey had this friend, an acquaintance really, who used to try and pass herself off as black. She was white, English, maybe if she was lucky she had some Italian in her background, a grandparent or something. She had black curly hair and thick black eyebrows above brown eyes, like the girl in the Douglas Sirk movie *Imitation of Life*. She wasn't passing, but that was as black as she got. She was actually very beautiful and perhaps that was why she managed to get away with her fantasy without anyone hitting her.

Nan used to go out a lot to clubs, to pay-parties, she was always right on top of every trend. She got into places free because everyone liked her and she looked so good, even though people, including non-groovers like Audrey, knew that, basically, she was a lunatic. Audrey met her a few times at parties, and it got so they would always speak. She was friendly to Audrey, as though she thought being a journalist was interesting or worthwhile. Maybe, like Shereen, before they met she thought Audrey was black because of what she wrote. They would have a chat somewhere beneath the thudding bass and booming voices; they would talk about what was happening around London. She had lots of ideas for things that Audrey could write about, good ideas, and she seemed to feel it was her duty to give these ideas away since she would never write them herself. Audrey appreciated that. Ideas were, after all, the way she made her living.

It must have been the third time they met that she told Audrey she was black. Audrey couldn't remember how she did it, it was very oblique, in code, but clear. She felt shocked that this woman was black and she hadn't known. They had another drink and she went off to dance. Jack came and sat beside Audrey. He sank down into the great cushy thing on which she was sitting and planted a kiss on her neck. They were both a little drunk. Jack had come to the party without Shereen, and they were pretending they were both there coincidentally, which Audrey kind of enjoyed. Later they'd go home together by accident. She asked him if he knew that Nan was black.

'Oh yeah,' he said, 'and I'm a cracker.'

'No, really, she just told me.'

'I'm surprised you haven't heard that one before. Nan has been going around saying she's black for years now.'

Audrey could see her out on the dance floor, her curly head and skinny shoulders moving up and down amidst all the others. 'How do you know she isn't?'

'Everyone knows. She just isn't.'

'Why doesn't someone stop her?'

'What's the point?' Jack said, tightening his grip around her waist. 'She's not hurting anyone. No one cares.'

8

Audrey never had higher ambitions as a journalist. It took ambition enough to get there, do it, make the phone calls, get the writing done, get the work published. Once she'd established a market for herself it never really occurred to her to move on. She wasn't interested in editing, nor commissioning, she didn't want to be anybody's boss. Journalism is always ephemeral, the world is full of rubbishy newspapers and magazines, good for cat trays, budgie cages, wrapping up fish guts and broken glass. This was Audrey's life now, get the commissions, do the work, see Jack occasionally. Things did not feel that different than they had before.

*

The second term at UBC passed quickly. Audrey found exams like epic nightmares, except real, all the anxiety and tension and forgetting everything she had learned happening in actual time, without the relief of waking. She went into the campus employment office one afternoon. There were jobs on the bulletin board for the summer – Audrey noticed that BC Highways were recruiting. She filled in a government form for a labouring job, she knew they hired women, and in the middle of her exams she received a phone call asking her to come into town for an interview. She took her revision with her on the bus, and kept on studying right up until the moment she was asked into the recruitment office, and then studied all the way home again. This too could have been a dream, except she got a phone call the next day offering her a job on a road crew.

So she finished her exams, took all her stuff home to Victoria on the weekend, and headed back to Vancouver. Her father was pleased about the job, the pay on the highways was very good. Audrey's mother said she was sorry that her girl – 'my girl' – wouldn't be home for the summer, but Audrey felt they had got used to living without each other rather too quickly. She had been hired for all four summer months, on a paving crew that was resurfacing Highway No. 3 over the Hope-Princeton, down into Keremeos.

The crew was based near a camp in Manning Park at the top of the pass and, though it was warm May days in Vancouver, up there as soon as the sun went down, winter cold arrived. There were four women and ten men on the crew, they slept in two wooden huts filled with bunkbeds, the women in comparative luxury. The toilets were outhouses built over freshly dug holes of lime, one signposted 'Fillies', the other, 'Bucks'. There was a cold-water shower rigged up next to them. A travelling caravan cooked enormous fried meals up and down the highway, and they worked a twelve- to sixteen-hour day, depending on how far from camp they were placed. The first night, Audrey woke at the sound of an animal crashing through the trees outside the hut. She shivered in her sleeping bag and realized she had to pee. When she could wait no longer, she grabbed her government-issue black rubber flashlight, pulled on a sweater and her boots, and went to the door of the cabin.

Outside, the moon cast a strong light, and it took Audrey a moment to realize that the landscape glittered because it was covered in a thin layer of snow. There was no sign of the noisy animal. Her breath froze in little clouds as she walked, and she was so amazed and pleased by the wintry scene she forgot to be afraid. Steam rose up from beneath her as she pissed, and she kept the door of the outhouse propped open with her boot, more afraid of what lay beyond a closed door than an open. Then she crunched back over the snow to her cabin, and her sleeping bag felt very warm, the room filled with women's sighs. By morning the snow was gone and the others wouldn't believe it had ever happened.

Audrey and the other women – Kathy, Donna and Marie – were slightly disappointed to discover that they were regularly assigned the most basic, undemanding, jobs of sign-holder and director of traffic, but they decided not to object. 'Better for working on our tans,' said Marie. 'I only want an easy life,' agreed Donna. In the morning the foreman drove everyone out to where the tarring equipment had stopped the night before and, while the men started up the heavy machinery, the women, two on each site, would begin the job of pacing out the cones. Audrey's own equipment included a walkie-talkie and she could communicate with her partner at the other end of the roadworks through this. For most of the day she stood in one place holding up a sign that read 'Stop' on one side, 'Go' on the other, turning it around at prearranged signals. If there were no cars, no sign of traffic, she sat on the soft shoulder and contemplated the trees which were dense and endless. During the course of the day the temperature rose and rose and she stripped for the forest, jeans, long underwear, parka, sweater, shirt, down to her T-shirt and shorts. As the weeks passed the days grew hotter and hotter, and they moved from camp to camp out of the mountains down into the Okanagan Valley. Sometimes at night the crew would build a fire, sit around and drink beer fetched on a run into the nearest town.

Audrey worked every day; highways employees were supposed to work ten days on, five days off, but most of the students among the crew organized themselves into three or four months of solid work. There was nowhere to spend any of the money she made, it was deposited directly into her bank account. She went into a ladies' shop in Princeton one afternoon, thinking she would buy a new pair of shorts, and she scarcely recognized herself in the full-length mirror, she was so dark from the sun, and her body had changed shape, tightened and lined from the heat of the tarmac, as though she had been slow-cooked, or baked. Some days, as they got closer to Keremeos, down into the Okanagan Valley with its parched sagebrush hills, the heat haze off the road was so vivid and shifting that she would stand in place holding her sign high above her head, unable to see the cars, hoping that they would see her.

It could have been very boring out on the road, but somehow it never was. When she had a line of cars stopped there was usually someone who wanted to talk, and she was happy to pass the time of day, discussing the works, or the weather, or the most recent baseball game. She had a transistor radio and she'd listen to the CBC or a local music station, sometimes she'd sing into her walkie-talkie to entertain Kathy or Marie. And when there were no cars she'd prop her sign up with a few rocks and run to the side of the highway and scramble down to grab handfuls of wild raspberries that dripped dark red juice down her legs as she ate. There was always a slight edge of worry to the day, in case a bear or a wolf wandered out of the forest, there were plenty of terrible stories that circulated through the road crews, but she saw no sign of any wildlife.

She had an affair with one of the guys on the crew. He drove the big roller and had long legs on which the tendons showed clear as if his skin had been flayed. He was watching her, and she noticed, and they snuck into the trees one night while the others were sitting around the fire. He made love to her urgently up against a pine and Audrey discovered something new then, she discovered that sometimes we are humbled by sex, by the strength of our own desire. Ted came from Lillouet, and hadn't finished high school, and had a fiancée back home who was four months' pregnant. They were getting married at the end of the highway summer season, and that made Audrey feel safe. Sometimes when she was standing at the end of the line with Donna singing at her through the walkie-talkie, she felt the ground tremble beneath her feet, and then she'd hear it, and it would be Ted on top of the roller, rolling her way. How he managed to escape on the ten-ton piece of equipment without the foreman noticing always baffled Audrey, but he would jump down from the burning plastic seat and chase Audrey into the trees. They were lucky that the traffic was light that summer, and they didn't cause any pile-ups and Marie's traffic did not meet Audrey's on the single track that was all that was left of the highway.

But then autumn came, and they felt the change in the temperature at night, in the last few days of August. They said good-bye, Ted gave Audrey his favourite checked shirt, and it wasn't until she got back to Vancouver that she noticed how it was faded by the sun, stained by his sweat, and how it smelt of tar and paving.

*

The thing Audrey liked about Jack Campbell was that he was wicked. He wasn't afraid of being horrible, he didn't care if people didn't like him. Audrey knew she was not that way, she wanted people to like her, she wanted everyone in the entire world to be her friend. She knew that was why she had never been all that successful as a journalist; she loathed being harsh or cruel in print. Jack couldn't give a fuck. If he disagreed with you he told you so. And if he liked you he showed that as well, although in evil ways, teasing, baiting, laughing. Anyone who leaves me, thought Audrey, has got to have something wrong with him. Even if he does come back.

Audrey saw now that she didn't really know Jack. She used to think that she did, but she could see that the hours did not add up. They hadn't spent enough time together. She knew his body fairly well, she knew what he liked best, what he enjoyed. But beyond that – it would have taken years of a proper, full-on relationship. Dinners, nights together – that wasn't enough. They would have had to have been married or, at least, to have lived as though they were married, holidays, boredom, happiness, intimacy. And maybe there would have been further, deeper, silences between them even then. She didn't know about that.

Audrey kept working for Professor Cronin. Her trips to the library were like little reminders of where she came from. Sometimes she felt as though the academic was her last tie to Canada. In her most recent letter Shula had mentioned she was giving a paper at a big conference on national sovereignty taking place in Ottawa, but Audrey had not heard from her since then.

One day she had a phone call from Carol Lumbank. They arranged to have lunch. Carol told Audrey the news from the High Commission, which Canadian writers and artists were coming to Britain and when. Half-way through the meal, Carol blanched and put down her fork.

'I've just remembered. Are you still working for Shula Cronin?'

'Little bits here and there – I met her in Toronto earlier this year.'

'You did? Well, there's been another scandal. Did you hear?'

Audrey shook her head.

'She gave a paper at this conference—'

'Oh, yes, I knew she was going to do that.'

'She caused an uproar!'

'She did?' Audrey laughed. 'Good for her.'

'She has damaged her career, some say this time it's irreparable.'

'What?'

'Her paper was called "Quebec and the Bogus Notion of Racial Purity".'

Audrey laughed again, but Carol shook her head gravely. 'She attacked everyone. The Government of Quebec – she maintains it isn't possible for the province to form an independent government, claiming sovereignty over territory still disputed by land claims. She said that the native people of Quebec have more right to form a separate government than the Québecois themselves. She said that all real Quebeckers are part Indian anyway. That the *coureur des bois* and the *voyageurs* all took native wives, that the Catholic missionaries fathered great numbers of illegitimate children, that white hostages taken during the Indian wars married and settled into native communities. That the links between Quebeckers and native people run deep, much deeper than either side is willing to admit. And that cross-border allegiances between tribal communities make a mockery of all borders anyway. And that the water in the rivers in northern Quebec, the hydro-power that is the province's economic base, the only thing it has of value to the Americans, belongs to the Cree.'

Carol finished her summary and took a gulp from her wine glass. She spoke again before Audrey could think of anything to say. 'Well, the native studies academics took her to task. There was a verbal bloodbath, apparently. Do you know any Quebeckers?'

'Me?' Audrey thought Carol seemed rather angry, as though somehow personally affronted by Shula's ideas. 'No, I lived in BC all my life, then I left. I don't really know anything about the situation.'

'Well, if you did – if Shula Cronin did – you would know that lots of Quebeckers claim mixed blood as a badge of honour, they love to go around saying their grandmother was Mohawk or whatever. My ex-husband was a perfect example of that, I mean he still despised Indians, but he found the idea of "savage" blood exotic. But the truth is that, in fact, Quebec has made greater efforts on behalf of indigenous people than any other Canadian province. They signed land claims treaties in James Bay as far back as 1975. It's just a sanctimonious stick that English Canada likes to think they can beat the French with, because of Oka, because of that disaster, the armed siege, when in reality the French have been much more progressive than anyone else.'

'What is Shula up to?' Audrey asked. 'She's an academic, not a politician.'

'Academics like to get down in the dirt too, sometimes, you know. I think she has some kind of weird grudge because of what happened to her last book. Perhaps she was retaliating in some obscure way. She spent years on her research, then was accused – by the very people she had lived with and studied – of stealing Haida mythology. But she can't attack the Haida – that would be unthinkable – so she's going for Quebec instead.'

'What happened?'

'She was booed off her platform during the question and answer period. She's a nutcase – the issues are so complex, too complex, she's got some kind of bee in her bonnet. If I were you, I'd stop working for her.'

'But I like her. At least she speaks plainly, says what she thinks. She needs my help . . .'

'She's a nutty old woman, and now she's put her foot in it.'

'Carol—'

'I know, but really. It's hard enough to keep the issues straight without having people like her stirring things up. I'm sorry I ever introduced you. Let's hope she doesn't put your name in the acknowledgements of her paper.'

After lunch, Audrey went home. She calculated the time difference, and rang Shula's office in Toronto, but reached an answering machine. She left a message, saying hello, inventing a question to do with the British Library. Then she sat down and wrote Shula a letter, diplomatically asking her to explain what happened, asking for a copy of the paper.

★

Back in Vancouver, Audrey felt sure that her second year of university would be more interesting than the first. She got her old job back, and registered for classes, concentrating as far as was possible on Canadian history, the history of the west. She did not have any particular reason for this interest. Apart from the big compulsory classes, the seminars were all fairly small and this appealed to her.

She had opted to live outside the halls of residence this year, not wanting to go back to the rowdy atmosphere of the dorms. She got a room in an apartment in Kitsilano, the neighbourhood nearest the university. In the sixties Kitsilano was a centre for students, hippies, radicals and American draft dodgers. In the intervening years those people cut their hair, got proper jobs and redecorated their houses; Kitsilano moved upmarket. Audrey's landlord was a stockbroker, a man in his late twenties, who was often out of town, and who rarely ate at home, so Audrey was free to do as she pleased. Her room was small, and at the back of the apartment, which was on the top floor of a converted 1930s house, and she overlooked a garden to which she had no access. But at the front of the house there was a balcony off the sitting room, and from that balcony Audrey could look down the street to the beach.

Living off campus was a little bit more isolated, but Audrey spent long hours in the university library, and at the student union bar in the evenings once she had rediscovered her friends from the previous year. She resumed reading on the history of British Columbia, fascinated by the place-names and events that to her seemed from so long past, but that her professor kept assuring her were recent history.

She discovered the university Museum of Anthropology and spent afternoons there, gazing at the artefacts, porcupine-quill headdresses, ceremonial masks, elaborate wooden carvings, totem poles, an enormous seafaring Haida canoe.

She took the bus downtown from time to time, and went into the big bookstore on Robson to stare at all the novels she hadn't the time to read nor money to buy. One friend had become an accomplished shop-lifter, specializing in books, and Audrey was looking at a copy of Robertson Davies's *The Deptford Trilogy*, contemplating crime, when she heard a man say her name. She turned around, and David, Mr Dumont, was standing right next to her.

'Have you read that?' he asked. 'You really should.'

Audrey laughed, she felt like a different person than the girl who used to borrow books from her English teacher. 'How are you?' she asked.

'I'm okay,' smiling his crooked smile, brushing back his hair. He seemed younger to Audrey, the gap between them had narrowed somehow. 'Let's have a coffee?'

Audrey went to put the book back on the shelf, but David took hold of her wrist. 'Let me buy it for you,' he said. 'I remember what being a student is like, I'm sure you don't have any money.'

So she let him buy it, and with that purchase, something was altered between them.

In the coffee shop they sat at a little table and David stretched his legs out, and Audrey leaned back and remembered why she had always found him sexy. 'How is school?' she asked, then felt embarrassed by her question, sorry to have mentioned it, as though she couldn't help childishly dwelling on the past.

'Oh,' he waved his hand, 'same as always.'

'What brings you to Vancouver?'

'I come over fairly often. I've got a friend from university back east who lives here, I stay with him. Get a dose of the big city. Victoria is lovely, but there's no grit there. Vancouver is nice and dirty.'

They talked, Audrey kept hoping for a topic to settle on, something they could sit there and talk about, relaxed, not worrying. She began to tell David about her studies, and this interested him. As she spoke she found herself thinking about Jane, and she determined not to mention her. Here she was, in a Vancouver coffee shop with David, this had nothing to do with Jane.

After a time he said he had to head off to meet Ben, his friend. Seeing David made her feel a little homesick, and confused. He was one of the reasons she had gone away; he was one of the things she missed most.

'Give me your phone number,' he said. 'I'll be back in Vancouver in two weeks. I'm going to a concert on the Friday with Ben, but I'll be around the rest of the weekend. Why don't we meet for a drink?' He laughed. 'It will be like old times.'

Audrey went back to college and didn't think about David, caught up as she was in the library. But a few days before he was due back in town she found herself staring at her own reflection in one of the glass cabinet displays in the Museum of Anthropology. It was November, and the rain had arrived, the sky was low, and every morning a heavy fog rolled in from the sea. Getting to university on the bus was like travelling underwater, except without the aid of scuba gear. David rang Saturday morning; her landlord banged on her door to wake her up, she had worked late in the union bar the previous evening. They had arranged to meet on campus, David was curious about the university. They had a drink in the bar, Audrey slightly worried she would run into her friends, trying to think of a way to explain David. She thought she might just say he was a friend from Victoria, and field the questions later on, the next day. But in the end there was no one around whom she knew, and as they left the bar she felt slightly disappointed.

David had his car, so they drove across town to a billiard room on Commercial. It was a good idea, Audrey felt nervous about spending the evening on her own with him, and the physical tension of the pool table suited them both. They drank beer while they played, smoked cigarettes leaning over the table. David paid, insisting, once again, that he understood her poverty. She told him stories about working on the highways and he told her about his own days at university, in Winnipeg where he came from.

'I had a motorbike, and when things were really bad, when I had too much work and was way behind, I'd drive out onto the prairie. Have you been there?' Audrey shook her head, no. 'Well, it's very flat, and the roads are long, straight, and empty. I used to get the bike accelerating, and then stretch my body out behind the handlebars, along the seat. I'd get the bike going as fast as possible, 100, 110, 120. I'd travel in an absolute straight line and I tell you,' he leaned back, banged his pool cue on the floor, 'it really was like flying.'

'Sounds wonderful.'

'Dangerous. But amazing.'

David had a difficult shot to make, he leaned over the table. Audrey stood behind him. She watched him move, the way his shirt pulled away from his jeans, his hair just touching the collar, one cowboy boot in the air as he balanced on the other leg.

They were evenly matched at pool, neither very able, but as the evening wore on, they improved. The billiard hall was large and it had a jukebox that played a weird mix of old country standards and last year's rock. At the very back was a small dance floor, and every once in a while there was a flurry of movement. At around midnight Audrey found herself on it, dancing with David. He moved stiffly, as though his hips needed oiling, and Audrey felt compelled to dance with great energy, as though to demonstrate her youth. They fell together onto a bench at the dark rear of the room, David's thigh pressed against hers. Audrey's mouth and throat went dry. She was drunk, and horny.

'Well, I guess we should go,' said David.

'You're too drunk to drive.'

'Me? What an allegation. I'll have a cup of coffee.'

They made their way to the front of the hall, past all the women in skin-tight jeans who were winning their boy-friends' wages off them. There was an espresso machine up front, and David had two cups, 'just to be on the safe side'. Audrey had another glass of beer.

Outside, the rain was dense as jelly. The car was parked half a block away, and they slid into it, soaked and laughing. David drove very carefully, sticking to residential streets, slowing at every corner. When they reached Audrey's house, he parked the car and turned off the engine. The rain fell steadily, rhythmic on the roof. Audrey could smell him, familiar, boozy. Neither of them said anything for a while, then Audrey began to find the silence oppressive.

'Come inside for another drink?'

'If I have another drink I'll never get to Ben's place.' He looked at her.

Audrey pushed her back along the inside of the door of the car. She felt as though she had some power. She ran her tongue over her teeth, her mouth still dry, her breath shallow. She was cold and sweating at the same time. 'Come inside for another drink,' she said smoothly.

David followed her up the stairs and into the apartment. They whispered in the kitchen so as not to wake the stockbroker, and stole two of his beers from the fridge. They went into Audrey's bedroom, and she put a record on low. It was an album she had bought recently, an old Curtis Mayfield, nothing like the records David used to play. She sat at her desk chair, David on the bed, there was nowhere else to go. The next day she couldn't remember what they had talked about, but they had talked, and laughed, making an effort to keep their voices down, for another hour or more. David moved from sitting upright, to leaning back on his elbows. Then he pulled off his boots, and moved further up on the bed, his head on Audrey's pillow, the pillowcase her mother had given her, his arms behind his head.

At around four in the morning Audrey asked, 'David, what are you doing here?'

'I'm waiting for you to come to bed.'

Audrey got up and went down the corridor to the bathroom. She brushed her teeth and looked at herself in the mirror. Maybe when she went back he would have left. He was thirty-two years old and she was twenty.

When she went back into the room, he was still there. She lay down beside him on her small bed. He smelt old, she thought, old and sexy. They kissed, and as he began to unbutton her shirt, she realized she had not thought once about Jane.

In the morning David was awkward and tired; they hadn't slept for more than an hour or two. He said he would call, or write. Audrey told him she'd be back in Victoria for the Christmas break, which was only three weeks away. He said that was good, he would see her when she came over, she should call, they could arrange to meet. Audrey wondered if he seemed a little shamefaced. She had gone to sleep expecting the morning after to be sweeter.

She carried on with her studies, and her Friday-night job, and her commute from Kitsilano onto the campus. In one of her classes she was studying the period when British Columbia became a part of Canada; the old Governor, Douglas, had retired, and the new administration was taking the region into confederation. The province was emerging into modernity, blinking, a federalism hewn out of the great river canyons, and the trees. She found a book in the library about the history of Highway No. 3, and she touched the pages as she read about the stretches of road she knew so intimately. David did not occupy her thoughts, but he hovered in the background like a demon. She was determined to look forward, guided by the light over her desk. Sometimes, late at night, when she picked up *The Deptford Trilogy*, he came more clearly into view. From time to time she might lose herself in the luxury of her sheets, thinking of how he had lain there with her. This term she hadn't had boyfriends like last year. No reason, she thought, nothing to do with Ted of the summer, she was busy with her studies, too preoccupied, that was it.

She went home at Christmas, and did not call David. She was frightened of what he might say. Sometimes she thought she had imagined the whole thing. She knew he wouldn't call, paranoid that one of her parents might answer and somehow guess the truth.

She went out for a drink with Jane, going round to the place she shared with Frank beforehand. The little apartment was clean and neat and Jane complained that Frank never did any housework. Less enamoured of her life than she had been the year before, she was in the same job, but making the long trek to work on the bus because she couldn't afford to run a car any more. She seemed ground down by this adult life.

'I thought I might call David,' Jane said once they had left her apartment and driven to the bar. 'For a long time I thought I would run into him somewhere, but I haven't. Or that he'd come into the restaurant again. I'd like to know how he is, to see him.'

Audrey swallowed hard. 'Good idea.' She realized then that she wasn't going to tell Jane. She had stopped communicating with her parents long ago, and from now on she would refine the art of not telling her friends important things, the art of keeping it to herself. How could she possibly tell Jane about David anyway?

'Yeah, I don't know, I've known Frank for so long, I'm sure we'll always be together. But I'd like to see David again.'

'Call him,' Audrey said, changing the subject. She saw disappointment wash over Jane's face. What was there to talk about if they couldn't talk about David?

Christmas was quiet and miserable like it had been the year before, though her mother showered Audrey with gifts – everything was signed 'Love Mum and Dad', but Audrey's father was just as surprised as Audrey each time she opened another parcel. Audrey had bought both her parents books, and she remembered only now that they did not read. They looked pleased anyway. She went back to Vancouver in time to spend New Year's Eve with friends in the union bar. Her mother drove her out to the ferry, and when Audrey kissed her cheek she felt a surge of love before she moved away.

Once the boat had left the dock, she got a handful of quarters from the shop and rang David on the radiophone. The connection was dim and scratchy.

'I'm on my way back to Vancouver.'

'Why didn't you call?'

'I don't know, it felt strange to be in Victoria, I wanted to get away.'

'I would like to see you.'

Audrey couldn't decide if he sounded more like a lover or an ex-teacher.

'Listen,' he said, 'why don't you come back over later this month and spend the weekend with me? Here, at my cottage.'

Audrey's stomach turned over and tightened. 'Come back?'

'Yeah – your room's so small, your bed's so small,' he laughed, 'if you came back here we could relax, not worry.'

'But my parents—'

'It's possible for you to come to the island without telling

184

your parents. No one has to know. I for one won't be telling anybody,' he laughed again.

'Okay,' said Audrey, 'when?'

★

In London, Audrey was losing her grip. She felt shunted between work and Jack, and was spending too much time alone in her flat. She avoided her friends because she didn't want to have to explain about Jack. She began to clean out her filing cabinets, throwing away research notes, unpublished articles, endless copies of magazines and newspapers. She got down to her file marked 'University'. This was where she kept the material she had worked on during her third – and last – year of university. She had embarked on a research project after reading about the Hudson's Bay Company post at Fort St James, Stuart Lake. She titled it, 'Sir James Douglas and His Wife Amelia'. She had fiddled with the title a lot, unhappy with the lordly 'His Wife', yet wanting to get Amelia's name in there somewhere. The professor did not like the sound of 'James and Amelia Douglas' – 'He was the important one, the Governor, after all,' he had said as an explanation. Chauvinist old git, Audrey thinks now as she looks at it, although she wouldn't have thought that then. She took the file and put it on her desk and threw everything else away.

One morning as she went through her post, she found a letter from Shula Cronin. It began, 'Dear Audrey, It happened like this,' and Audrey expected to read an account of the disastrous Ottawa conference that Carol Lumbank had told her about. She was intrigued to hear Shula's side of the story.

Dear Audrey,
    It happened like this.
    It was 1976 and I was flying back to BC, to Prince Rupert

185

to see my father who was then in his eighties. I had never been afraid of flying, I thought it a perfectly wonderful way to make the world smaller. I loved the fact I could live in Toronto and yet get to my father in just one day. The early pioneers would have been amazed.

We touched down in Edmonton – this was August and in Edmonton it's either so cold at the airport that the plane's hold freezes up, or so hot that the tyres give way. Anyway, we sat on the tarmac for longer than expected, but then took off as though everything was fine. I guess they thought everything was fine.

We crossed the Rockies, and I remember it clearly, I had a window seat at the rear of the aircraft – I still smoked then, and they still allowed it – and the mountains were magnificent, the view wonderful. I never understood people who could read on airplanes, I always wanted to look out the window, even if all there was to see was endless clouds, cloud castles, a flat cloud plain.

We flew over Fort St John and I saw the Peace River twisting its way through the earth. I guess things began to go wrong there because they put on the seat-belt sign and told us to return our drinks to the stewardesses. I always drank a lot on aeroplanes, that was part of the fun. I didn't want to give up my drink. Rum and Coke.

Things got worse from there. The stewardesses – why do little girls all want to do that job? – began to go through the emergency landing procedure and we were told to put on our lifejackets. Everyone remained calm, even the fellow seated next to me, and he had never flown before. He turned to me and asked, 'Is this normal?' I said no. He said okay.

I looked out the window and the ground was coming towards us very quickly. Our dive was sudden and extreme, as though the plane had lost the will to go on. The odd thing was that we were still moving very smoothly – there was no bumping, no thrashing from side to side like you see in the movies. I don't know why we didn't turn south to Prince George and land there. I know that area so well, I could see the highway from my window – I thought, why didn't we land on that, the cars would get out of our way. But then the pilot announced we were going to land on water. 'Think of it as an adventure,' he said, 'something to tell the folks back home,' and we laughed, we actually laughed.

I knew where we were heading. We were going to land on Stuart Lake. I turned to the man beside me and said, 'It's all right, it's Stuart Lake.' I looked back out the window and saw the wing was coming apart. Breaking up, like river ice in the spring, making the same noise, booming, cracking, heaving. Our ride got bumpy then.

We began to hit the tops of the trees and the plane turned on its side and all our belongings fell out of the overhead racks and onto the people across the aisle. The oxygen masks came down, I looked out the window and saw only blue sky, looked to the other side and saw we were ploughing through the water. People were shouting now, but somehow I couldn't hear them, it seemed very silent to me.

Eventually the plane came to a stop. Someone in the row behind me – everyone was so extraordinarily calm – opened the rear exit door and I climbed over the seat and out onto the side of the plane. Then we were all popping out of that door, one after the other, like marsupials expelled from the pouch. The plane had begun to sink and I looked for the shore and found I knew precisely where I was. It was like I had revisited my childhood and was sitting on a float in the middle of the lake, feeling the sun on my face.

About two-thirds of the passengers survived, the rest drowned because the plane sank so quickly. The pilot and co-pilot were killed on impact. A number of the steward-esses died, in their little scarves and their matching skirts. The plane finally rested too deep to salvage but they tell me that on a clear day if you fly north of Fort St James, over

Stuart Lake, you can see the outline of the wrecked plane down in the water, like a shadow of the one you are in.

So there you go. Now you know.

I am going to retire after all, not going ahead with the book. Thank you for all your help, Audrey. Enclosed please find a cheque. Also enclosed is an article about Douglas that you might find of interest, given the work you did on him when you were a student.

Yours,
Shula Cronin

Audrey put the letter down. Her heart was beating a little fast. This is awful, she thought. How unspeakable. She thought Shula Cronin should be forgiven for whatever it was she was meant to have said at the conference. People survive the most extraordinary things.

She picked up the article that Shula had photocopied for her. It was called 'Some Further Notes on the Douglas Family', by Charlotte S. M. Girard. Audrey had done a fair amount of reading on Douglas at university, although nothing too substantial, she had dropped out just as she was getting really interested. There was a mystery about Douglas's origins, she had picked up on that. The early biographers and historians claimed he was born in Scotland; Douglas's youngest daughter, Martha, who lived well into the twentieth century, had been interviewed and she herself said her father came from Lanarkshire. But later writers cast doubt on this claim. In Hudson's Bay Company journals James was often referred to as 'the Scotch West Indian', and they picked up on this and began to look for clues. However, the truth was very obscure. Apparently Douglas had seen to that.

Audrey read the paper. The writer had done an enormous amount of research, in Scotland, and in Georgetown, Demerara, British Guiana, now known as Guyana. There she found traces, bare watermarks really, of Douglas's mother, a 'free coloured woman' named Martha Ann Ritchie, whose own mother was a freed slave, Rebecca Ritchie, and Douglas's father, John, a Glasgow merchant with shipping interests in the Caribbean.

Due to the vagaries of the global postal system, James did not receive the letter from his sister until the day before she arrived. He was sitting on the verandah in the thin early-morning sun, drinking tea – both the tea and the teacup imported from China – before starting the day, reflecting, as was his wont, on all he had achieved. His daughter, Martha, ran up the footpath clutching the post, dress ribbons flying.

'Papa,' she said, 'Papa, look at the stamp.'

And indeed, the stamp was a glorious thing, coming, as it did, all the way from British Guiana. Martha handed James the letter, then flew away again. Her father received a tremendous weight of correspondence and a letter, even with such exotic markings, was not an unusual thing.

But the postmark gave James a shock. He stared at the unknown handwriting, then opened the envelope carefully. The date of the letter was six months past. He glanced at the bottom of the page. 'All my love, Your Sister, Cecilia.' His sister, whom he had never met, was arriving in Victoria. His sister, Cecilia. Tomorrow.

A ship was due from San Francisco the next day, but James had not planned to meet it. He stood, and the letter slid from his lap to the porch. He reached down to retrieve it and saw his hand was shaking – what would Cecilia's arrival bring? How much of Demerara would she carry with her?

James walked into the house. He found Amelia in the kitchen, supervising the day's menus. She would never become accustomed to having staff. At his beckoning, she followed him into the parlour.

'Cecilia will be here tomorrow.'

Amelia clapped her hands together and smiled, mistaking his words for news of their eldest daughter.

'No, Cecilia Douglas – Cecilia Cameron – my sister.'

'Your sister?' Amelia knew James had a sister, and half-sisters, she knew the names of all James's family, but no more than that. 'From Lanarkshire?'

'No. Demerara. British Guiana. The West Indies.' James sat down and stared at the letter. His wife took it from him gently.

Amelia was puzzled. James had never spoken freely or easily about his early past, though he was now full of reminiscence of the fur trade. She knew only of the hated Scottish boarding school, and of the father James did not love. An unknown sister, from far away, tomorrow. Amelia did not tease James for more information, but busied herself preparing a room for this woman who was to arrive, it seemed, from out of nowhere, with her English husband. She would wait for James to tell her his story.

That night James was unable to sleep and wandered the house without resting. He went from room to room, surveying his possessions as if they might show him who he was. She had traced him here, perhaps through his father's wife to whom James had sent the most formal of greetings every year since his father's death. He had never corresponded with Cecilia, and knew of her existence only because his father – their father – had written to him at school. James could still recall the letter, how his father's sparse hand had brought memories of his mother rushing to him. 'Martha Ann Ritchie of Demerara, your mother,' it said, 'has given you and your brother a sister. She is called Cecilia. The girl will stay in Demerara, to be with your mother.' John Douglas had continued with news of his own Glasgow family, the half-brothers and half-sisters, the wife, from whom James had always felt exiled, even in Scotland. A sister of his own. A sister he would never know. He had been glad of the news, even though it concerned people who might as well have been strangers to him.

The boat was already anchored in the harbour when James rose the next morning. He pulled on his clothes quickly, pausing to pass his hand through his hair in the mirror, then he walked down the muddy street to where the small boats were bringing the ship's cargo to land. A tall woman in a bonnet stood on the quay, surrounded by boxes and crates. On the largest tea chest perched two little girls. They were watching the men unload the craft.

'Cecilia?' James thought his own voice odd.

She turned quickly, and he forgot what he had been about to say, the speech of greeting he had spent the night composing. It was like looking into a fractured mirror, his own face reassembled, womanly.

'Governor,' shouted one of the men, 'the price of that land up towards Beacon Hill . . .' But James did not hear him.

'James?' asked Cecilia, breaking into a smile. 'My own brother, the self-same one?' James returned her smile and felt something inside fuse with tenderness and grief. Her husband stepped forward to be introduced, and James shook David Cameron's hand while Cecilia talked happily. 'We've heard it's a new land here, and a good place, so we have come to try our luck. David never liked the swampy mangroves of Georgetown. Do you remember it, James, do you remember our house? Our mother spoke so often of you, I feel I have known you always.' Her voice was melodious and full of emotion, and her accent, the cadence and phrasing of the Caribbean, fell gently on James's ears. It was his mother's voice, which he had not heard since he was a boy of six. Cecilia was laughing, her broad shoulders shaking, and James heard his mother and felt a pain so deep and disguised he thought he might fall into the mud and be unable to rise. But he led the couple and their children up the hill as though he was daily accustomed to greeting long-lost family.

There she was, in all her glory, Cecilia Douglas Cowan Cameron, his sister, a woman who had spent all her life in the West Indies, with one daughter from her first marriage, another of her second. She was darker skinned than James, and with her arrival the long-held rumours about James's parentage were confirmed for all of Victoria. The epitaphs – half-caste, mulatto, quadroon – were true, he could hear the gossip rumble down the street already. Cecilia Cameron proved it, but James did not speak of it, he brought silence to bear on the subject as always. He made it clear to Cecilia that the family stories – the stockpiled news about his mother, herself long dead, which he longed for and dreaded at the same time – were for themselves alone. They struck a bargain, although it was not spoken of as such: Governor Douglas appointed David Cameron the first Chief Justice of the Vancouver Island Supreme Court. He had no judicial experience and there were myriad complaints from the burgeoning citizenry, but James quashed dissent and moved on. In return, Cecilia Cameron did not speak to anyone outside the Douglas household of Martha Ann Ritchie, the coloured Demerara woman, daughter of a freed slave, who was mother to herself and to James.

But inside the house, once the children had been put to bed, and all the guests gone home, James and Cecilia, and often David and Amelia too, would sit in the parlour and talk into the night. James was full of questions, Amelia saw now he had always been full of questions. Cecilia had answers to give. She spoke with great animation, her words made them feel as if the curtains floated on a Demerara breeze. John Douglas, their father, had returned to Georgetown regularly for many years after her birth, long after he shipped his sons to Britain and made his Scottish marriage, and she had known him well. And her childhood, in the manzanilla, the rice paddies, and the sugar cane, was light; she had been loved, and she had known it, and she spoke of it freely. The Scottish boarding school was far, far away.

James listened carefully, and Amelia watched him listening. And when they went to bed, having exchanged fulsome goodnights with Cecilia and David, Amelia looked on as James tore at his pillow, his body creased and twisting. He was fifty-four years old and he could not stop sobbing. But his sorrow was silent, and the tears did not flow, and when Amelia touched him she thought his skin aflame. There was nothing she could do to ease him, so she sat with him until he fell into a fitful, fisty sleep.

PART FOUR, an interlude

Between

*The story of Inkle and Yarico was
one of the most often repeated and most
popular narratives of the eighteenth
century . . . The story itself can be
reduced to the four moments common to
almost all its versions. Inkle, an
Englishman, is shipwrecked and separated
from his companions; he is succoured by a
native girl, Yarico, who falls in love
with him and for whom he professes love;
they are rescued by an English ship; and
they arrive in Barbados where Inkle sells
Yarico into slavery.*

Peter Hulme, *Colonial Encounters:
Europe and the Native Caribbean,
1492–1797*

9

Atlantic crossing, 1799

For many days after the ship left the Mersey he was troubled by sea-sickness. This is a phenomenon which no medical man John Douglas ever met could satisfactorily explain, and the only advantage he had derived from conversation on the subject was to collect a few facts. Sea-sickness is most likely to occur if you stand still upon the deck and watch the motion of the sea. If your eyes are closed, so that the dancing of surrounding objects cannot be perceived, you are less liable to be sick. If you lie horizontally the rocking of the ship is almost imperceptible, hence the most effectual way of avoiding sea-sickness is to lie down on your bed. By these means John Douglas often passed in a few minutes from the most dreadful nausea to a state of perfect ease, and could eat, talk, and read as well as if he was on shore. This, however, was only a temporary escape from sickness, for as soon as he came up to the deck again he found he was as much affected by the motion of the ship as at first.

On the 27th of January the ship saw snow on the Peak of Tenerife, and John Douglas knew this was the only part of Africa he was ever likely to behold. Three of his horses died in this neighbourhood – it had been his brother Archibald's idea to ship horses. J. T. & A. Douglas & Co. had held sugar interests in Demerara for a number of years, but John Douglas was on his first voyage to that country.

From there the ship pressed on across the mid-Atlantic. On the 7th of February they were surrounded by flying-fish. Several of them lit on deck. John Douglas ate one for his supper and found it not unlike herring. These fish fly, it seems, in order to cool themselves by evaporation; they do not rise in the night, and always plunge back into the water the moment their wings are dry. The heat had become excessive and as the ship voyaged further south and west, each day brought John Douglas some new sight – the nautilus sailing with its fan, the cerulean brilliance of the dorado moved by golden fins.

After a passage of seven weeks one of the seamen from the foretop-gallant masthead gave the joyful warning, 'Land ahead'. The day was serene, with a tropical transparency of atmosphere. Captain Barrow told his passengers that the river to windward was the Courantyne, situated between the Berbice and the Surinam, and that the ship lay about a hundred miles to the eastward of Demerara River, their ultimate destination. He ordered a sharp lookout to be kept, as the coast was infested with privateers from the Orinoco.

The next morning John Douglas could see the thin line of land himself, without the aid of the glass. It was low and perfectly flat, and appeared quite wild and uncultivated. Large forests of trees extended along the coast even to the beach, which apparently consisted of mud, with a few intervals of sand. This prospect was not flattering, but it being the end of his journey, and the first land he had seen for several weeks, John Douglas beheld it with glad eyes, and thought it a most delightful place.

Highly gratified by this verdant scenery and, having completely recovered from his remaining sea-sickness, he retired once more to his stateroom, but not to sleep. The watch being set, the careful mariner pacing the deck, universal silence reigned, interrupted at intervals with the hollow yet pleasing sound of 'All's well,' and the chiming of the half-hour bells. John counted eight when the starboard watch was called, and again visited the deck. The flood-tide had come up and, having raised the anchor, the ship drifted a little, and the seamen were veering out more cable. The breeze which had before been so brisk died away and left a perfect calm, the swell and roughness of the sea had subsided. Nothing was heard but a rippling against the vessel's side, and the voices of the seamen singing 'Yo heave ho'. The moon was just descending below the horizon, the air was mild, and John Douglas found that repose on a hen-coop on deck which his bed had denied him.

It was not until ten o'clock the next morning that they were under way again. A light breeze from the north-east soon brought them off the mouth of Berbice River. Here the scene began to vary: the river appeared to be about two miles broad, and in the middle of the channel was an island which, from a chart he had on board, John Douglas learned was called Crab Island: the Captain said it abounded with land-crabs. With a glass he discovered ships lying at anchor, and small craft sailing about in shore and coastways were clearly perceptible to the naked eye from the deck. The coast to the eastward of the river was as wild as that he had seen the day before off the Courantyne. The land to the westward appeared to be cultivated, and John Douglas had the pleasure of beholding habitations on firm ground, interrupted at intervals with clumps of mangrove trees.

The plantations ranged regularly on the coast. The foliage was quite remarkably green, and there were clusters of little cottages and some detached buildings. Some of the houses, of two, three and four storeys high, were painted white, and the red-boarded roofs gave every plantation the air of a separate village. The passing and re-passing of schooners and other colony-boats considerably enlivened the landscape, and John Douglas felt himself swell with life once more, as though his body had shrunk down for the duration of the voyage. This character of country continued all the way to the Demerara. The ship went over the bar safely, but as night was coming on, they were obliged to anchor about one mile from the river's mouth, and did not get in till the next morning, when a pilot came on and took charge of the vessel, which he brought to anchor under the guns of Fort William Frederic.

That last night aboard ship, John Douglas sat on deck and surveyed the new country as the sun set upon it. Now that the breeze blew over land it carried with it the fragrance of oranges. A number of windmills appeared at work both on the east and west side of the Demerara and there were several handsome and spacious mansions with look-outs on the beach. John Douglas watched, alert to all changes in the air, and wondered what the next day would bring to him.

In Stabroek, a mucky huddle on the Demerara River that would soon be called Georgetown, Martha Ann Ritchie washed out her petticoat by candlelight. She had come from Barbados, where civilization was much more advanced. She and her mother, Rebecca, had travelled here not long before, lured by the prospect of a good living, housekeeping in the houses of the merchants of Demerara. Rebecca Ritchie was a freed slave, given manumission by Martha Ann's father, an impulsive white planter who then washed his hands of the pair. Martha Ann was sixteen, and wise with her age. Both she and her mother sought work, but neither would consider employment on the plantations, among the slaves. They preferred the hurly-burly of Stabroek with its grand wooden buildings, porticoes and balconies, its marketplace, and its criss-cross of stinking canals which they had heard were built by Dutchmen in the image of a perfect, distant city.

Martha Ann and Rebecca lodged with a coloured woman who had made a business of feminine importation, bringing women from Barbados for introductions to the gentlemen of Demerara. Elizabeth Drury's traffic in women was highly successful on all accounts – the women were as anxious to leave Barbados for new positions as the men of

Demerara were to receive them. Once they were resident in her house, Elizabeth would provide opportunities for newly arrived ladies to meet gentlemen. Stabroek was a place of wild sociability, although as yet there were no inns or taverns. But concerts and balls were held in the army camp at regular intervals – each gentleman could purchase a ticket for the price of twelve dollars which would include introductions to two ladies of colour. Elizabeth Drury handled these negotiations adroitly.

Rebecca Ritchie thought it might be difficult to secure a post as housekeeper owing to the colour of her skin and the infelicities of her past, but she did not trouble Martha Ann with her worries. For the time being she paid Elizabeth Drury for their keep by hawking oranges in the market, oranges purchased from another freed slave, a tall black-skinned man whose shirtless back was too ridged and scarred to look at. Rebecca could get a better price from the market than this man who had a tendency to glower and rage at passing white men.

Martha Ann was a determined person, beneath her surface youth and tenderness. She was excited by the prospect of life in Demerara, and felt herself on the edge of something completely new. She had already proven herself an adept seamstress; the riot of coloured cloth available in the marketplace of Stabroek inspired her, and Elizabeth Drury commissioned new dresses nearly every week. In anticipation of the forthcoming ball to which Elizabeth assured her she would be invited, Martha Ann was constructing a dress for herself as tasty and extravagant as anything she could imagine. She would look splendid, and the thought of this made her happy.

John Douglas landed about noon at the American wharf, ferried from the ship on a flat-bottomed punt. It spread like wildfire that a boatload from one of the off-standing vessels had arrived, and Captain Barrow was soon surrounded by the whole band of hucksters and pedlars belonging to the town. Here were all manner of people, bawling and vociferating in what seemed to the new arrivals a wretched jargon, half Dutch and half English, each trying to hitch himself closer than his neighbour. Not liking to be enclosed within this stifling ring of people, John Douglas slipped away, leaving Barrow in the midst of his assurances that he had plenty of goods for sale. Seeing some fine oranges Douglas asked for six-pennyworth; to his surprise Rebecca Ritchie gave him thirty, but they did not consolidate their acquaintance any further.

Stabroek was a new sight to John Douglas. He recollected no Scottish nor English town which bore the least resemblance. It stood on the flat strand, and in the canals children plunged about like dippers, while wooden houses, shaded by projecting roofs, were orderly arranged at spacious intervals. Nowhere the glitter of a glass casement; Venetian blinds, jalousies, closed every window, and rooms projected in all directions to catch the luxury of a through-draft of air. There were no trees in the streets, and the roadside where he walked was strewn with casks and bales, as if every road was a wharf, and numerous warehouses intermingled with the dwellings. Even the public buildings were of wood. Here and there a white man in a muslin shirt and gingham trousers was to be seen smoking his cigar, and giving directions from under an umbrella to his black messengers, who travelled on errands clothed only in blue pantaloons. A noonday sultriness and silence prevailed, every motion performed with tranquillity for fear of kicking up a dust – one would suppose the very labourers at work in a church during service. John Douglas walked slowly through the thick air until he found himself at the door of his own offices, J. T. & A. Douglas & Co. emblazoned across the wood.

Douglas arrived in Demerara at the tail end of the rainy

season – the wet months had been particularly dry this year and, as a result, the mosquitoes had not attained the usual level of dominance, although Douglas would not have recognized this. Shortly after his debarkation, the dry season arrived as well, a season which, in Demerara, is beautiful. A fine clear blue sky prevailed throughout the day, making its appearance from the east between the hours of four and five a.m. The morning twilight was gradual and long and John Douglas often rose early to make the most of this cooler time. In the evening the sun went out at six instantly, as if covered with an extinguisher, leaving the country in sudden darkness. The greatest heat was from seven to ten in the morning, almost intolerable in its strength. Much of life came to an oozy halt then, even the plantation slaves were allowed to cease their toil for an hour or so. After that, the sea-breeze began to set in, restoring to nature all her animation, and blowing with increasing spirit until dark, decreasing about ten at night.

Along with the pattern of the alien climate, John Douglas quickly began to grow accustomed to Demerara life. He found his business well-attended to, Tom Barnett, his manager – a Highlander – well organized with a list of planters ready to come to the house for business. Douglas surveyed his property and was pleased by what he found, his house among the small number of tall white dwellings built of wood imported from America, the roof of a more local red mahogany. Barnett informed Douglas that he would need to hire a new housekeeper, the previous one having departed abruptly when she learned it would be John Douglas and not his brother Archibald who travelled from Scotland to Demerara this year. John Douglas was mildly startled by this show of loyalty to a brother he himself had always found ill-tempered and prone to violence. When he enquired about the most efficient method of hiring staff in this region Tom Barnett laughed and told Douglas that all gentlemen seemed to find their housekeepers by drinking and dancing with them at the not infrequent balls held in the officers' mess at the army camp of Fort Frederic.

So, ten days later, John Douglas made plans to attend his first ball. His ticket had been purchased through Elizabeth Drury, whose glittering smile had caught Douglas by surprise. He was a single man, and singularly inexperienced in the ways of women, having only had the company of Glasgow whores on two occasions. Elizabeth, thinking of her gown being tailored at that moment by Martha Ann Ritchie, had agreed to procure John Douglas the two ladies that his ticket allowed him to escort to the occasion.

When Douglas and his manager had departed Elizabeth trolleyed herself up the steep painted staircase to the room where Martha Ann sat sewing.

'I've a gentleman to take you to the ball,' she announced with a flourish.

Martha Ann's hands dropped to her lap. She grew very still. She had been waiting for this news, and was made sombre by its arrival.

'He's very tall, and Scots, and his name is John Douglas. He has not been in Demerara long, and he is without a housekeeper.' Elizabeth moved forward in the room, and adjusted her hair. 'How is my dress?'

'It is nearly ready, Elizabeth,' said Martha Ann. 'What about Mama? Will she come with me?'

Elizabeth shook her head. 'I've made other arrangements for your mother. You will be accompanied by Rachel,' another recent young migrant along Elizabeth Drury's feminine highway.

That evening, all of Demerara society emerged from its houses and made its way to the ball – all of society deemed suitable to attend. John Douglas, in his best nankeen trousers and jacket, took his place among the other merchants, planters, overseers, company officers, ship captains and ranking soldiers – the Demerara River sheltered a great herd of nations and in attendance were Dutch, German, Prussian, Russian, Swedish, Danish, Spanish, French and American patriots, as well as the swelling population of Brits. The gentlemen's companions were a bastard ensemble, mulatto, quadroon, free coloured women, not one of pure African lineage. Places were staked in the dancehall, in the backroom tables bowed under the supper banquet, while drinks were served by all manner of freed men, freed women, and older coloured women. Rebecca Ritchie, Martha Ann's mother, had the task of wielding the ladle over the enormous bowls of sangaree and pineapple punch. In a confrontation with Elizabeth Drury that afternoon it had become plain to Rebecca that, as she had worried, by Demerara standards she was considered too old for a position as housekeeper, her back too stooped, her visage too imprinted with her slave past. In the few hours that had since passed Rebecca had made shrift of her own ambition and constructed a future for herself that rested upon the success of her child in finding a much-longed-for position. Rebecca had had many things stolen from her during her life; she had lost much in her journey through the middle passage, and now she wanted to ensure her daughter would not suffer such bare robbery.

John Douglas found Martha Ann Ritchie especially appealing. Sixteen, and such calm brown eyes, small hands appearing from within her sleeves – and such a dress! Yellow and blue, high-waisted, low-cut; John Douglas would have liked her for the dress alone, he thought, as Martha Ann smiled at him boldly before lowering her gaze to the floor.

After much dancing and drinking and a late supper of Muscovy duck and thin slices of roast beef, John Douglas accompanied Martha Ann Ritchie down the lamplit main street of Stabroek. Rebecca followed them outside and, unnoticed, watched as they left. Even in the darkness, each footstep raised dust from the ground as there had been no rain for several weeks.

Rank water moved slowly in the canal alongside where they walked, so separate in their histories. John Douglas felt he should make some attempt to woo this pretty young mulatto, even though their contract was a simple one. She was not like Scottish girls, not like the daughters of other merchants, whom Douglas had met in the parlour rooms of Glasgow's great houses. She spoke English with a strong accent that could have been thought musical, and she seemed shy and unastonished, even if she was not as formal and well-mannered as she might have been.

Housekeeper, mistress, mistress, housekeeper – the words were interchangeable, in Demerara they amounted to the same. Elizabeth Drury had not made this plain to Martha Ann and Rebecca, although Rebecca knew of the equation. Martha Ann felt as calm as she appeared. Accustomed as she was to sudden changes in her life, to adapting to new surroundings and situations, she had realized when Elizabeth Drury introduced her to John Douglas that evening what the nature of their arrangement would be. She was not naive, and in the marketplace she had made the acquaintance of a number of other merchants' housekeepers, young women who were proud of their light-skinned children and who spoke freely of the day their master would take his sons back to Britain for education. None of these women would lower themselves to assignations with men of their own race or blend of races; their mobility was upward, forward, and the only way to secure a future for their children was with a white man. Martha Ann had accepted this code as if it was cast in stone. She had enjoyed the dancing at the ball, she found the swirling crowd of half-familiar faces enthralling. John Douglas was tall and white and spoke in an accent she found difficult to decipher, but he was very polite. When they reached the doorstep of his tall white house, Martha Ann's breath caught and she lifted her hand to her throat: lit from within, it was as though the house was shining.

In the bedroom John Douglas undressed quickly. Martha Ann observed that he attempted to keep his eyes lowered as she herself began to disrobe, and she observed that he was unable. She did not mind his eyes upon her, she felt warmed by his gaze, while the night air was cool on her skin. She slid beneath the cover of his bed, a bed far larger and more luxurious than any she had seen before, a bed she could scarcely believe herself allowed in. John Douglas moved swiftly from where he had stood gawping at her to between the covers, and he was upon her just as swiftly. Martha Ann willed her body into compliance, and she was not without her own curiosity. He lifted her legs apart – her thighs were brown and strong – and pushed himself into her. Martha Ann felt his cock like she had felt nothing else before. This is what it is like, she found herself thinking, this is what it is like to do this. She raised one hand and placed it on the small of John Douglas's back; his skin was damp. He had not kissed her, but she reached up and kissed his chest where it hovered above her, like a new sky, she thought. Martha Ann clenched her fists because, truth told, John Douglas was hurting her. But she did not care.

Douglas came suddenly, stifling a cry. He fell forward and felt Martha Ann's small body beneath his, her breasts full circles pressed against his skin. Sweat trickled off his brow and onto the pillow as he felt himself convulse inside the girl once more. He rolled over, and Martha Ann smiled at him. John Douglas thought Demerara a rough paradise.

The next day Martha Ann was instructed in her duties by the manager, Tom Barnett, and Elizabeth Drury who had been asked to attend by John Douglas who saw that she was sturdy on household matters. Douglas himself had been fetched before first light by the owner of the Bel-Air estate, one of the largest and most successful of Demerara plantations, who took the young merchant on a tour of his land. They travelled by tent-boat, powered by six slaves, along the canals of the watery country until they reached the estate. Hemmed as it was by reclaimed land and a sea-wall on the narrow sea frontage, the estate extended back past the great house, wind, water, and cattle mills, on to the cultivated land itself, sugar cane backing onto savannah. Each plantation formed a kind of flat island, with a wharf, or landing-place, on the sea-front opposite the dwelling-house, and canals ringing the length of the property, a dam at the rear. These trenches and their sluices answered two purposes: to drain off the superfluous water on the estate, and to harbour boats while loading or discharging. Douglas was impressed by the industry all this represented, and he said as much while the planter cast his arm wide to display his land and the slaves who worked it. There had been a revolt in Berbice not fifteen years previously; control had been regained bloodily. The planter mused that his own slaves had it easy, that their lives here were a tenfold improvement on what they had been in Africa, and John Douglas was inclined to agree.

All that water and mud and heat, Demerara plantations built on reclaimed swampland, the few remaining man-groves attesting to that former soupy state; John Douglas, although robust, was not acclimatized and that very afternoon he contracted a bilious fever. By five o'clock he was reduced to shivering and painful diarrhoea, and by seven in the evening he was insensible.

The master, John Douglas, had fallen ill, and Martha Ann was new to her position. He was carried from the tent-boat to his house, and it fell to the girl to nurse him. Day after day she sat by his bedside, opening the blinds and parting the mosquito net only to be shocked by the sallowness of his complexion. Martha Ann kept his brow and his lips wet, and followed the advice that rained upon her from other housekeepers, women long resident in

Demerara who were so familiar with this fever that they referred to it as 'seasoning' – once seasoned, the sick emerge with greater immunity. Every day Martha Ann slipped her small supple hands between his sides and his arms to lift his body and give him ease. John Douglas, in his fever, knew nothing, but when, nearly ten days later, he opened his eyes, he saw the young woman Martha Ann, her own eyes wide in her face. He could scarcely remember who she was after their one night of acquaintance, but he felt soothed by her presence. Martha Ann ministered to him, alert to his needs. She was pleased by her intimate proximity to this man, her importance in his life.

And John Douglas grew stronger, and the mark of his strength was the way his eyes began to follow Martha Ann as she moved around the room; she felt his eyes upon her. And soon looking was replaced with touching, his hands upon her now, drawing her down into his bed.

John Douglas's house was spacious, airy and open, the shuttered windows allowing the air to move. Martha Ann was given her own room downstairs at the back which she shared with her mother, Rebecca, who continued to hawk goods in the market for the scarred freed slave when she was not required in Douglas's kitchen. Martha Ann and John Douglas developed a system of private signals – when he wanted her to come to him at night he would leave his bedroom door ajar. Some nights the door remained firmly closed while, behind it, John Douglas longed for Martha Ann – he felt it advisable to deny himself gratification at least some of the time. He was not troubled by the questions his new arrangement might have begged had he and Martha Ann lived in Glasgow, but he worried that the hazy pleasures of Demerara might unlock in him an uncontrollable indolence. He had been slightly affronted by the arrival of Rebecca Ritchie who slipped into the house as though she had been invited, but when he mentioned this at the Exchange where the merchants and planters gathered to gamble at whist and talk of an evening, he had been rebuked and laughingly informed of his duties of husbandry.

Martha Ann quickly caught the rhythm of the house. From a relieved Tom Barnett she took over domestic organization. The previous housekeeper had built up the house stocks of linens, china and other fine white goods, placing orders through the Douglas network of shipping contacts and, on occasion, Martha Ann would pass time simply touching these things in the same way she touched John Douglas in his sleep, as though she might learn or absorb the world's secrets in this manner.

Her favourite tasks revolved around the formal evening meal prepared whenever John Douglas had guests. She lingered carefully over the menus, the place settings, the Madeira wine decanters. At dusk she would light the spermaceti candles, placing them within their protective cones of blown glass as the breeze came through the shutters and cooled the dining room. Of course Martha Ann was never invited to grace Douglas's table, not even on the evenings he and Tom Barnett had no company, but this had not yet occurred to her; white women were scarce and the table was often crowded with men.

At night Martha Ann luxuriated in the arms of John Douglas, featherbedded and at ease. She gave herself to him without question, and he did not cease to marvel at that. In the dark their cries filtered through the jalousies, through the walls of the house, hovering over the heads of all who slept there. Rebecca Ritchie heard them, and with every moan she felt more secure, less concerned with the past, and the future.

She waited out her pregnancy in the shade of the balcony. The master, John Douglas, had left for Scotland weeks before she realized she was going to have a child.

Martha Ann felt healthy in her confinement. Now he was gone she slept each night in the back room with her mother, entering John Douglas's room only to raise the dust and turn the mattress to protect it from the humidity. Without Douglas the house ran quietly. Tom Barnett attended during the day – at night he went to his mistress, another of Elizabeth Drury's women. The house slaves returned to their quarters and the place felt empty around Martha Ann and her mother. The baby kicked and turned and the young woman smiled as she waited for John Douglas to return from across the sea.

Martha Ann was seventeen, nearly eighteen, by the time the baby was born. He tore through her flesh, but she survived. His skin was very fair, almost as pale as the skin of John Douglas himself, but his hair was dark like Martha Ann's, his eyes a luminescent brown. She gazed at him happily, and found herself dreaming of his life, and of her own life with John Douglas.

This first child: Alexander.

John Douglas returned to his old life in the great stone buildings and parlours of Glasgow, taking his place at the card tables of the Green Cloth Club as though he had never left. There were Scottish girls to court – they amazed him, these women, with their petticoats and their conversation – and business to conduct with his brothers. Douglas did not think often of Demerara; he knew he would soon be returning there. Sometimes at night he craved Martha Ann's body, but then he fell asleep, blameless and sated.

Douglas's second journey to Demerara was not nearly as arduous and nauseating as the first. Seven weeks was still a long time to be aboard ship, but he passed the days more happily. Once off the boat, he slipped through the excited crowd and walked quickly to his house, the swampy mangrove sights and sounds of Demerara familiar to him. Tom Barnett opened the door and greeted him, then immediately left to organize the retrieval of Douglas's goods quay-side.

John Douglas walked to the back of the still house. It felt altered, as though in a deep sleep. He entered the room of the two women. There sat Martha Ann, much changed, and in her arms a pale baby whom Douglas recognized straight away as his own, his heart pushing up in his chest. Martha Ann laughed when she saw John with Alexander, she rejoiced as he stuttered with amazement and called the baby his own.

Douglas installed mother and child in a large room on the first floor of the house, leaving Rebecca in her old chamber. For a day or two he pampered Martha Ann, until she pushed him away with her broad smile, telling him she was strong enough for them all. At night, John would send for Martha Ann. They pressed themselves together, time and time again, while they listened for Alexander in the next room. Martha Ann's young body was taut and giving as before and John Douglas took great pleasure in her.

Two years later, a second son, James Douglas was born.

Stabroek grew, the main thoroughfare was cobbled. Britain gained control of the territory around the Demerara. In Europe, slavery was becoming untenable, economically and, some were arguing, morally. The plantation-based sugar trade began to change. Sugar made Demerara, its history was sugar-coated and, like tar, sugar sticks. Over the generations, J. T. & A. Douglas & Co.'s interests had moved from tobacco to cotton then to sugar and soon the company would transform itself yet again. But a residue, a gritty, burning, crystalline stickiness, would always remain, coating the profits from Africa to Demerara to Glasgow and away.

John Douglas travelled to Scotland, and then returned to Demerara once more. Martha Ann licked the taste of sea-salt from his skin. Beneath that he tasted very sweet.

Years passed, John Douglas divided his time between the

northern isles and the southern world, so utterly different that keeping the two separate was no task at all. Both boys were pale, yet Martha Ann saw herself in them too. She nursed them, they were hers, and John Douglas so often gone.

During one of his spells at home in Glasgow, John Douglas met Jessie Hamilton at a Green Cloth Club evening party. Jessie Hamilton's *décolletage* was very white, the dip between her breasts powdered and smooth, and John could not keep his eyes from returning to her. Their courtship was swift – he had no patience, any longer, for the convoluted social rituals of seduction; as with many aspects of life, he felt the Demerara way to be more honest, more true. But this Glasgow woman would make a good wife.

And of course his trips to Georgetown continued, and his life there went on as though nothing had changed. The year of his Glasgow marriage, John Douglas arranged for his Demerara boys to be educated in Lanarkshire. His bride was unsurprised when he returned with his sons, James and Alexander. Scottish merchants and their West Indian 'interests'; it was well known what they produced out there, as well as cash. She was not expected to treat these boys as her own. The school to which they were sent was not the school her own children would attend. Jessie Hamilton did not dread John's trips to the Caribbean although from time to time she worried he might bring back more sugar children, more evidence of his life out there.

John Douglas told Jessie Hamilton nothing about the other woman, his other family in fact, across the Sargasso Sea. And he did not mention his new domestic arrangements to Martha Ann either, although once he made plans for the boys to go, she understood. There was never any communication between the two women, but they knew of each other, they dreamt of each other, they saw themselves reflected in those dreams. North. South. Old. New. Empire and colony.

At the age of six, James Douglas made the long Atlantic crossing, south to north, west to east, a distance much greater than its mileage could indicate. In Scotland James began to unlearn his mother, to forget her and, in the act of forgetting, remake himself.

But, for a while in that Lanarkshire boarding school, he did long for his mother, transfixed by the ice which formed in swirling patterns on the river in winter. He longed for the soft and sudden changes of the Demerara air, his mother's hand on his brow. Years later, when he reached Vancouver Island, his 'Eden', he woke one summer morning with the uncanny sensation of having returned to his mother's house.

PART FIVE

An experimental tour

*For the Governor of Vancouver Island
has been in the Company out here ever
since he was a boy about fifteen years of age
and now he is a Man upwards of sixty years –
so you may say he has been all his life
among the North American Indians and has
got one of them for a wife so how can it
be expected that he can know anything at
all about Governing one of England's last
Colonies in North America.*

Settler Annie Deans,
29 February 1854

Dear Shula,

Thank you so much for the article that you sent to me about James Douglas. I wonder if my mother would have been so pleased about 'our relative' if she had known about his lineage, but perhaps I am too harsh. Sometimes it feels as though all colonial history, all of modern British history, somehow leads back to slavery. The very fabric of the cities in which we live. James Douglas went to Canada, where he thought he could escape that legacy, which was so directly his own. And for much of his life he was free of it. But, in the end, he was his parents' boy.

As I'm sure you know, Amelia Douglas's father, William Connolly, married *à la façon du pays* the Cree woman Suzanne Pas de Nom. In Demerara that same year John Douglas fathered James with his housekeeper, the 'free coloured woman', Martha Ann Ritchie. I see now how William Connolly's life mirrored John Douglas's and how this haunted James; both men left one family and started another, left a dark woman for a white, rendering the previous liaison without currency, illegitimate. Perhaps it was straightforward at that time of great sea-voyages to far-flung outposts of Empire, perhaps it was usual to have one family in the cold country and another in the heat. John Douglas abandoned Martha Ann in the sugar cane, and James was determined that his own children would not face the ignominy of illegitimacy as he had done. He made his marriage vows to Amelia Connolly not once, but twice. When James thought of himself, did he think of his own so very Caribbean history? Or did forgetting come easily to

James Douglas, whose young life was full of abrupt and complete leavings?

Audrey hadn't heard from Shula since the long letter about the aeroplane crash. She'd written to her a number of times, and tried to phone her. At the university in Toronto, another academic had taken over her direct line; he was curt, saying he didn't know where Shula could be contacted. On her home number, Audrey got the answerphone; the announcement on it was electronic, so she didn't even get to hear Shula's voice. She left a couple of messages, but then stopped. Shula was nowhere to be found, she had gone to ground. It was as though that plane resting on the bottom of Stuart Lake had claimed her at last.

Audrey stopped writing for a moment and went to her shelves. She pulled down a book, a history textbook she had kept since her days at UBC. In it she found a photograph of Amelia in her old age: she looked buried in layers of dark clothes, long full skirt, petticoats, high embroidered bodice, long sleeves, lace cuffs, bonnet, ribbons. She was seated at an odd angle, almost reclining, and she was small in stature, little. Her face was wizened, like a dried apple dolly. She looked both Cree, and not Cree, white, and not white, James's Little Snowbird, a soft, story-telling granny.

James Douglas never wrote of his past; in all the copious letters, diaries, notebooks, company reports and government correspondence he produced, he never mentioned his place of birth nor the journey he had made as a small boy, aged six – old enough to remember, Audrey thought, old enough to make himself forget. In all the mountain of paperwork he left behind he mentioned his mother only once: July 1839, he recorded the date of her death. What could it have been like to live like this, wanting to hide his illegitimacy? What would have happened had he lived openly with the fact that his grandmother was a freed slave?

Audrey wondered if that possibility had disappeared the day that James set sail from Demerara, the day his mother, and her mother, were banished from his life, the day he was cast out from theirs.

Alexander (1801), James (1803), and Cecilia (1812).

Audrey lined up the names and dates on bits of paper in front of her on the desk.

It is nine o'clock in the evening, end of the twentieth century. When I think about them now it feels to me as though James and Amelia provided a direct physical link between Britain and its colonies. It's as though these two people were bridges from the past into the future, James descended from both slaver and slave, Amelia from conquered and conqueror, their bodies spanning the abyss. They were it, it was them, they were Empire at its most emblematic and contradictory. They were the conduits over which Europeans could walk into the new world, they provided the passage, they made it easy.

Did they have any regrets, I wonder, were there Cree customs, ways of being, that Amelia preferred to those of the white people? Did James feel he was his father's son or was it his mother's character that moulded him? Did James envy Amelia and her facility for moving between cultures, Cree and European? Even after Suzanne was exiled to Red River, Amelia had a proximity to her mother that James had been denied. He had sailed away from that part of himself, the Caribbean, his mother's body. Perhaps James journeyed west in an effort to find his mother, a trans-migratory passage through the trees. He arrived at Amelia, his own children, his sister, and life in his 'Eden'. In that sense he was lucky.

And it comes full circle to me. Somehow I feel I'm implicated in all this. I don't know why – not just because of the family connection, that light is dim. But through whatever it was that brought me to London, to this place.

I'm going to keep on writing to you, Shula. I had a friend who disappeared once, a long time ago. And, over the years, I've lost friends, not just misplaced them, but lost them completely. I know we only met once but, well, I hope that you are okay.

Audrey turned the pages of the textbook she'd taken from the shelf, scanning the pencil notes she had made in the margins. She could remember sitting in the university library and turning pages in this same way. She had not regretted not finishing her degree, although she had missed the intensity of studying, the absolute absorption into the detail of other peoples, other times. She closed the book and went to return it to the shelf, but as she did a piece of paper fell from the pages to the floor. She bent down to retrieve it.

It was a snapshot of herself with Jane. They were both wearing sunglasses, and they were kissing, their arms flung backwards away from their torsos, fingers splayed. Their bodies did not touch, only their lips. Jane was wearing cut-offs and a T-shirt, Audrey was wearing jeans and a short-sleeved check shirt. Audrey could tell the two girls in the photo were laughing; she could not recall the circumstances in which it was taken. Yet there they were, their previous selves.

Audrey wondered how much she resembled herself at eighteen. She knew she was thinner now, parched. Her hair was completely different, it was long and curly then, she and Jane both wore their hair long, and now it is short, with too much grey. Her face, yes, the shape of her face could well be completely different. Hollower cheeks and she used to wear glasses before she got contact lenses. And she had wrinkles now, new lines where before there were none, her face moving in different directions than it once did. The way she spoke was different, perhaps even the timbre of her voice had changed.

She purged herself of the old Audrey when she arrived in London, getting rid of what she thought were her provincial ways, adapting to the big, foreign city. Since Jack left, and she became his other woman, she had felt her old self, her childhood self, more strongly. She had been surprised by how good this felt. Now she wondered if perhaps she hadn't changed as much as she thought, as much as she had wanted. I'm the same old Audrey, she thought, those added layers rapidly shed.

And maybe James Douglas found himself the same old James, his mother's boy, the Demerara boy made good, after all those years away. Maybe this was something they had in common, Victorian patriarch, *fin-de-siècle* girl runaway.

★

At UBC the winter term workload was heavier, and Audrey drifted deeper and deeper into the library stacks. She was writing a paper on the gold rush, and the period was vivid to her, the anxiety of the speculators and miners as they scrambled upriver for cash, the Governor's struggle to keep control, waves of miners flooding Georgia Strait, Fraser River, Barkerville, Lillouet, each swell larger and more avaricious than the last. Under Douglas's leadership the resources of the region began to be exploited as the fur traders gave way to true colonizers who quickly recognized the province's raw potential. Beaver, gold, then coal, copper, lumber, salmon: the land was to become a place of company towns. Her professor was encouraging. Audrey felt there was a great well of knowledge available and she had only just dipped her bucket into it.

Time passed quickly and then on the last Wednesday in January Audrey realized she had agreed to go to Victoria to see David on the forthcoming weekend. She half hoped that he had forgotten, but the phone rang that evening.

'I'll come out and meet the ferry – which one will you be on?'

Audrey calculated. 'I guess the six p.m.' Already the arrangement felt completely illicit.

'I'm pleased you're coming, Audrey,' he said, but she was unable to reply.

She took a seat by the window on the boat, and hoped there'd be no one she knew on board. She had had no difficulty getting a friend to work her shift at the bar, even though she had left it until that afternoon, her one attempt at creating an obstacle. She told her friend she was going home to see her parents. That felt like a terrible lie. The hour-and-three-quarter boat trip, which, on other occasions, felt interminable, passed too quickly. Before disembarking she went into the ladies' room and looked at her face in the mirror. She had never learned how to apply make-up properly and wore only mascara, no lipstick. She thought her face looked naked and plain, and roundabout twelve years old, not a face a conscientious barman would serve without asking for ID. Not a face that did this kind of thing.

When she got into the terminal building, there was no sign of David, so she walked out to the car park. It was dark, but she could see his car, and him in it. As she went towards it, he opened the door and got out. He wore a thick wool scarf and a denim jacket lined with sheepskin, and she thought he looked like the Marlboro Man. She smiled. His blond hair was a little longer than before. She said hello and went towards the passenger door without going near him, throwing her small bag into the back seat.

He got in the car and sat down before speaking. 'I'm really glad you came.'

He sounded a little too sincere, she thought. She felt her guts constrict once again. 'Me too,' she claimed.

When they drove through Colwood Audrey couldn't help herself, and gave in to her impulse to slide down in the seat, so that no one on the road could see who she was, who she was with. She was sure every other vehicle contained her parents, and on the Metchosin Road David overtook a car that Audrey was convinced was driven by her parents' friend Dorothy Jones. David could not have helped but notice what she was doing, but he did not say a word, and she understood that he was nervous as well, and that did not make her feel any better.

The cottage looked the same, tiny and sunk down into the mossy sand. It was late, after nine, by the time they pulled into the drive. David had forgotten to leave a light on – he had come to the ferry straight from school – and the headlights reflected off the bedroom window when they came to a stop. He turned off the engine and they sat in the dark, not speaking. The night air was cold, harsh, salty. In the distance Audrey could see the searchlights at William Head Prison flashing over the point. She got out of the car and felt a powerful *déjà vu*; she was with Jane, her best friend – and they were going to visit their teacher. At the top of the path to the front door, David put his arm around her. She leaned into his hard body and tried to feel confident.

Inside, the dog, Suzanne, jumped up on Audrey before David had a chance to put on the lights. She placed her paws on Audrey's chest and stretched languidly, as though she remembered her from previous visits. David sent the animal out into the dark, and then they were alone again. He lit the fire, put on a record, offered something to eat, a drink. When he went into the kitchen to get things together, she sat on the settee. It was very difficult not to think of Jane. Audrey could almost hear her voice. She stood up and went into the narrow kitchen. David had his arms in the sink. She spoke to him, he turned and dried his hands on a towel, and then moved forward, pushing her against the wall, grabbing her hips. He kissed her, he bent down, his teeth clicking against hers. The thing about him, Audrey thought as he undid her zipper, is that he's a man;

all the others were boys. Then she laughed at herself, and David ran his tongue along the tilt of her neck. They fucked there, standing up in the kitchen, and Audrey felt herself drain out, into him. And yet even then she struggled against Jane, her name on her lips, despite her mouth being full of David.

They slept a long, dark sleep, and in the morning it took several moments before Audrey understood where she was. They got out of bed, and walked on the winter beach, and the day passed quickly. They played cards in the afternoon, and were careful with each other, polite, keeping an erotic distance, brushing hands, legs, not kissing. They listened to the radio, and David cooked things – they didn't need to go anywhere, they had everything they needed right there in the cottage. David talked about his past, about when he was a kid, but he was cautious in what he said, Audrey thought he did not want to make the gulf between their ages too big. He did not mention school, he did not mention his girlfriend. And he did not mention Jane. But she was there, right there, between them.

That night, they went into the bedroom when the tension grew too great. Audrey took off her jeans, but kept on her sweater, it was cold in the room, there was frost on the windowpane. David undressed slowly over by the wardrobe, his glance meeting Audrey's. His body was lithe, but it had a stiffness that she recognized from when they had danced together in the billiard hall, a stiffness that, she wondered, came with his age. When he was absolutely naked, he moved towards the bed, and he lay beside her, shivering, stroking her legs.

The last stitch of her clothing removed, he was on her, her hands on his back, moving with him, into him, Audrey looked up at the ceiling, and she couldn't stop herself from wondering if this was what it had been like for Jane. He pushed into her, whispering her name into the pillow. He made Audrey come, she felt herself burn and seize, and then when he came he cried out and Audrey was glad there was no one there to hear him.

In the middle of the night, a storm arrived, a stark wind blew off the Pacific, as though it had come tunnelling straight down from the Arctic. The wind woke Audrey, and she fell back into a fitful sleep. She dreamt she was in her mother's car, driving down the lane to see David. Tree branches thrashed the sides of the vehicle like rows of children reaching out to smack her.

Later, the storm shifted up a gear or two. Soon sea-wash was battering the front windows of the cottage and David, half-asleep, drew Audrey near to him. The noise was tremendous, Audrey thought it was as though the ocean was possessed, as though it was trying to reach out and suck the cottage in, as though it was trying to punish them. She lay awake for ages until it began to abate and then she fell asleep again.

They woke early the next day, drew open the curtains, and found the beach covered with a layer of snow. On an ocean front snow is strange, it makes the landscape – white strand, whitecaps, white sky – look impossibly other-worldly, like an over-exposed photograph. And lonely, thought Audrey. He must get lonely here on the beach. The snow was no more than an inch deep, no trouble getting in and out with the car, David said the main roads were probably clear already. So Audrey relaxed, and decided to enjoy herself, imagining they were snowed in, keeping warm, drinking tea, looking out to sea. By mid-afternoon, the snow was gone, and David drove her to the ferry.

The rest of the term passed in a flurry of papers and exams. Audrey found she had an enormous amount of work, and it was a struggle to keep up. Every weekend, every evening, except Friday nights when she worked at the bar, was taken up with studying. Her reading was endless, her head swirled with dates and facts and names. She enjoyed it, and she kept up, she had to do well in order to retain the scholarship money.

She didn't hear from David, and she didn't contact him, and she was getting very good at putting him out of her mind. She finished term, and was re-hired by BC High-ways. Before setting off for the summer she went home. While she was at her parents she had a phone call from Jane. The spring had been unusually warm. They met in a bar in the early evening, both hot and sticky from the drive.

Audrey could tell that Jane was unhappy, that she wanted to talk, but she kept preventing her, too tired to ask what was wrong, worried it might have something to do with David. She wanted to avoid the truth, in case she found herself lying. Finally Jane interrupted. Audrey had been rambling on about exams and money.

'Frank wants to get married.'

'That's great, isn't it?' Audrey hesitated.

'I guess so.' She sighed. 'I tried to see David.'

Audrey took a deep breath. 'What happened?'

'We met for a drink, downtown. He was very casual. He didn't seem to understand that it was a big thing for me, that it was difficult, arranging an evening out, not telling Frank. In fact, I lied, and said I was seeing you. That you were in town for the weekend.'

Audrey looked at Jane, and Jane returned her gaze.

'It was pretty sad.'

'Sad?'

'We didn't have anything to say to each other.' Jane stopped talking then, and turned to Audrey, as though she was about to cry.

'That's terrible,' Audrey said, trying to give her voice the right pitch.

'He told me he still thought about me, and that he fantasized we were together.'

'He did?'

'And then he said that we both had other obligations – Frank, whatshername—'

'What *is* her name?'

'Brenda. Dr Brenda Milroy.'

'Oh,' said Audrey, then added, 'That's a stupid name.'

'Anyway, I know he's right.' Jane put down her drink. 'Just because I started going out with Frank when I was fifteen I didn't know that meant I would be spending the rest of my life with him.'

'You don't have to stay with him, Jane.'

'You don't know Frank, Audrey.'

Audrey shivered at the look Jane gave her. 'Doesn't he make you happy?'

Jane turned to look at her again. Her eyes were circled with darkness, and she had begun to look older than her years. Audrey remembered how she had looked the week before Grad, and she was struck by the fact that she had no idea of what went on in Jane's life, what went on between her and Frank, and she had no way of knowing, no way of finding out, unless Jane told her the truth.

'No, he does not make me happy,' she said.

'Why on earth would you even think of marrying him?'

'You don't understand, do you Audrey?'

Audrey was shocked to be cut off in this way. But no, she saw now she did not understand. She couldn't fathom how anyone could feel so bound to another, she couldn't see how Jane could let herself in for this. They sat for a while without speaking. Then Jane said she had some beer in her car, and why didn't they go out to Mathiessan Lake to cool down. Maybe they could go for a night-time dip.

When they got to the car park, and switched off the engine, Audrey felt the dark night around them. When she got out of the car, she could hear the lake in the distance. Although she had been coming to this lake ever since she was a kid, she had never been at night. They fumbled across the gravel, looking for the footpath that led down to the water. The beer swung cold against her leg. Jane had a couple of towels on her back seat, but neither of them had swimming suits.

They giggled as they stood together taking off their clothes. The moon was only half full, but it cast enough light for Audrey to see the slopes and curves of Jane's body. Just as Audrey was thinking Jane looked a bit fuller, a bit more womanly, Jane said, 'I'm pregnant.'

Audrey stopped taking off her clothes, and straightened. 'Should you be drinking?' she asked.

'I don't care. What's good for me has to be good for the baby.'

Audrey nodded. 'What does Frank think?'

'He's happy. It proves he's a man, doesn't it.'

'That's great, Jane, it's really good news.' She put her hand on Jane's arm, and squeezed. 'You'll be the first of my friends to have a baby. You'll be a mum!'

'That's right,' Jane said. Her smile was weak.

The water felt wonderful, the same texture as the night, cool and smooth. They floated on their backs and looked up at the stars, splashing out, away from the shore. Around them the water was completely black. Audrey loved swimming in lakes although she was always slightly afraid. Who knew what lay beneath the blackness of the surface? She imagined she could see down through the clear water as she swam – dead trees decaying on the bottom, swaying water weeds, fish, sunken debris. Audrey kicked her legs and arms calmly and tried not to think. She could hear Jane breathing a few feet away.

Floating on her back, she looked at the stars. Pregnant, Jane was pregnant. She turned towards her to ask how it felt, if she could feel the baby move yet. Jane brushed against Audrey under the water. Her skin felt rubbery and cold, dead. Audrey shrieked, dived down under the surface and kicked hard, somersaulting, moving far away. She stayed under until she felt her lungs might burst.

When she came up for air everything was quiet and dark. It seemed that she was the only source of noise in the world, swimming and breathing, shaking water out of her eyes and ears. She swivelled around but couldn't see Jane, could no longer hear her. Everything was dark. It was as though she had gone through an underwater passage and emerged in another lake. She called out and her voice echoed against the hills. Jane had disappeared. Everything looked different, silent. The shoreline curved in the distance, trees, but she could not tell where they had entered the lake, she could not see the beach. She started to swim to what appeared to be the nearest land. She swam as noisily and as quickly as she could, hoping to attract Jane's attention and scare off anything else that might be lurking in the deep.

As she came in to the shore she scraped her leg against a submerged tree – she knew what it was even as it first touched her. She stumbled over sharp rocks and heaved herself onto the bank, falling into brambles, blackberry bushes, poison ivy. There was no beach on this part of the lakeside, the forest came right down to the water. She moved along as quickly as possible, keeping close to the shore, climbing over dead trees, grazing her skin against every conceivable obstacle, barefoot and naked, soaking wet.

Eventually, after long sweaty minutes and mumbled oaths that resembled prayers – 'Fuck, damn, fuck . . . Fuck, fuck . . .' – Audrey broke through the trees and into a clearing. She recognized the car park up ahead, and ran through the site across spiky gravel, back down to the beach.

In her hurry, she nearly fell over Jane. She was sitting beside their clothes, huddled beneath her towel. When Audrey realized it was her and not yet another obstacle she collapsed beside her, naked, winded and shaking.

'I thought you'd gone,' Jane said, her arms around Audrey after she wrapped her in a towel. Audrey's heart pounded, and Jane held her tight. 'Left your clothes on the beach and swum away. Left me here, by myself, left behind.'

That summer Audrey began working on the highway that runs up the coast, between North Vancouver and Squamish. This was less enjoyable than Highway No. 3. Their base was in the town, and the traffic was heavy, and it was cooler on the coast, more rain. Instead of working through the summer without taking breaks, she took a bit of time off, went to the Okanagan to see a friend from university.

In July she spent a night in a motel with David. He was on his way into the interior for a holiday. She had rung him from the pay phone in the camp canteen a few weeks earlier, wanting to see him, missing him for no good reason. The motel they chose was run-down and a little seedy, the neon sign flickering on and off. Their room had a vibrating bed. Put a quarter in the headboard and the mattress buzzed and shook and shivered. They used up all their quarters, and were not done fucking, before they had exchanged more than half a dozen words. He was impressed by her tan and her walkie-talkie, and she, by his stamina.

'This is great,' he said, when they had finished and were lying side by side.

'What?'

'The way we can be friends, and do this, and stay friends, and have it not get too complicated.'

She smiled and pressed herself against him, and thought, oh, so that's what we are doing.

She left early in the morning to get back to the crew. They hadn't made plans to meet again. Audrey went back to work, and to saving her money, holding up her sign that read 'Stop' on one side, 'Go' on the other.

At the end of the summer, she spent a long weekend with her parents. Her father had retired that spring, and she thought he was less relaxed, more unwell, than she expected, as though not working was ageing him in a way working never had. They had spent the summer working in their garden, and their freezer was full of vegetables and fruit pies and Audrey's mother offered to send her to Vancouver loaded down with produce.

Audrey went back to UBC, back to her room in Kitsilano. The workload of the first term of her third year – it was a four-year degree – was heavier than ever. She had managed to hang on to her scholarship, in fact they had increased the money they gave her.

At Christmas she made the pilgrimage home to her parents. By then her father was glum, scarcely speaking, he had had a bad autumn, pain in his gut, heart arrhythmia. Audrey concluded he was depressed. Her mother's face was brave. She did not contact Jane, nor David. In late December she took the ferry back to Vancouver.

It was raining hard when she boarded, dark, and the ferry was delayed while they waited for the storm to subside. After twenty minutes the rain and wind abated and they pulled away from Schwartz Bay, but as they circum-navigated the bottom of Saltspring Island a thick fog descended and the boat began to heave with the waves. Audrey paced the lounge, overhearing other passengers mutter about winter storms – much worse winter storms – they had weathered on the ferry. In the coffee shop she ran into Jane. They went to sit together in the forward lounge. It had windows on three sides but even in narrow Active Pass they could see nothing of the islands they travelled between. The foghorn blasted over and over and the ferry pitched from side to side.

Jane was now heavily pregnant, eight months. She was on her own on the boat, but Audrey didn't think to ask where she was going until it was too late. She looked terrible, drawn, grey-skinned, thin, apart from the bulge of the baby.

'You never told me about you and David,' she said

suddenly as Audrey sipped her coffee.

Audrey swallowed hard. 'No. I didn't.'

Jane looked at her reproachfully.

'I didn't know how.'

'I'm not stupid, you know.'

'I know, Jane.'

'It was between him and me. You knew that. He wanted me.'

'He did. But then he seemed to want me.' Audrey knew any explanation would sound pathetic.

'He did not. He did not want you. It was always me. He fucked you, but he was thinking about me. You were a reminder of me, that's all.'

'Okay,' Audrey said, as though she agreed. Besides, as soon as she heard these words, she was afraid they might be true.

'He told me,' she said, 'he told me everything.' Jane hunched down in her seat.

Audrey did not want Jane to cry. She couldn't think of anything to say. She felt as though she didn't exist, wasn't really there on that ferry.

'You took him away from me.'

'But I haven't got him.' Audrey spoke slowly, as though to a child. 'He is not with me,' she looked around to prove her point.

'You fucked him because you knew I was out of the way. You knew about Frank, you knew it was difficult for me.' Jane turned towards Audrey. 'I hate you,' she said, looking into Audrey's eyes. 'You know that? You betrayed me.'

Jane got up then, and left the lounge, her big belly making her slow and heavy. Audrey did not know what was true. She had had sex with David, but not much else, not a real connection, not like she had had with Jane. She sat and stared out of the window. The water was very rough, the wind stronger than earlier. The fog had broken up a little and outside Audrey could see the grey water boiling with rain. The deck beside the window was sluiced, streams of water ran off the rigging. After a few moments Jane appeared outside. She had no coat and was immediately soaked through, her shirt clinging to her stomach. She stood by the rail for a moment, then came towards the window where Audrey was sitting. She began to run her hand across the glass, as though to clear the rain, but Audrey could tell she could not see into the lounge, the glass was opaque. She passed her hand over the window again and again, like a blind person waving. Then she walked across the deck towards the outer handrail. At that moment, the ferry hit a trough in the sea and a great wave washed over the prow. Audrey saw the water rear up; the floor beneath her feet vibrated and shuddered. Her stomach rose into her throat as the ship went down into the furrow. She gripped the armrests of her seat, stared at a fixed point between her knees, and held her breath.

When Audrey looked out the window again Jane was not there. She had vanished. It was as though the sea had opened up and swallowed her, taken her away. Audrey stood, bracing herself against further squalls. She traversed the length of the forward lounge, but Jane was no longer on the outside deck. Audrey felt exhausted suddenly. She sat back down in her place. Jane must have come inside. She would go and look for her in a bit.

After twenty minutes the ship had made slow progress across the strait and the wind had begun to calm itself again. Audrey got up and went to find Jane. She would be able to explain what had happened, she would find the words, David had just appeared, it hadn't been planned, it was nothing – it meant nothing. She felt a full-bodied adult nostalgia for Jane then, for their old friendship, the link they had made. Everything would be okay if they could just be friends. She looked in the coffee shop, but Jane wasn't in there. She looked in the magazine kiosk, in all the other lounges. It was as though she just kept missing her, Audrey kept thinking she would be there, around the next corner. But Jane was nowhere to be found. She had disappeared.

As the ferry docked Audrey went down onto the car deck and got on the coach that would take her into Vancouver. From downtown she took a bus out to Kitsilano. She let herself into the apartment, her landlord was on an extended holiday in Hawaii. There was no post for her, no messages.

Her bedroom felt a little damp. Her bed looked hard and narrow. She stood on the threshold and contemplated her desk, the piles of books, her papers in their folders. She looked at the posters she had hung on her walls; among them was a postcard map of the London Underground that a friend had sent her the previous summer. That's where I'll go, she thought. That's where I'll belong. In London, I will come to life. In London, I'll be able to live.

A day highly suggestive of the past,
of fresh scenes, of perilous travel, of
fatigues, excitement and of adventures by
mountain and flood; the retrospect is full
of charms; images of the morning breezes,
the bright sky, the glowing sunrise, the
rushing waters, the roaring cataract – the
dark forest, the flowery plains, the
impressive mountains in their pure white
covering of snow, rise before me, at this
moment, as vividly as ever and old as I
am, my heart bounds at the bare
recollection of scenes I loved so well . . .
I can recall nothing more delightful
than our bivouac on a clear moonlit May
night, near the Punch Bowls – the highest
point of the Jasper Pass. The atmosphere
was bright, sharp and bracing, the sun set
in gorgeous splendour, bringing out the
towering peaks and fantastic pinnacles
dressed in purest white, into bold relief.
Our camp was laid and our fire built, on
the firm hard snow which was about twenty
feet deep. As the daylight faded away,
and the shades of night gathered over the
Pass, a milder light shot up from behind
the nearest Peak, with gradually
increasing brilliancy until at last the
full orbed moon rose in silent majesty

from the mass of mountains shedding a mild radiance over the whole valley beneath.

James Douglas's journal, 1862

The next time Jack came by Audrey cooked him dinner – he was impressed – and then she took him to bed. He had learned new tricks since he began sleeping with Shereen; she would show him that she was educated too. Once they were naked she was aggressive, rolling him over, gripping him tight, slapping his bum, urging him on. She opened herself up to him completely, she couldn't have opened any further if she'd taken a knife, cut out her own heart, and handed it to him. But he was caught up by the fucking, by the movement of flesh on flesh, and he couldn't raise his face to look in her eyes, he couldn't receive the message she was sending. It isn't his fault, really, she thought, I am complicit in all of this. He wouldn't be here if I hadn't invited him.

After both Amelia's parents had died, her eldest brother, John, fought for a share in William Connolly's estate in a celebrated litigation. When Connolly abandoned Suzanne Pas de Nom, when he placed her in a convent and repudiated her, he disinherited his children as well, all thirteen living and dead. They were left to fend for themselves for the thirty years – a whole lifetime, really – between the estrangement and Connolly's death. For Amelia, married to James, living in increasing comfort at Victoria, the damage was emotional; for her siblings, particularly her brothers, the consequences were fiscal as well.

The Montreal trial was lengthy and notorious. It was the mid-1860s, James had only recently received a knighthood and retired. Victoria was a long way from Montreal but, even so, news filtered through from the courtroom to the west and this served to sharpen Amelia's humiliation. She had lived with her father's abandonment for many years, it was a private, deeply felt, sorrowing thing. Now the calumny was made public.

During the period of the trial, Amelia rarely ventured beyond her house. James wrote notes on her behalf refusing invitations. 'Lady Douglas now being a great invalid . . .' 'Lady Douglas cannot be persuaded to leave the house . . .'

After long and dusty machinations, a settlement came to pass. The Canadian courts ruled that the marriage to Suzanne, *à la façon du pays*, was valid and William Connolly's second marriage to the white woman, Julia Woolrich, was not. The Douglas and Connolly families applauded this vigorous and original decision on behalf of the judiciary. Woolrich and her representatives appealed but a settlement was reached out of court. More than thirty years after William deserted Suzanne, Amelia's legitimate birthright was re-established. Julia Woolrich's children, the white babies she had borne Connolly in his old age, who were themselves now adult, were declared bastards. Amelia re-emerged, taking up her duties once again, the wife of the retired Governor, Sir James. James wrote a letter to one of the lawyers, condemning his father-in-law and one-time mentor. Amelia's brother had 'vindicated his mother's good name, and done justice to the high-minded old lady, now at rest in the peaceful grave – worthy of a kinder husband than poor Connolly.'

There is a story that Douglas once freed a runaway slave, a boy, at Fort Vancouver.

The black Church of Zion in California sent a deputation to Victoria. They were welcomed by Governor Douglas, and several hundred black Californians came to settle and seek gold. An all-black militia was formed under the sponsorship of James, the Victoria Pioneer Rifle Corps.

The first mercantile firm in Victoria was a black-owned business, Lester and Gibbs, a big dry goods store on Yates Street opened by Americans Peter Lester and Mifflin Gibbs. When a great banquet was organized by the city on the occasion of James's retirement, the organizing committee did not invite Lester and Gibbs – objections were raised, letters written to the press, but, in the end, the two men did not attend. At the reception organized for the incoming Governor ten days later, the Pioneer Rifle Corps was excluded from the welcoming parade. Two days later the black Rifle Corps organized its own welcoming salute outside the Government buildings.

In 1864, James embarked alone on a great tour of Europe, 'my experimental tour', he called it. He left the Pacific Northwest for the first time since he had arrived in Fort St James many years before. He crossed the Atlantic yet again, and this time, perhaps because of the presence of his sister Cecilia in Victoria, and all she had brought back to him, this time he let his mind return to the journey he had made as a boy. Sixteen when he left Britain, but that was not the voyage closest to his heart; six when he left Demerara. He remembered that first journey now, that primal journey away from the warm country. His mother, Martha Ann, had insisted on being rowed to the boat with her boys and their luggage, she had hugged them roughly in the little dippy wooden craft, straightened their coats and their hats, sending them on their way. Once on ship James thought he could hear his grandmother, Rebecca, singing to him from the shore, in her own African language, the language that she spoke to him at night. Rebecca was a veteran of boat journeys herself, she had been sold into slavery when she was no more than twelve, and she had told James, once, about the cargohold, the passage, and all she had seen, not a great adventure story, but a horror of proportions too great to comprehend.

James remembered this now, on the boat to England. He hadn't thought of his grandmother for many years, not even Cecilia spoke freely about the old black woman who hung about their father's house like a ghost.

But Rebecca had stayed on the shore, and Martha Ann had seen her boys get onto the ship before she was rowed away. James's brother Alex, who was older and wiser at nine, began to cry. Alex wept, in fact, on the ship that night, and called out for their mother, provoking their father's fury. 'You're my sons,' James remembered his father shouting, 'you belong in Britain with me.' He seemed to expect the boys to be reassured by his assertion and its vehemence. This was as close as the man ever got to a declaration of love and, as James saw it now, it was more a declaration of ownership.

But still, James had left Demerara, and then left Britain, and now he was returning for a European tour, not a prolonged reminiscence over journeys which were in themselves redolent of slavery.

Gone for just over a year, he travelled through Italy, France, Germany, Switzerland and Spain – Burgos, Rome, Versailles – keeping a detailed diary and writing letters home. Spending his first months abroad in Britain, he met with Hudson's Bay Company officials and men from the Colonial Office in London, where he was treated with deference. Then he travelled the country meeting his relatives, who welcomed the old fur trader and his knighthood in a manner they might not have done had he not met with such success; no one had forgotten that he left Scotland an illegitimate son. His father and stepmother were both dead, and it grieved James that John Douglas was not there to see for himself how the Demerara boy had been made. James returned to Lanarkshire for a few days, to his old school and village, but this visit did not pass so favourably.

27 January, 1865

My history is a rather curious one. I left England on leaving

239

school and have never returned to it till now – after an absence of forty years . . . Reflections on a return home after so long an absence – more painful than agreeable – the face of nature remains the same, but everything else is changed. I was advised of these changes, deaths and departures were duly reported, but it was only upon my return that I felt the stern reality. Before then I saw only the image of home as I left it, peopled with those who were dear to me, indelibly photographed as it were upon the mind. The vision is now dispelled and the past with its delusive hopes has for ever vanished.

Nothing is ever as it might have been.

The great tour lasted one year almost to the day and James returned to Victoria a man with a family, his connections to the 'old country' revived, proof to the world – and to himself – that he was a gentleman, not someone who had spent his life passing.

Amelia did not accompany her husband on this voyage. She did not see Notre Dame or St Paul's Cathedral. She was still the half-breed bride, best left to the places she knew, and not the great world which might look on her harshly. Curious as she was about this world, and the hints of it she had seen in those who had sailed it and arrived at port, she had not entertained thoughts of becoming travelling companion to James. She stayed at home with her children, and let James make peace with his past on his own.

Winter had arrived again. Audrey dressed carefully, her good suit, make-up, an ironed shirt. She dabbed perfume at her throat, her wrists, her ankles. Dark red lipstick. Jewellery.

Since she had started seeing Jack again, the phone calls from Shereen had stopped. She did not know if this was a coincidence, or if Shereen had figured out what was happening. She dialled her number now, surprised her fingers still remembered what to punch.

'Hello,' said Shereen.

There she is, thought Audrey, Jack's main squeeze. 'Hello. It's me.'

'Audrey!' she said, as though greeting an old friend who had been away.

'Yes.' Audrey spoke quickly. 'I thought I'd come around for a cup of tea.'

Shereen blustered. 'That would be fantastic! I didn't think I'd ever hear from you again. All those messages I left, I'm sorry, but I—'

'Never mind,' said Audrey. 'We can talk about that at your place.'

Audrey ordered a minicab, then moved around her flat picking up things and putting them into her handbag. A book she was reading, the day's newspaper. A notepad and pen. Her lipstick. Wallet. Keys. She looked for evidence of Jack's visits, something that she could offer to Shereen. But there was nothing, as always Jack left no trace. She wandered around opening and closing drawers. She wished she had a gun. She wished she could pull open her underwear drawer, push aside little bits of lingerie, and take out a handgun, a small one, mother-of-pearl handle, lady-like. She laughed out loud. Of course she had no such thing.

The taxi came and took her to Shereen's. She rang the bell. Shereen opened the door and came forward as though to embrace her, but Audrey stiffened and moved away. It would be too much to touch her, knowing Jack had touched them both. Shereen pretended everything was okay. She was effusive, nervy, welcoming.

Her flat looked different. 'I've redecorated,' she said, moving her arms back and forth to indicate what was new. 'I had a burst of energy, I did it myself.'

'That's what happens,' Audrey said, 'when you start seeing somebody. You get a whole new lease on life. Don't you?' She didn't mean to sound bitchy, just matter-of-fact.

Shereen pulled her arms close into her sides, across her breasts. 'Yes,' she said evenly, 'you do.'

'Well, it looks good.'

'Thanks Audrey, I knew you'd like it—'

'And your hair's different too.'

'Yes, I – do you like it?' Shereen turned her head, vaguely coquettish.

She really wants me to like her, Audrey thought, she really thinks I should be able to like her. She remembered the last time she saw Jane. On the ferry, during the storm. I wanted her to like me, I thought she should like me, I thought she would understand, that we could commiserate. But that was different. The circumstances were completely different. It was another time, another place. She shook her head.

'What's wrong? Don't you think it suits me?'

'Oh,' said Audrey, returning, 'yes, it looks great.' She paused. 'Does Jack like it?'

'Well,' Shereen blushed, tensed, 'you know what men are like. I don't think he noticed.'

'No,' she said, 'he didn't mention it to me.' Before Shereen could speak, Audrey turned and walked across the room. Hanging on the wall was a large framed colour print, a photograph of Jack and Shereen kissing. The room they were standing in was dark, and they were lit from behind as though with streetlight. They looked golden, a sheen of golden orange light suffused their hair, their skin, they looked like dark angels. It reminded Audrey of the time she had seen them, or thought she had seen them, kissing at Jaime's party.

'He didn't mention it to you?'

'No.' Audrey turned on her heel to look at Shereen.

'Why would he have done that? I mean, when would he have had the chance?'

'I don't know. Actually, we never talk about you, I don't know what made me say that.' Audrey could feel something hard and glassy inside herself, every word she spoke polished and shiny.

'Do you see Jack often?' Shereen was beginning to sound lawyerly.

'Yeah, Tuesdays, Thursdays, sometimes Sundays too.'

'Every week?'

Audrey watched as the other woman began to crumple. She could see a trace of sweat on her upper lip. 'Yes, every week. Since he dumped me, he's like a tiger in bed.' She laughed at her own cliché. 'Like he's had a whole new lease on life.'

Shereen took a step towards Audrey, but Audrey wasn't afraid. She didn't know why she had come, why she wanted to tell Shereen about Jack. She took another step. She looked as though she was in pain. Audrey wondered if Shereen were going to hit her. Maybe she kept a gun in the drawer of *her* desk. Audrey thought it might be a good thing for Shereen to kill her. She didn't want to die, it was more that she would be happy to stop here, to bring the whole thing to a halt. She could go to the Dolls' Hospital and have her string fixed. Her father, her mother, they had both escaped, in fact her mother had got off lightly, dying well before she reached any kind of real difficulty with age. Her father – it had been much worse for him, it had all gone wrong when his foot hit the accelerator instead of the brake. Actually, it had gone wrong for him well before that. When he retired, and fell ill. Or perhaps when he had a child. Or maybe long before that. Audrey had no idea. Her parents' lives were as mysterious to her as that of James and Amelia Douglas. Really, she thought, the real problem here was Jane. Audrey did not know what had happened to her. On her infrequent trips home before her mother died, she had not tried to track her down. In the decade since that ferry trip, Jane had not contacted Audrey. She wondered now, as Shereen stood there in front of her, she let herself wonder if Jane had truly disappeared that day. If she had been washed overboard by that great wave. If she had let go of the handrail and been swept away, her body tossed up, baby dead inside, on an island beach when the storm ceased. People jumped off those ferries all the time. It was a popular suicide. Was I responsible? Audrey wondered. Was it all my doing? Could I have altered the course of our lives the last time I saw Jane? Or was she alive somewhere, happy with Frank and one, two, three children?

Shereen clapped her hands together. Audrey flinched, her memories fled. 'We should kill him!' Shereen said, as though she'd thought through Audrey's revelation and formulated a brilliant plan. She was smiling.

'Why?'

Now she looked aggrieved. 'Because he's a . . .' The words died before she could form them. She sounded as though all the air had left her lungs. She paled and sat down.

'I'm not really up for sisterly revenge, Shereen,' said Audrey.

'No,' she said, 'I guess not.'

'In fact, we should probably carry on just as we are.'

'What do you mean?'

'I don't mind, so much, being the other woman. It frees me up. I still get fucked, without being fucked, so to speak. At least now I'll know he isn't deceiving you as well.'

'No,' said Shereen, drawing herself together, shaking her head. 'No. It's not right. It's not what I want.' She stood and crossed the room. 'I want to get married.'

'Oh,' said Audrey. She thought of James and Amelia.

'No,' Shereen shook her head, 'Audrey, we can't have it this way. He can't have it this way. It's too much.' She looked around the room, as though appraising it. 'I want to get married,' her tone was firm. 'I want to be one of those people who gets married and stays married and is happy. I want to exchange vows and introduce our families. I want that piece of paper, and all it means.'

'With Jack?'

She looked shocked. 'Of course. Not just anybody.' Her

expression grew fierce. 'I love him, Audrey.'

'Of course,' Audrey said, 'you love him.'

'I do,' she said, 'I really do.'

Audrey felt embarrassed for her. Hadn't she loved Jack too? Did he love Shereen? Perhaps he did. Maybe it worked for him, being with Shereen. But then, why was he still fucking me?

'I really do,' Shereen said again.

'Okay,' she said, not knowing what she meant, 'okay, Shereen.'

'Will you stop seeing him?'

'Oh,' Audrey spoke slowly, as though considering the request. 'I don't know. Maybe. Ask him.'

'I think you should stop seeing him,' Shereen sounded definite.

'Oh,' said Audrey. 'We'll ask him. We'll see what he thinks.'

They stopped talking then and Shereen went into the kitchen. Audrey heard cupboards opening, the fridge door closing. Shereen was making drinks. After a while she came out clutching two glasses. Audrey sniffed hers, gin and tonic.

'No lemon,' said Shereen, 'sorry.' She returned to the kitchen, and brought out the bottles, placed them on the coffee table. Both women sat down, opposite ends of the sofa, gingerly.

'Maybe he's not up to it, Shereen.'

'Marriage?'

'Yes.'

Shereen didn't reply.

'Where is he?' Audrey asked.

'Working. He's coming over later.'

'We'll wait for him then, shall we?' We are like two wives, Audrey thought, a harem. Maybe there was something good in that.

Outside it was dark, and raining. Audrey thought about all those messages Shereen had left for her, all those inches of answerphone tape she had consumed back in the bad old days. Perhaps now she could reply.

All at once, Audrey began to talk. She didn't know why she was talking. It was as though something inside her had been switched on, a lever that had been jammed suddenly came free, the engine started running. At first she faltered, but then her voice grew smooth. She told Shereen about Jane, and David. She talked about her parents, she told Shereen how each had died. She described the car accident as though she'd been there, and, in the telling, she felt relieved of something, as though she had carried a heavy object with her for a long time and had finally put it down. She talked about Jack, and what came between them, what brought them back together, not sparing Shereen the details. 'Maybe it is this thing about whiteness,' she said, 'the social construct of whiteness, white femininity. And black masculinity.' It drew them together, it forced them apart. And this led her to James and Amelia. Their story was like a rich seam of ore, just below the surface in the geology of history. She could mine it, she could study its composition, she could attempt to decipher its mineral codes. She could use it however she wished. It was part of her material world. And she felt reassured by that, comforted.

Audrey knew now what had drawn her to the story of James and Amelia; it was the very idea of a marriage that had been consecrated both in the forest and in the church. She had been drawn to this image of fidelity. It was so unlike anything in her own life, circled, as she was, by Jane and David, and now, Jack and Shereen. James and Amelia were the perfect couple, perfect parents, their commitment to each other and their family absolute, complete. And James was the perfect father, the perfect colonial father; he would not desert her, unlike Jack, David, her own father, he could not desert her, he would be there always, embedded in the past. Or, at least, that was how it seemed to Audrey.

And yet, perhaps it didn't matter who 'our relative' was,

his wife, their mothers, their grandmothers. James Douglas, representing the Crown, Queen Victoria herself, had been an active agent for Empire; he was, Audrey thought, an imperialist in the working sense of the word. A Company man who became a Government man. Audrey had seen that most biographical portraits of James and Amelia obscured and bleached-out their origins, made them both white and British, good colonial rulers, their Caribbean and Cree mothers erased. Sir James Douglas ensured that things turned out the way London demanded; he secured his place in official history. 'It made no difference who his mother was, nor his wife's mother,' said Audrey, 'these women had no influence on the course of history.'

'A little like us,' Shereen interjected.

Audrey laughed.

She had been kept separate from Jack, from Shereen, they were different, they each had something she did not, she had something they didn't. But that was not the whole truth either. Jane and David. The impossibility of connecting, reality's betrayal of fantasy. As she got older it seemed more difficult to have friends, to keep friends, to be with people. Long gone were the days of hanging out, hours spent together, time and trust accumulating like heavy, soft, blanketing dust. And Audrey had never been good at accumulating.

She kept talking, she kept showing herself to Shereen, as though she hadn't had an audience before. And Shereen was her witness, mostly quiet, refilling her glass occasionally. They sat in her sitting room with the curtains pulled shut, one low lamp in the corner behind them. The radiator across the room sent out its steady warmth and, Audrey thought, this sitting room couldn't be anywhere but here, in London. This city. This feeling of being tucked up on a wet night with the city all around us. It wasn't something she could feel anywhere else. And maybe she was at home in that. Somehow. Some way.

ACKNOWLEDGEMENTS

I am indebted to the following people, organizations, books and articles: Simon Mellor, Rachel Calder, Catherine Byron, Alixe Knighton, Percy and Margaret Pullinger, Grazyna Krupa, Mandy Rose; the MacDowell Colony, the Arts Council of England, the Provincial Archives in Victoria, BC, the British Library, Faculty of English at the University of Reading, and HMP Gartree; *Many Tender Ties* by Sylvia Van Kirk, *Strangers In Blood* by Jennifer S. H. Brown, *The West Beyond the West: A History of British Columbia* by Jean Barman, 'Some Further Notes on the Douglas Family' and 'Sir James Douglas's Mother and Grandmother' by Charlotte S. M. Girard, *Colonial Encounters: Europe and the Native Caribbean, 1492–1797* by Peter Hulme, *A Voyage to the Demerary* by Henry Bolingbroke, *Kinship and Class in the West Indies* by Raymond T. Smith.

Kate Pullinger was born in Canada and has lived in London since 1982. Her first book, *Tiny Lies*, a collection of stories, was published in 1988, and was followed by the novels *When the Monster Dies* and *Where Does Kissing End?*, as well as, most recently, a new collection of stories, *My Life as a Girl in a Men's Prison*. She has written for film, television and radio, and co-wrote the novel based on the film *The Piano* with director Jane Campion. Her work has been widely anthologized and translated.